CROSSING the LINE

SIMONE ELKELES

An Imprint of HarperCollinsPublishers

HarperTeen is an imprint of HarperCollins Publishers.

Crossing the Line

Copyright © 2018 by Temple Hill Publishing LLC

All rights reserved. Printed in the United States of America.

No part of this book may be used or reproduced in any manner whatsoever without written permission except in the case of brief quotations embodied in critical articles and reviews. For information address HarperCollins Children's Books, a division of HarperCollins Publishers, 195 Broadway, New York, NY 10007.

www.epicreads.com

Library of Congress Control Number: 2017962471

ISBN 978-0-06-264196-0

Typography by Michelle Taormina

18 19 20 21 22 PC/LSCH 10 9 8 7 6 5 4 3 2 1

❖

First Edition

For Mindy

because when God was passing out friendships I won the lottery

ONE

Ryan

When you die, it's game over.

There is no coming back, no re-spawns or do-overs.

I'm sitting in the last row of the funeral home, watching as people file past me to pay their respects to Max Trieger's widow. She's clutching on to her two little daughters tightly. One tearfully asks if her daddy is in the wooden box in front of them, and all Mrs. Trieger can do is nod slowly through her sobs. Her son sits stiffly with his arms folded on his chest a few feet away.

I'll always remember Max as being a tough-as-nails border detective. A few of the Mexican kids at our school were wary of him, afraid he might start snooping around and asking questions about their parents or immigration status. But his goal wasn't to sniff out anyone who crossed the border illegally. He made it his mission to crush the criminal drug trade so the next generation wouldn't have to carry that burden.

Supposedly Max Trieger was in the middle of some secret operation with the Mexican authorities and the DEA to take down *Las Calaveras*, the cartel operating between Mexico and the US, and he got shot for it. In his face. Nobody knows who did it but even if they did, the motto in our Texas border town is "snitches get stitches."

Or worse.

I stare at the wooden casket and wonder if Max had known beforehand that he'd die and leave his wife and kids behind, would he have carried out whatever secret operation he was involved in?

Probably.

"Ryan, come sit with us," my mom urges from the front row. She's frantically waving me over as I contemplate how much alcohol she downed before she showed up here.

I shake my head with the hope she'll stop focusing her attention on me while I try to blend in with the crowd. I put my head down so I don't have to make eye contact with her or anyone else. It's a trick I learned a long time ago to escape situations. Sometimes it works.

Other times it doesn't.

I can tell this is one of those other times, because after a few minutes I feel a hard tap on my shoulder. "Yo, loser. Your mom wants you to sit up front with us," my whiny stepbrother PJ sputters in a voice that could shatter glass.

Instead of answering, I shoot him a level stare as a warning to leave me alone.

"Suit yourself," he says in a clipped tone. "I didn't want you to sit with us anyway."

Everyone here knows we're not related by blood. It's no secret I'm the troublemaker stepson of Loveland's beloved sheriff. Nothing I do is about to change that.

PJ trots up to his dad, who's standing guard in front of the casket, and whispers something to him. It doesn't take a genius to figure out that he's tattling on me, which is so pathetic for a kid who's about to turn seventeen. My stepfather, Paul, otherwise known as Sheriff Blackburn, looks in my direction with pure disgust while PJ flashes me a small, triumphant smile.

I ignore them and bow my head as I do the only thing I came here to do. Pray for Max Trieger.

A few months back Max found me sitting on a park bench with a pocketknife in my hand. It was late at night, nobody else was around, and I stared at the shiny blade as if it were my salvation. When Max walked up to me, he didn't interrogate me or demand I hand over the knife. As if he knew what I was about to do, he parked his butt on the bench next to me. We sat in silence for a long time until he said in that calm, cool voice of his, "What if it gets better but you never knew 'cause you gave up?"

"What if it doesn't get better?" I asked him as I stared at the blade.

He shrugged. "Law of averages says it will, and I'm a guy who knows a thing or two about laws. Why don't I hold on to that blade for a little while, Ryan? It'd be a shame if you accidentally cut yourself waitin' for things to get better." He held out his hand and I gave him the knife. "If you ever need me, don't hesitate to call me anytime. Or my partner, Lance Matthews. He's rough around the edges, but a good guy." He handed me a card with both of their numbers on it.

Even though I knew I'd never call, I stashed that card in my wallet as if it were my lifeline to sanity.

Max Trieger saved my life that day. Max was a hero, unlike my stepfather.

I look at my mom's husband, wearing his dark blue Loveland sheriff's uniform with its shiny gold star pin and name tag engraved with the words PAUL M. BLACKBURN, SHERIFF. He loves that heavy polyester uniform, but not because of what it stands for. He loves it for the ego trip it gives him.

Paul is now greeting mourners at the entrance. Summer break just started and it's hot as Hell here in southern Texas. I wonder if they notice the droplets of sweat on his face. Probably not. Some look at him as if he'll single-handedly protect the entire town from harm. Truth is, he doesn't give a shit about anyone but himself. He lets guys like Max and Lance do the dirty work while he hides in his big office at the Loveland police station and takes credit for every drug bust and arrest as if he's the only competent person on the force. He dismisses the federal border patrol agents as irrelevant wannabes even when some police departments in border towns are notorious for employing crooked cops who are paid by cartels to look the other way.

I glance over at my mom sitting in the second pew next to Allen and PJ, Paul's two obnoxious sons from his first marriage. Mom's wearing a little black lacy dress from some designer store in town and she's got her hands folded neatly in her lap. I know she's drunk, but my mom is a pro at hiding it. Hell, I bet even Paul doesn't realize she downed her daily dose this morning.

Or maybe he doesn't give a shit.

In his sleazy mind, having a trophy wife by his side just enhances the hero image. Having to deal with her bastard son who doesn't conform to his perfect image pisses the heck out of him.

As the flood of mourners starts to dwindle, a bunch of girls from Loveland High appear. They're all wearing similar short, strappy dresses and they cluster around each other as if they're a herd.

"I'm not sitting anywhere near Ryan," their self-appointed leader, Mikayla Harris, announces loud enough for me to hear.

I flip her off.

She glares at me and mumbles "Jerk" before fingering her fiery red hair and leading the girls to the opposite side of the funeral home.

When I first moved to Loveland a year ago from Chicago, Mikayla and I hooked up at a party. I warned her that I wasn't looking for a girlfriend because I was in training to move up the ranks as a boxer, but I guess she expected me to change my mind once we started hanging out. When I didn't agree to worship the ground she walked on, Mikayla made sure everyone knew I'd been to juvie back in Chicago for assault and grand theft auto. I don't know how she found out, but that didn't matter. Pretty much everyone at school avoided me after that.

Paul, who just abandoned his post, is suddenly in my face. He reeks of cheap cologne. "Go sit next to your mother," he orders through clenched teeth.

"Why? So we can pretend to be a cohesive, happy family?" Fuck that.

"No, smartass." He flashes a tight, thin-lipped smile to a couple who just walked into the place before turning his attention back to me. "It's so your mother doesn't have to answer questions about why her son chose to sit with strangers at a funeral. Just once, spare her from having to make up excuses for you."

I glance at my mom and feel a pang of guilt. It's not like she's been the doting mother all my life, but I don't need to give her yet another excuse to get plastered.

Pushing past my stepfather to sit with my mom, I cringe when he pats me on the back as if we have some kind of affection for each other. It's just a show. If everyone in this funeral home knew how he ripped on Max behind his back, they'd get a small glimpse into the real Sheriff Paul Blackburn.

Commotion in the front row brings me back to the reason why I'm here. Max's twin girls are still crying. When Mrs. Trieger tells her son to sit closer to her, the kid shakes his head.

"I don't want to be here!" the kid shouts.

His mother reaches out to console him but he twists away from her and runs outside. The kid has the right idea. I don't want to be here, either.

While mourners and Max's partner, Lance, rush to comfort the distraught widow, I sneak outside.

It doesn't take me long to find the kid. He's around eleven or twelve, a crappy age to lose a dad. Hell, I lost my dad before I was born and that was pretty crappy too. That's not exactly true because my dad left. He disappeared right after my mom told him she was pregnant. Supposedly he took all the money they'd saved up and ran off with some bimbo stripper he'd met at a dive bar.

My dad was one helluva jerk.

Trieger's kid peeks his head out from behind one of the trees and eyes me curiously. "No matter what you say I'm not goin' back in there."

I shrug, then pull out a cigarette from the pack I have in my pocket. "Listen, kid, I don't give a shit if you go back in there or not." I light the cig, then sit on a picnic bench near the tree. "The way I see it, you can stay out here and hide behind that tree all day long."

"I'm not hidin'," he says, stepping out and revealing his skinny body and a blotchy red face from crying.

I take a drag and the smoke burns the back of my throat. It's a harsh reminder of why I hate the damn things. "Looks like you were hidin'."

The kid tentatively perches himself on the edge of the bench. "You're Sheriff Blackburn's son, aren't you?"

"Stepson." I'm quick to correct him.

He focuses his gaze on the cig. "That causes cancer."

"So does eatin' hot dogs. You ever eat one of those?"

"Yeah."

I take another drag, then smash the cigarette on the bench. I started smoking at about this kid's age when my mom left a box of Newports on the kitchen counter and went out for the night. I gave up smoking when I started boxing and working out, but every once in a while I have one when I'm stressed out. Today definitely calls for a few drags. "Sometimes it's fun to do shit that's bad for you," I tell him.

"Did you really go to jail for stealing a car?" he asks.

"I didn't steal it, kid. I borrowed it."

"Why?"

"You want the truth?"

He nods.

"To piss off my mother's boyfriend at the time." I gesture to the funeral home. "Why'd you walk out?"

He reaches for the collar of his stark white shirt and pulls it away from his neck as if it's about to choke him. "I just . . . I don't want to see that coffin. I'm not an idiot, I know he's dead. I just don't want to be reminded of it. And I don't like everyone starin' at me now that my dad is gone." He kicks the leg of the bench and keeps his head down. "Did you ever just want to disappear?"

"All the time. The law of averages says that when you're at your lowest things will start to look up. Your dad told me that a while back." I glance at the parking lot where my old, beat-up Mustang is waiting for me. "Running away isn't gonna fix your problems." I toss a rock, hitting a tree in the distance. "And if you run away you'd be alone, and I gotta be honest with you. Those girls in there, your sisters . . . they need you. Your ma needs you."

"I don't want to be needed." He finds a rock and follows my lead, trying to hit the same tree I did.

"I get you, but sometimes . . ." I think of Max's coffin with the Texas flag draped over it. "Sometimes you got to man up before

8

you're ready. Trust me, I know from experience."

The kid picks up another rock, but instead of aiming it at the tree he's suddenly focused on something behind me. I turn to see my stepfather walking up to us with a stern look on his face.

Oh, hell.

"Charlie, the service is starting," Paul says in his high-pitched voice that's supposed to sound authoritative but instead sounds like nails on a chalkboard. "Get inside."

The kid sighs.

"Go on," I tell him. "Man up."

The kid hands me the rock before heading back inside the funeral home.

Paul glares at me with cold, beady eyes. "What did you say to Max's kid?"

I boldly stare back, because I know he hates that. He'd rather have me cower and be intimidated, but that's not gonna happen. "Nothin' much."

We're at a standstill, but he refuses to back off and leave me alone. He's too predictable. Any minute now the insults are gonna fly.

Paul gestures to the pack of cigarettes lying on the picnic table. "What the hell are those?"

I slide one of the cigarettes out of the pack and light it. "I offered it to the kid, but he refused."

"That's illegal, Ryan."

I take a drag and release a stream of smoke into the air. "So?"

"You're such a loser," he tells me as if I don't already know it. Insult number one, check. But he's not done. "You should feel mighty lucky I let you live in my home instead of sending you to live with your father." The side of his mouth twitches. "Oh, yeah, that's not an option."

Insult number two, check.

"I thank my lucky stars every day that you're so generous, *Paul*," I say. I take another hit and blow it out slowly, immensely enjoying the fact that it's annoying him.

He wags his finger at me. "I don't want you talkin' to Max's boy. You hear me?"

"Give me a break. He just lost his old man and needed someone to talk to."

"Let him talk to someone who treats people with respect." He stands tall as if that'll somehow make him appear intelligent. It doesn't. "Someone with *honor* and *integrity*."

Insults number three, four, and five, check.

Damn, he's on a roll.

If this guy weren't my mom's husband, I'd probably knock him out. He thrives on insults and is the least qualified person to spout words of honor and integrity. "Whatever, man," I say. "You're not my father and you're not family."

"Thank the mighty Lord for that. If you were, you'd be sittin' up there with your poor mother, wearin' a respectable suit and tie instead of"—he gestures to my dark jeans and black T-shirt— "that."

Paul is more than aware that I don't have money to buy a suit and he sure as hell wouldn't offer to gift me one.

Enough insults for one day.

"I'm out," I say as I smash the cigarette on the bench and start walking away.

"That's littering," Paul calls after me.

"Arrest me," I respond as I head to my car.

I can hear the words of the pastor as I pass the window of the funeral home. "Today we say good-bye to our dear Max Trieger, a man who lived without fear and was a hero to us all . . ."

Hearing those words reminds me of my motto in life . . .

Fuck being a hero.

TWO

Dalila

The good thing about listening to my favorite *música* loudly is that you can drown out everything else around you. The bad thing about it is people can sneak into your room unnoticed, like my little sisters. They have this annoying habit of thinking I need to be surrounded by family at all hours of the day.

"You're wearing *that?*" my sister Margarita yells above the gravelly voice of Atticus Patton, the lead singer of my favorite American hardcore punk band Shadows of Darkness. My parents don't understand my fascination with American music and would rather have me listen to Mexican bands and Spanish music, but my brother Lucas and I used to sneak out of the house and blast it in my dad's car.

I look down at my jeans and black tank. "What's wrong with what I'm wearing?"

Margarita twirls around, her pale blue skirt flying around her like a windmill. "Papá said we should look nice because Don and Doña Cruz are coming over with their son Rico tonight. You're dressed like you're about to go hunting with Tío Manuel."

"And you're dressed like you're about to go to a *quinceañera*," I tell her as I walk over to my dresser and pick up the tiara with sparkly crystals I wore at my own *quinceañera* more than two years ago. "Here, you can wear this."

Placing the tiara on her head, Margarita struts over to my mirror as if she's royalty. "Does that mean I look like a *princesa*?"

"*Sí*. All the *hombres* in Panche will be lining up to dance with you one day." If Papá allows it. Mexican dads aren't known as the most lenient parents and Papá is no exception. He's super strict when it comes to who his daughters can dance with, talk to, or date.

I should know. I'm the oldest daughter of Oscar Sandoval, one of the most sought-after lawyers in Mexico, famous for representing powerful businessmen and politicians. His clients pay him generously to get them out of trouble. Needless to say, he's brilliant at his job.

Margarita stands in front of my mirror twirling her long, curly hair as if it's not already perfect. "Don Cruz's son is nineteen now, you know."

"Yes, I know." Our families get together every year. When we were younger Rico and I would play games and get into trouble. Our parents joked that we'd be a perfect match for each other, but for the past few years Rico has been distracted and distant. Last year he was more interested in texting other girls than talking to me, so I'm not really looking forward to tonight.

"He's a *papacito*, Dalila! You should date him."

"I'm not looking for a *papacito*," I tell her.

"What if you're alone the rest of your life? Yuck." She laughs, a giddy sound that often echoes through the halls at La Joya de Sandoval, the estate where I was born and which I will always consider home.

Lola, our housekeeper since I was five, comes bursting into my room. Her cheery smile always brightens my day, especially when she sings songs while she works. I swear she makes them up. Sometimes they're in Spanish and sometimes in English. She knows both languages because she was born in the tourist town of Puerto Vallarta. Papá went to a university in New York on a scholarship when he was younger. He insists we speak English as much as possible in case we need to be bilingual for any job we might have in the future. He even sent me to a private school in Texas for middle school.

"*¡Hola, niñas! Su mamá quiere que bajen en cinco minutos. La familia Cruz estará aquí para la cena*," Lola announces.

"They'll be here in five minutes? *¡Dios mío!* I've got to get ready." Margarita practically skips out of my room, those curls of hers bouncing with each step.

"She's got enough energy for five people," Lola says as she pulls off my dirty bedsheets and grimaces as another song blasts from my speaker. "Turn that *música* down before your *mamá* starts complaining. You know she doesn't like that crazy yelling disguised as a song."

"That's because she doesn't listen to the words."

Lola cocks a brow. "Words? Is that what they're calling it these days? Sounds more like nonsense to me."

"You're old fashioned," I tell her. "You still expect men to pay for everything and open doors for females and—"

"There's nothing wrong with a man showing respect for a *señorita*, Dalila," she replies with utter conviction. "One day you'll understand."

Sure, it's nice when a guy opens a door for me, but I'm not about to park myself in front of a door and wait until a man opens it when I can easily do it on my own.

"Lola, does it look like I'm about to go hunting?" I ask as I check my reflection in the mirror. My hair is secured in a long ponytail so it won't fall into my face the entire night. I've put a little eyeliner and mascara on, but it's so hot outside I don't dare put on more for fear it will start melting and make me look like a clown.

Lola shifts her head to the side, contemplating my question. "You're the daughter of one of the most important men in Mexico," she says, abandoning her task as she walks across my room and stands in front of my closet. "Jeans and a tank top aren't appropriate for greeting guests."

"I don't want to show off."

"It's not showing off, Dalila. It's representing yourself with dignity." She pulls out a short yellow dress that Mamá bought for me when she traveled to Italy last year. "*¿Que tal esté?*"

It still has the tag on it. "That's for special occasions, Lola."

"Reuniting with Don Cruz's son might be a special occasion."

With a hefty sigh, I take the dress from her and rip off the tag. "Why do I get the feeling like everyone in *mi familia* wants to parade me around like some kind of attraction?"

Lola bundles my bedsheets in her arms and starts walking out of my room. "They want to see you happy."

"I can be happy without a boy in my life," I call after her.

"Of course, *señorita*. But being in love softens a woman."

Softens me? *¡Que asco!* Yuck!

I don't need to be soft. And I don't need a boy to make me happy. I have *mi familia* and my studies . . . and La Joya de Sandoval. My entire life is planned out and it doesn't include time for a serious boyfriend. At least not until I'm almost done with medical school in nine years.

I gaze out the window at the colorful gardens below. *Mi mamá* works hard to make sure they're well maintained to show off the vibrant colors of the flowers native to Mexico. I think it reminds her of her *abuela*, who used to sell flowers in the markets in Sonora to put food on their table. She's especially proud of her *cempasúchil*, the colorful orange marigolds that we use in traditional celebrations and holidays.

Mamá makes all of us aware that we live a privileged life now, one that many people in my country only dream about having.

After slipping into the dress Lola picked out for me, I walk down our winding stone staircase with colorful pieces of ceramic artwork cemented into each step. Every detail of La Joya de Sandoval was designed by my parents to create a sanctuary for our family.

As I pass my father's study, I hear him in a heated discussion with Don Cruz.

"I already took him on as a client," I hear Papá telling Don Cruz in a brisk tone. "I won't betray him."

"You need to give us the information we need, Oscar," Don Cruz replies as I peek into the room through the slightly open door. "Show your loyalty to an old friend."

"We're not discussing this," Papá states sternly as he crosses his arms on his chest. "You're like a brother to me, Francisco. Don't force my hand ever again."

His stern expression softens quickly when he sees me in the hallway watching their interaction. "Ah, you finally made it, *cariño*," Papá calls as he walks out of his office and leads me to the courtyard with Don Cruz in tow.

"What were you and Don Cruz talking about?" I ask.

"*Nada*, Dalila," he says. "Just boring business stuff."

I want to pry, but we're joined by everyone else when we reach the courtyard.

"Every year you grow even more beautiful than the last, young lady," Doña Cruz declares.

All three of our guests sit in cushioned chairs around our open courtyard while Mamá serves them some kind of amber-colored brandy. Don Cruz has his signature full mustache and is wearing a gray suit with a red handkerchief that screams of wealth peeking out of his front pocket. Doña Cruz looks like she's been at the salon all day just to attend this small dinner party. Her hair is in an intricate updo and her dress has sequins sewn in it that sparkle in our courtyard lights.

Their son, Rico, definitely changed this past year. He's obviously been working out and taking care of his body. Instead of wearing casual clothes like most nineteen-year-old boys I know, he's wearing a tailored suit designed for his slim physique. He's got short hair that makes him look confident and tough. It's a dangerous combination.

Rico acknowledges me with an appreciative nod. "Remember when we knocked over one of your mother's flowerpots playing hide-and-seek when we were kids?" he asks. "You were so into those flowers, but I guess your interests have changed. My father tells me you're going to the university next year to study medicine."

"Yes. I'm going to be a heart surgeon," I tell them.

"Wow," Doña Cruz says, clearly impressed. "Ambitious."

Mamá pastes a warm smile on her face. "We're proud of Dalila."

I know she's thinking of my older brother, Lucas. If it weren't for his heart murmur he would still be alive today. Even though he's been gone three years, I think of him every day and wish he were here. I know she does, too.

Don Cruz turns to Papá. "It's a good thing I don't have daughters. I wouldn't let them go to university or even out of the house without a bodyguard."

"My sisters and I are more than capable of taking care of ourselves," I retort back.

"I'm sure it's easy to take care of yourselves when you live in Panche," Rico chimes in with a cocky grin. "But Panche isn't the real world."

I raise a brow. "Are you saying my life is fake, *señor?*"

"I'm saying there's an entire world out there that you don't know exists."

I'm about to challenge him when Mamá puts a hand on my knee signaling me to keep quiet.

Lola appears and announces that dinner is ready and I breathe a sigh of relief. Hopefully the topic of conversation will change as soon as we start eating. Before I can follow everyone else to the dining room, Rico steps into my path. "I didn't mean to insult you, *señorita.*"

"You didn't insult me," I tell him. "I just don't like being seen as weak."

Rico holds his arm out for me to take. Obviously he hasn't gotten the hint that I'm not looking for special treatment. "My father tells me to treat women like delicate flowers."

I try to hold back the chuckle that escapes from my mouth, but I'm painfully unsuccessful. "*En serio.* That's the most ridiculous thing I've ever heard. I'm not a flower and I'm not sheltered. I'm a tough *chica* who can kick butt if I need to."

"Really?" He gives me a once-over. "You think you're tough?"

I nod. "*Por supuesto que sí.*"

He crosses his arms on his chest. "Okay, *Doña* Sandoval. Why don't you show me how you can defend yourself from a guy like me."

"Here?"

"Sure."

"Not here," I tell him. I'm all for proving myself, but not when it will embarrass my parents.

"I belong to a boxing gym down in Sevilla," Rico says. "How about I take you there and you can show me that you're not a flower. I can even give you boxing pointers. Do you like boxing?"

"Boxing is like a religion in my house." I was brought up watching fights with Papá and Lucas.

Rico holds his head high and puffs out his chest. "I'm a semipro about to move up in the ranks."

Now it's time for me to give him the once-over. "You, a semipro? Aren't you the boy who cried when he got a paper cut making a paper airplane?"

"That doesn't count. I was five."

"Even so, you could never convince my papá to allow me to go to a boxing gym." I'd love to get out, even if it's with Rico, a guy who stupidly thinks women are delicate flowers. I'll show him I'm not as weak as he thinks I am.

"*No hay problema*," Rico says assuredly. "By the end of this dinner your papá will agree to let you go. He thinks of my father as family. Trust me."

During dinner, Rico talks to Papá about taking me to the gym.

With a raised brow, Papá eyes me curiously. "You want to box, Dalila?"

"*Sí*," I tell him. "I want to show Rico that I'm not some delicate flower."

I'm a tough *chica* who can hold my own.

THREE

Ryan

Lone Star Boxing Club in Loveland, Texas, reminds me of the gym
I trained at in Chicago. They're both gyms where dedicated boxers
train in the hopes of going pro one day. Most guys who come here
daily are like me, trying to get in as much training as possible.

"Where the hell have you been, Hess?" steroid-addicted Larry
calls out from behind Lone Star Boxing Club's front desk as I walk
in the door. "Usually you get here at the butt crack of dawn."

"Life happened," I tell him.

"I hear ya, bro."

He tosses me a white corner towel that's been washed so many
times the logo is peeling off. I catch it in one hand and head for the
small locker room on the other side of the gym. After that talk with

Paul earlier today, I definitely need to be here. It's the only place where I belong, where I'm in control of my destiny. Boxing used to be my escape, but now it's part of my life. I don't mind the sweat, and I ignore the pain. When I'm fighting my mind is at peace and I can focus without being distracted or inhibited by anything or anyone.

After changing, I find an available punching bag. Most guys here aren't into chatting, which is just fine with me. I don't usually talk unless I got something to say.

"Lookie here! It's our resident delinquent, Ryan Hess, in the flesh," my friend Pablo calls out. He's oblivious to the unwritten no-chatting rule. He works out here a couple days a week and goes to Loveland High with me. "Thought you'd be at the funeral," he says.

I hit the bag and start to warm up. "I was."

"Why'd you duck out early?"

I stop punching. "I didn't duck out, Pablo. I was there. I left. End of story."

He grins, his chipped front tooth a sign that he doesn't always play it safe. "You know what you need?"

"I'm sure you're gonna tell me, whether I want to hear it or not." I would ignore him, but I left my headphones in my duffel so I can't zone out.

"You need to work on your social skills."

Whatever. "Maybe I don't want to be social."

I punch the bag again.

And again.

Pablo says, "You need a crew because you can't fight the world on your own, Hess. You're not an island."

What the fuck is he blabbing about? An *island*? "You've been readin' too many self-help books, Pablo. Why don't we go in that ring and spar?"

He chuckles, the sound echoing throughout the gym. "You ain't gonna find me in the ring with you, Hess. Rumor has it you knocked out Roach last week," he says. "And Benito the week before that."

"They lost focus."

His mouth twitches in amusement. "They're two of the best damn fighters in this place, *pendejo*. At least they were until you came along. You fight like you've been throwin' punches your whole life."

Little does he know I used to be the resident wimp when I was younger. In elementary and middle school in the western suburbs of Chicago, I got beat up a lot. I didn't talk much and my clothes came off the rack at Goodwill. I was an outcast, a kid who didn't fit in. Hell, I still don't fit in. And I still don't talk much. But I learned pretty early on that getting beat up sucks.

One day in seventh grade Willie Rayburn was chasing me after school like he always did. With the bully hot on my trail, I wasn't paying attention when I ran right into this high schooler named Felix. He lived in the trailer next to ours.

He asked me why I was scared of Willie. I shrugged.

He asked me if I wanted to learn how to fight. I nodded.

After that, I'd meet Felix on the small patch of grass behind our trailer park every once in a while and he'd teach me how to box. He said his father was a boxer and told me if I learned how to throw a punch like a pro, guys like Willie Rayburn would leave me alone.

I remember the first time I fought Rayburn. It was glorious.

It went down in the school cafeteria. I'd been talking to a pretty girl named Bianca. Willie came up and told Bianca that I was trailer trash whose mom was an alcoholic whore. I hated when people found out I lived in the old dirty trailer park on the edge of town. My mom had a history of bringing random guys to the trailer, but she wasn't a whore. She was hoping one of them would stick around long enough to take care of her. All they ended up doing was giving her black eyes and aiding her alcohol addiction.

I hated my life, my absent dad, my mom, and Willie Rayburn.

That day everything I'd been holding inside me burst like a volcano. I wasn't gonna feel sorry for myself and play the victim anymore.

Before he could punch me or push me to the ground, I whacked Willie with a solid left hook. Willie fell and I was immediately on top of him, punching him repeatedly as frustrated tears streamed down my face. My fists kept flying until three lunch supervisors hauled me away.

I didn't care that I'd broken his nose and was suspended a week from school. After I came back the kids wouldn't even look at me for fear I would do to them what I'd done to Willie. Instead of upsetting me, it was empowering. I liked that people didn't mess with me and thought I was tough.

Even if I was still an outcast.

The gym is suddenly quiet as Todd Projansky, the owner of the gym, walks in with four guys who look like they're seasoned fighters.

"Who are those guys with Projansky?" I ask Pablo.

"The guy in the middle is a fringe contender named Mateo Rodriguez," he answers in a low voice. "Supposedly he trains at a gym in Mexico where Camacho gives pointers to a couple of guys. I've seen him fight. He's good."

Wait. My brain has a hard time processing what I think I just heard. "Back up. The dude knows *Camacho*? Are you talkin' about Juan Camacho, the boxing legend?"

"The one and only." Pablo shrugs. "At least that's the latest rumor."

Damn. Juan Camacho is a world-famous Mexican boxer who was the heavyweight boxing champ in the seventies. He didn't only win it once. He dominated for years. And then he disappeared without a trace. He's got to be in his sixties by now. He was an old-school fighter who used to train like a beast.

When I started boxing I'd watch videos of him and mimic his moves. Hell, I'd act out entire matches of his, copying his quick jabs and the way he moves around the ring. If this Rodriguez guy knows him . . . "I'm gonna see if it's true."

"Don't." Pablo grabs my shoulder and holds me back. "You don't just walk up to a guy like Rodriguez."

"You might not, but I do." I make my way across the gym with one goal on my mind. Finding out if the rumor is reality.

Mateo Rodriguez has black hair and he's wearing a plain white tank and shorts as if he's ready to fight. He's not crazy muscular and doesn't look intimidating, but then again I learned a long time ago you don't assess anyone's skill unless you see them in the ring.

He's watching two guys spar with his arms crossed on his chest like he's analyzing cattle. When I stand in front of him, he raises a brow.

"I heard you know Juan Camacho," I say without any hesitation. "Is it true?"

He doesn't answer right away and instead eyes me curiously. "Who is this *gringo*?" he asks Projansky.

"Ryan Hess. He's a new fighter from Chicago," Projansky explains. "Moved up here last year when his ma married Sheriff Blackburn."

His jaw twitches as he turns back to me. "Look, kid, Camacho doesn't sign autographs."

"I don't want an autograph," I tell him. "I want to meet him and see if he'll train me. What club is he affiliated with?"

"Train you?" Rodriguez lets out a low chuckle, then stares me down. "Camacho isn't affiliated with anyone. And he sure as hell doesn't have time to screw around with young *pendejos* who don't know shit about boxing yet think they can throw down in the big leagues."

The problem Rodriguez is that he made the mistake of judging my skill before seeing me in a bout.

"Go three rounds with me," I challenge. "If I win, you introduce me to Camacho."

"Are you challenging me?"

"Yes."

The side of his mouth quirks up in amusement. "And if I win?"

I look him straight in the eye. "You won't."

"You're a cocky motherfucker, aren't you?" I can feel all eyes on us. Guys like Rodriguez won't back down from a challenge, because their masculinity is at stake. Some guys'll risk everything to save their precious egos, inside the ring and out. "Tell you what, Hess. I'll make it easy on you." He winks at his friends. "We go thirty seconds. If you land one solid punch, I'll take you to Camacho."

One punch in thirty? "What's the catch?"

He holds his arms out wide. "There is none. If you don't got the skill to land one in thirty seconds, you don't got what it takes."

I hold out my hand. "Deal."

He shakes it. Deal is done.

I walk back to Pablo. "You gonna be my cornerman? You said you had my back."

"I didn't say I had your back." Pablo shakes his head so hard I think he's going to give himself a concussion. "I said you should be more social so you have a *crew* to have your back. I'm not a crew."

"Well, you're all I've got."

He cranes his neck to look over at Rodriguez and his buddies who are now in the ring prepping him for the fight. "You think you can land one in thirty seconds? Don't get me wrong, you're a great fighter, Hess. But he's got more time in the ring than you have. He can just dance around for thirty seconds and make you look like a damn fool."

"I'm not planning on looking like a fool. I know I can do this. You with me?"

Pablo loosens his shoulders as if he's the one about to fight. "Yeah. I'm with you."

When I take my place in the corner in full gear, the owner of the gym comes up to me. "You're a decent fighter, Ryan," he says. "But Mateo Rodriguez is no joke. You let up for one second or get distracted, he'll pound you like you're a piece of raw meat. Those thirty seconds will feel like thirty minutes."

I nod. "Did you give Rodriguez the same speech about me?"

Projansky shakes his head. "No. You're the underdog."

I've been the underdog my entire life, so his words don't faze me. If anything, they make me stronger and more focused on my goal. One solid punch. That's all it'll take.

"He's a slugger, so watch out for the power of his hits," Pablo tells me when Projansky joins the spectators outside the ring. "I saw him knock a dude out with one punch in the first round. Don't get that close to him."

"If I don't get close, how am I supposed to land a solid punch?" I ask.

Pablo shrugs. "Beats me, man."

When the bell rings signaling the fight is on, Rodriguez and I dance around the ring. He hits the air a few times as I duck his jabs. One of those air bombs gives me an opening to get a liver shot, but I just clip him as he backs up.

"You think you can do this?" Rodriguez taunts as we move around the ring.

"No sweat." I motion for him to come closer with my gloved hands. "Why don't you come at me?"

"I'm waiting for you to make a move. We're about ten seconds in and you haven't landed shit."

"I got time," I say confidently.

"Ticktock. Don't forget to keep your hands up," he says in a condescending manner as if this is my first bout.

He has no idea the ring is where I feel most comfortable. When I'm here, nothing else matters.

I'm usually a patient fighter, analyzing my opponent. That way I can be unpredictable. Sometimes I stay at a distance and sometimes I prefer to close the gap and hit hard and fast. One technique doesn't fit me and I like switching it up. The problem is this round isn't the usual three minutes. It's thirty seconds. I've got to make my move now.

Pablo says Rodriguez is a slugger, which means he might be slow but crazy powerful. I'll let him think he's got a shot at knocking me out. Then I'll go in for the prize.

I close the gap and can see the hunger for blood in Rodriguez's eyes. I know his punch is gonna sting, but I'm ready for it.

He thinks he's got this.

He lands an uppercut and I stumble backward to let him think he's got the best of me. I'm obviously tougher than I look, and a better actor than he is an athlete.

Guys with inflated egos celebrate too soon.

As he turns to his friends to flaunt his victory, I quickly regroup and throw a solid hook to his jaw just as the bell echoes through the gym. Now it's Rodriguez's turn to stumble backward.

"Next time don't forget to keep your hands up," I joke.

I hold out my gloves for him because there isn't any more animosity. Rodriquez was trying to make me prove myself. He set a bar and I met it. Now I get the prize.

He taps my gloves, a boxer's handshake signifying respect. "You're tough," he says. "Most guys would've been out with that uppercut."

"I'm not most guys."

"Obviously."

After taking my gloves off, I meet Rodriguez and his crew beside the ring. "All right, *gringo*, you earned it," he says. "You want to spend the summer training in Mexico?"

"Of course. I'm ready."

"All right, man." He hands me a piece of paper with instructions to a bar across the border. "Meet me at this bar in a week and I'll get you a meeting with Camacho."

Wow, that was easy. "Thanks so much, man. I really appreciate it."

"Just stick with me and you'll move up."

After shaking his hand, I've got a renewed sense of purpose. All I have to do is break the news to my mom and Paul that I'm going to Mexico for the summer. I know it won't be met with enthusiasm, especially because Paul feels a need to break me down and prove to my mom that I'm as worthless as he makes me out to be.

I nod. That's four days from now. "I'll be there."

Max Trieger told me the law of averages says things will get better. Maybe the guy was right. I look up and give him a silent thanks.

Outside, Pablo drapes his arm around me. "We have to celebrate your win, Hess."

"How?"

Pablo grins wide as if he knows he's going to annoy the shit outta me. "Friday night we're going out to party. Don't even try arguing, because I won't take no for an answer. You owe me one."

"And if I don't pay up?" I ask him.

"Then you'll lose your one-man crew."

FOUR

Dalila

Girls Night Fridays have become a ritual. Sometimes my friends go to salsa clubs in town or to the movies. Other times we just hang out and pamper ourselves with spa treatments.

My friend Soona and I arrived at Demi's *casa* an hour ago with nail polish and exfoliating face masks we bought online. Demi's parents are in Monterrey for the night at their "city" residence, so we've got her entire house in Panche to ourselves.

Demi, with her short, pink-streaked hair, is the definition of *linda*. She's fun and always happy. I love hanging around her because her enthusiasm for practically everything is infectious. One night we were bored and crashed a wedding at a fancy resort near the beach. Another time we traveled to Mexico City and camped out for two nights to be the first in line to witness the inauguration of our president.

Soona is the friend who keeps our outrageous ideas and adventures to a minimum. She's conservative and completely neurotic, but Demi and I think it's fun to try to get her to venture out of her comfort zone.

"Tell us the truth, Dalila. Are you interested in Rico as more than a friend?" Demi asks me.

"No," I insist. "He's taking me to some boxing gym. It's not even a date."

"When is this non-date taking place?"

I shrug. "Next week sometime."

"I think you need a boyfriend," Soona chimes in. "You haven't dated anyone since Antonio. That was two years ago."

Antonio and I met at a private school I attended for a few years. We dated for six months, until I found him cheating on me with some girl he met online. "I don't want to be involved with a guy right now. I'm too focused on school."

"You're lucky you don't care." Soona's face turns pensive. "I want a boyfriend so bad."

"Why?"

"I don't know." She shrugs. "I guess I'd like to be held and know there's someone out there thinking of me."

Demi looks at her as if she's got two heads. "That's because you're needy, Soona. I never want to be a resentful old married hag."

"Damn, Demi," I say. "To you marriage sounds like prison."

"It is for my parents. But enough about depressing thoughts like marriage." Demi stands on her bed as if it's a stage and clears her throat. "Girls, I have an *anuncio* about what we're doing tonight."

"An announcement? I thought we were staying in," I tell her as I scan all the nail polishes and snacks we've gathered.

"No. This is just the beginning. We're going to celebrate your birthday, Dalila!"

"My birthday isn't for a week," I say even though a bolt of energy starts rushing through me at the thought of finally turning eighteen.

Demi grabs her treasured pink stuffed teddy bear and tosses it in the air. "Consider it an early birthday celebration."

Soona and I look at each other with curious expressions on our faces. Demi can definitely come up with crazy schemes. If my papá knew how mischievous I can be sometimes, I think he'd forbid me to hang out with them.

But what he doesn't know won't hurt him.

Soona waves her hands in an attempt to dry her newly painted red nails. "What's this great idea of yours? I'm nervous."

Demi holds her hands up as if she's a preacher about to say something important. "The three of us are going to Texas tonight."

My heart kicks up a beat. "Texas? What do you want to do in Texas?"

Demi's eyes light up. "You ready for it?"

I get up on the bed with her. "Yeah, I'm ready. ¡*Dime!*"

"Okay." She braces her arms on my shoulders. "Shadows of Darkness is playing in Loveland, Texas, and I got us tickets for their concert tonight!" Demi lets out a squeal of excitement.

My breath hitches. "You're lying."

Their song "One Night in Crazy" is the last song I listened to with my brother before he died. Lucas used to tell me their lead singer, Atticus Patton, wrote it after his girlfriend broke up with him. He did all of these *loco* things to destroy his life, but he came out of it stronger instead of weaker.

Jumping off her bed, Demi opens the drawer to her bedside table and pulls out three tickets. "Here they are," she says, tossing one to each of us.

"Wow," I say, staring at the ticket as if it's a piece of precious gold. "This is the best present ever! There's just one *problema*."

Demi's eyebrows furrow. "*¿Qué?*"

Soona and I lock eyes knowingly. "If you haven't realized," Soona says, "we don't just walk around with our passports in our purses."

Demi dismisses Soona's concern with a tilt of her head. "That's not a problem. I'll drive by each of your houses so you can pick them up."

"I know where my parents hide our passports, but they won't let me go to the US without their permission," I tell her.

"Mine are the same." Soona's frown deepens. "And if we tell them we're going to a punk concert, they'll never let us go."

"So don't tell them, Ms. Neg." Demi calls Soona Ms. Neg, short for Ms. Negative, whenever she picks apart our fun plans. "You have to learn how to take chances in life. Just go home and snatch your passport without them finding out."

"That's not taking chances, Demi. That's stealing," Soona challenges.

"It can't be stealing when it belongs to you," Demi counters. "Right, Dalila?"

Suddenly a sense of rebelliousness rushes through me. Lucas would tell me to do it, because he was carefree and hated to follow rules. "Let's do it, *chicas*. I'm in," I tell them.

"Me, too," Demi says. "Soona, what about you?"

Demi and I nod, willing her to go along with our adventure. "Fine," Soona finally says, "but if my parents find out, just be aware that I might be grounded for life."

The three of us jump on Demi's bed like we used to do when we were little kids, getting excited for an adventure. Even Soona starts talking about how much fun we're going to have.

Crossing the border tonight will only be the start of our journey. I can just imagine this evening ending up being One Night in Crazy, just like the song!

FIVE

Ryan

I'm standing in front of The Cage auditorium with Pablo. He's looking up at the posters promoting the concert tonight.

"Are you aware that Shadows of Death is a punk band?" he tells me in a pained voice.

"*Alternative* punk, Pablo," I counter. "And it's not Shadows of Death. It's Shadows of Darkness."

"That doesn't even make sense." Pablo scrunches up his face. "I hate to break the news to you, but Mexicans don't do crappy alternative punk. We listen to good music."

"You said we could go anywhere I wanted. I want to listen to SOD." It's no use telling him that the crowd is going to be louder than any other concert he's been to. He'll probably end up wishing he'd brought ear plugs.

When we take our place at the end of the line, Pablo's eyes go wide at the sight of a couple with piercings attached to chains traveling from their ears to their lips. He shakes his head in confusion. "White people. Most of these dudes look like they need heavy doses of therapy."

"Are you saying Mexicans don't need therapy, Pablo?"

"You know what would happen if I came home with chains attached to my face, Ryan? My old man would kick me out of the house, not tell me I need to talk my feelings out by seeing a shrink."

I wonder if my dad would be strict or more like a buddy. Maybe he'd be one of those lenient parents who let their kids do whatever they want. I try not to think about it too much.

There are about five people in front of us when the guy at the ticket counter announces, "Sorry. We just sold out."

A collective groan echoes through the line of people behind us waiting to buy tickets.

"Sorry, man," Pablo says without any remorse. "Maybe we can go to a normal club and dance to normal music."

But I don't want normal music. I want to hear Shadows of Darkness. When I had no friends the lead singer Atticus Patton was there to share my pain. "Listen, can't you just sell us two tickets?" I ask the guy at the ticket counter.

The dude looks up at me through his long bangs resembling a mop that practically covers his entire face. "No."

While the lucky crowd with tickets shuffles into The Cage, I shake my head at my lack of luck. This sucks.

"We could always go to a movie," Pablo suggests as Mop Head closes the sales booth and disappears.

I'm almost about to give up hope when I see a Dimitri's Catering van pull into the alley behind The Cage. I tap Pablo on the shoulder. "Follow me."

Pablo follows me to the back alley. The van parks by the back exit and my idea springs into action.

"You're late," I bark at the two guys inside the van. "The band wants to know where their food is and I've had to stall them." I act real jittery so they think I'm about to lose it.

"I couldn't help it," the driver says as he jumps out. "Traffic was a bitch and we've still got two more deliveries tonight."

I blow out a frustrated breath. "We need to get this food to the band right away. The boss man sent Pablo and me to find you." We follow him to the back of the van.

"Help us, then. Here," he says as he hands us trays of food. The other guy pulls out another tray and we all head for the back entrance of the club. I knock as if I own the place and think if we can pull this off, it'll be a miracle.

Some big guy with tats all over his arms answers the door. "Catering," I tell him.

He scans us and then opens the door wide to let us in. I'm completely at a loss as to where to go, so I wing it.

"Not there, you idiot!" some skinny white geek with slicked-back hair cries out as I find an empty room to set the tray down. "It's for the band!"

I follow the geek down a brightly lit hallway to a door with a star on it. He opens the door and I'm suddenly face-to-face with none other than Atticus Patton. He's wearing black jeans and a T-shirt with the band's name on it. His jet-black hair is spiked in the back and the front covers half his face, his signature look in every Shadows of Darkness video. The rest of the band is here, too, sitting on the couches, completely chilling. It's so surreal being in their presence, I almost drop the tray.

"It's about time, man," Atticus says in a lazy drawl. "We're fuckin' starving."

I set the tray down on an empty table while Pablo and the caterers follow suit. Pablo looks uncomfortable, like he fears being caught.

"Thanks, guys," the geek says as he takes out his wallet and hands all four of us twenty-dollar bills.

The caterers look confused as to why Pablo and I would get tipped, but they shrug and leave the room.

Not one to be shy, I walk up to Atticus. "I'm a big fan," I say. "Your song 'Fight for It' got me through a rough time."

He smiles. "Glad to hear it, man. What's your name?"

"Ryan. And this is Pablo," I say, gesturing to my friend.

"Nice to meet you, guys." He holds out a hand for me to shake. "Hey, you guys can stay and watch the show if you want. Unless you got more deliveries."

Pablo and I look at each other, then back at Atticus. "No more deliveries," Pablo mumbles.

I clear my throat. "Um, yeah, that was our last delivery. It'd be awesome to see the show, man."

Atticus nods to the skinny dude. "Brian, get them some passes," he orders.

Brian waves for us to follow him through the corridor. I think we're about to be busted when I see Mop Head walk by, but luckily he's focused on texting someone on his phone and doesn't notice us. We're led past security guards to the massive crowd gathering in front of the stage. The place is packed.

When Brian leaves us in the front row, I glance behind me at the massive number of people here. It's standing room only. I nudge Pablo. "This is fucking amazing."

"For who?" Pablo eyes the oversize speakers so close we can touch them. "Um . . . Ry, I think we're too close."

"No. This is perfect, man."

The crowd starts roaring as the lights go off and the opening band sets up. It's a lesser-known punk band called Psyclones. It isn't long before the stage lights burst with a flash of bright colors. The crowd moves even closer and we're practically on top of each other, but I don't care. The floor is vibrating to the beat and I'm fist-pumping and jumping to the music. Usually I'm reserved and shut down, but this music seeps into my soul.

Pablo shakes his head and seems amused, as if he can't believe how much I'm letting go.

The lead singer of Psyclones is singing to someone on the other side of the stage. I follow his gaze and see a Latina girl with long, brown hair with a blue streak who looks like she's having the best time. She's got two friends with her and all of them are smiling and enjoying the punk music.

I grab Pablo by the elbow and point to the girls through the crowd. "See? Mexicans enjoy punk music," I tell him.

He shrugs. "They're hot *chicas*, but they must be *loco*."

Loco? I don't think so. I glance over at the girl with blue-streaked hair. She's jumping up and down to the music, completely uninhibited, as if she doesn't have a care in the world. I can't take my eyes off her.

After Psyclones is done with their set, the place goes dark again and the energy in the room picks up a notch in anticipation of Shadows of Darkness.

"Can we leave now?" Pablo asks. "I think that girl over there with the spider tattoo on her face just grabbed my ass. I feel violated."

I raise a brow. "Violated?"

"Did you take a look at her? Dude, I'm afraid of spiders. Can you imagine kissing her and opening your eyes to a giant spider tat up close and personal?" He pretends to gag. "I wouldn't be complaining if we were standing next to those hot Latinas you pointed to on the other side of the stage."

"Then let's go," I tell him, but before we can push our way over to the other side, bursts of colorful flames appear and Shadows of Darkness is on the stage.

Atticus Patton is at the foot of the stage, holding the microphone tightly.

"Yo, Texas!" he screams at the top of his lungs and the crowd goes wild.

The drummer starts playing a beat and then Atticus starts singing "Chaos," a song about a guy whose mind races at night with random thoughts.

My head starts bangin' and my world starts shakin'. Atticus's voice rises above the fast beat of the music.

As if the song inspires the crowd into chaos, suddenly everyone clears a spot in front of the stage and a mosh pit forms with guys who are willing to get bumped and pushed around. It doesn't scare me. It's more like a challenge. I'm immediately tempted to get in the middle of the chaos.

Chaos!

What the fuck is wrong with me, these thoughts of mine don't let me be.

Chaos!

I nudge Pablo and gesture to the mosh pit. He takes one glance at the crush of fans violently bashing into each other and his eyes go wide. "Hell to the no!" he says.

When the crazy comes out, that's when I'm free!

Fuck the rules, fuck society!

"We're going in," I yell to Pablo over the pounding music.

He shakes his head, but in that instant, someone pushes him into the mosh pit. I shove my way in there, too, thriving on the mass of people just letting go. Atticus Patton is right. To hell with convention and rules. Who cares about the danger. Life is about being crazy and losing your inhibitions.

Pablo goes from being cautious to laughing as he gets jostled from one end of the sweaty mosh pit to another. We're a bunch of stupid, crazy guys, taking it to the brink of danger. This mosh pit is not for the weak-hearted, but as I glance into the center of the pit I notice a girl is tossed in the fray.

The girl with the blue streak in her hair.

Oh, shit.

This isn't good. She bumps into a guy and is practically catapulted into the air on contact. She's got to be terrified with guys twice her size crashing into her.

Someone's got to save her, and while my motto is "fuck being a hero," I'm not about to watch a girl get hurt or killed because some idiot decided to shove her into a mosh pit.

I rush through the rowdy crowd, heading for the girl before she gets trampled on.

It's time to play the hero for once.

SIX

Dalila

The people in the mosh pit are sweaty and loud. They're jumping around like they're being electrocuted.

And I'm loving it!

This was worth sneaking into my house and grabbing my passport without permission.

Atticus Patton is screaming the lyrics as if he wants the entire state of Texas to hear him . . . and Mexico, too. I was watching the mosh pit from the sidelines, but then I decided to join in the fun. At home I play the perfect daughter. Here, I can be anyone. I'm getting tossed around in the chaos, but it just makes me feel free and wild.

Until I'm halted by an iron grip on my waist. Suddenly I'm

whisked out of the pit by some jerk with rock-hard biceps and a solid wall of a chest.

What the—

When he sets me down I whip myself around and am met with the bluest eyes I've ever seen. A satisfied smile is plastered on his perfectly chiseled face. What does he think, that because he's cute he can pick me up like I'm some rag doll?

He leans down and says loudly, "You can thank me later."

Thank him? "For what?" I yell over the music.

"Saving you."

A chuckle escapes my mouth. Saving me? Is he kidding? I'm so annoyed my first instinct is to chastise him in my native language. "I don't need saving, *pendejo!*" I declare with irritation laced in my voice. "I can take care of myself, Mr. America."

He just stands there as if he's suddenly frozen in time.

Not wanting to miss more of the fun, I push past him and fling myself back into the mosh pit. Atticus is singing the next song, one about celebrating your uniqueness called "This Is Me."

This is me, I'm not gonna change for you.

Take me as I am or I'll find someone new.

Being flung from side to side somehow releases all the stress I've been feeling lately. Stress from my parents to make the right decision on my future, stress because I don't know if I can meet their expectations, stress because I want to make up for Lucas not being here anymore to ease their pain.

Suddenly they start singing "One Night in Crazy." I close my eyes and try to remember what it was like in the car with my brother. I remember him always tapping the dashboard as if he was playing drums and encouraging me to join in. Between songs, he used to tell me about his hopes and dreams of becoming a doctor. He wanted to help others who couldn't help themselves. I took on that role after he died.

One Night in Crazy was all it took,
You stole my soul with just one look.

When the song ends, I leave the pit and head for the bar area. "Hey," a dorky guy with short-cropped hair and a round face says to me. "This concert is insane!"

"It is," I agree.

He leans down. "I'm Skyler," he yells in my ear so loud my eardrum starts ringing. He's got short legs and his stocky build reminds me of a cartoon character.

"I'm Dalila."

I'm bobbing my head to the music as I wait for the bartender to come over so I can order something to drink. My mouth is so dry I'm seriously tempted to reach across the bar and chug water directly from the tap.

I wave at the bartender but there are so many people crowding around he doesn't notice me. Ugh.

"I've been trying to get a beer for five minutes," Skyler says. "Can I buy you one?"

I shake my head and point to my hand, the one that doesn't have an OVER 21 stamp on it. "Just a *Coca* for me," I tell him. "If the guy ever comes over here."

Craning my neck, I see Soona at the other end of the club talking with the same guy she's been chatting with for the past twenty minutes. Her eyes are bright and attentive and she laughs heartily at something he says. She's definitely having a good time.

Demi is catching the attention of the Shadows of Darkness guitarist, who's smiling down at her from the stage like she's a goddess. He probably thinks she's going to be some groupie that'll go backstage with him, but he'll be sorely mistaken. Demi might be a major flirt, but she's not into one-night stands or hookups.

Skyler taps me on the shoulder. "Here," he says, handing me a clear plastic cup. "Coke, right?"

I nod and take the drink from him. "Thank you."

"Do you live around here?" he asks.

"Not really."

"Me, either." He takes a swig of his beer, and then I feel his hand on the small of my back. I take a small step away from him to create some distance. "I drove down from Nevada with some of my frat brothers. We're staying at a hotel around the corner."

"Cool." As I lift the cup to my mouth, that guy with the blue eyes who rudely whisked me out of the mosh pit rushes up to me and bats the *Coca* out of my hand. It flies in the air and the contents splash all over me.

"What the hell is wrong with you?" I yell, then look down at my drenched outfit.

"Yeah, man," Skyler says, puffing up his chest like a peacock ready for a brawl. "She's with me."

Before I can blink, Mr. America's fist connects with Skyler's jaw.

The guy stumbles backward and falls to the floor.

"Are you insane?" I yell at Mr. America as I clumsily push him away.

"He slipped something into your drink," Mr. America says in a calm, steady voice.

"What?" I glare at Skyler, who's still on the ground. "Did you?"

Skyler's eyes are wide now as he presses his palm to his reddening cheek. "I didn't put anything in your drink! I swear!"

"Dude, I fucking saw you!" Mr. America grabs Skyler's collar and pulls him up. "Stay here," he growls through gritted teeth. "I'm calling security."

Panic settles in my chest as I look over at the security detail. Oh no! I recognize one of them as Gerardo, a bodyguard who my papá hires for parties and corporate events. I can't be questioned by him. What if he tattles on me to my father that I crossed the border without permission? I'll be in so much trouble. As soon as Mr. America turns to summon security, I put my hand over his mouth.

"Don't do that," I tell him.

He pushes my hand away. "Why not?"

"Because it's not a big deal."

"It's not a big deal that he was about to drug you?" he questions.

"Forget it."

With our attention diverted, Skyler runs through the exit doors and disappears.

Mr. America swears under his breath. "Looks like you don't

know how to take care of yourself as much as you think you do," he tells me.

I poke my finger into his chest. "You need to—" I stop talking because out of the corner of my eye I see Gerardo pushing through the crowd, heading toward us. Onlookers are circling us now, soaking up the drama that just unfolded.

I'm trying to find a way out of this mess and to ditch the attention, but it's no use. A uniformed officer is blocking my path. He's a big guy with sharp eyes and a pointy nose.

"What's going on here?" he asks in a gruff voice.

"Nothing." I grab Mr. America's hand and lean into him to shield my face from Gerardo. "Right, baby?"

"Right," Mr. America replies in a monotone voice.

The officer lingers for a minute. In an attempt to urge him to leave, I rise up on my tiptoes. Praying Mr. America plays along, I bury my hands in his thick hair and touch my lips to his. I'm determined to make this make-out session look convincing.

Instead of repulsion, the touch of his soft but firm lips against mine sends delicious sensations zinging up my spine. I've kissed boys before, but I've never felt goose bumps all over like this. It feels too nice and comforting. It's obvious this boy is not an amateur in the kissing department.

When we come up for air, his eyes are locked on mine. I'm barely aware that the officer is gone and Gerardo's attention is elsewhere. I clear my throat and let out a long, slow breath to make my heart stop racing from that amazing kiss. For a second I forget where I am, until I hear Atticus singing again.

Death is knocking at my door,
Don't you come around no more.

"Isn't this convenient," a girl with bright red hair snarls at us. She eyes our hands that are still entwined. "Just a little piece of advice," she says to me over the music. "He only does one-night stands. In the morning this loser will dump you and never look back."

Mr. America takes his hand from mine. He looks less than thrilled to be in this girl's presence. "Mikayla, we're not—"

"We're not a one-night stand," I interrupt him, then grab his elbow affectionately. "Because we've been dating for two months and we're planning on going to college together."

Before he can respond, Mikayla laughs heartily. "College? Ha! That's a good one." With her giggle still lingering in the air, she leaves us to join a bunch of her friends witnessing our interaction.

"Now we're even," I tell Mr. America as I take my hand off his arm. "You saved me from that guy who spiked my drink and I saved you from that mean girl."

"You're wrong," he says in a husky tone. "I helped you hide from that security guard over there and distract the cop. It's obvious you're hiding from the law. Are you considered armed and dangerous?" he teases.

I push my shoulders back and stick my chin out, attempting to project an air of confidence. I'm trying not to focus on his soft, full lips that were on mine a minute ago. "You don't know what you're talking about. I'm not hiding from anyone."

He leans on the bar stool and crosses his arms on his chest like he doesn't have a care in the world. "Then why'd you kiss me?"

Come up with something quickly, Dalila. "I thought you'd be a good kisser," I tell him, then add, "but I was wrong."

With that, I turn on my heel and weave through the crowd. My heart is thumping as fast as the beat of the music. When I find Soona, she's still talking to that same guy she's been attached to all night. *"Dios mío,* are you okay?" she asks in a worried tone as I find a spot next to her. "Your clothes are soaked! And your face is all flushed."

"I'm fine," I lie. I'm beyond embarrassed that my heart is still racing from that kiss. "I just need some air."

SEVEN

Ryan

I was on my way to the bar when I saw the dude at the bar slip something into her drink. I practically shoved everyone out of my way so I could get to her before she chugged it. Instead of making sure the jerk got arrested, she protested. It was obvious when I waved security over that she was hiding something.

Then she kissed me.

I've kissed my share of girls before, but those full, sweet lips woke something in me that I thought was dead a long time ago. Maybe it's this place and the crazy concert. This entire night has been surreal.

I glance across the sea of people and see Pablo waving me over. When I manage to get closer to him, I realize my mistake. Pablo is talking to the blue-striped-haired girl and her friends.

I settle next to them but immediately feel all eyes on me.

"Who are you?" her friend asks as if I'm intruding on their private discussion

"It's cool," Pablo tells her. "He's my friend. Ry, this is Soona and her friend Dalila." He points to a girl a few feet away. "And that's Demi."

The girl with the blue-streaked hair, Dalila, won't even look at me when Atticus starts singing "Lost but Not Forgotten." It's like I've suddenly turned invisible.

You may be gone, you're far away.
God's angel, don't let me go astray!
Memories of you will never leave,
This heart is yours every day I grieve.

"Dalila, are you okay?" her friend Soona asks her.

Dalila shrugs. "This song reminds me of Lucas." She swipes at her eyes. "I need to get out of here," she says.

Pushing past us, Dalila heads for the exit.

"Dalila, wait!" Soona calls out, but Dalila doesn't turn back. After flashing an apologetic glance at Pablo, Soona rushes after her friend.

"I forgot to ask Soona for her number," he tells me.

The last thing I want to do is be accused of stalking the chick. "I'm not following those girls."

"Come on, man." Pablo puts a hand on my shoulder. "You're my wingman. You're my crew. You're my—"

"Fine. Just get her number and we're out."

He raises a brow. "What's the problem, Hess? You don't want to talk to her friend Dalila? She's cute."

"Not my type," I blurt out.

"What is your type?"

I glance at the girl with the spider tat on her face. "That."

He laughs. "Arachnid Girl? I don't think so."

Outside, we see all three girls standing by the streetlamp talking to each other. Soona smiles wide when she eyes Pablo. I'm standing here with my hands in my pockets trying to act cool. The attempt doesn't go smoothly, especially when Mikayla Harris walks by with her group of friends and sneers at me.

When I look up, Dalila's eyes meet mine. I immediately look away and tap Pablo on the shoulder. "Let's go, man," I tell him. "Now." I'm not about to have Mikayla call me out in front of everyone.

After Soona and Pablo exchange numbers, Dalila whisks her friends away from the venue. But just because the girl is out of my sight doesn't mean I stop replaying that kiss in my mind. On the ride home Pablo won't stop talking about Soona and how amazing she is.

"I'm glad you made me go to Shadows of Death tonight."

"Shadows of Darkness," I correct him.

"Whatever. I might have met the girl of my dreams," he says. "Soona was great, wasn't she?"

"Sure, man. Whatever you say."

"Maybe you can date one of her friends." His eyes light up. "Wouldn't that be cool?"

"No. Get out of the car."

"You liked that girl with the blue-streaked hair," he says. "I saw the way you were lookin' at her. I haven't seen you look at any girl like that."

"You don't know what you're talking about. I think you had too much to drink tonight."

"I didn't have anything to drink, man." With an amused laugh, Pablo steps out of my car and I head home. This entire night was like a Shadows of Darkness song—chaos and a total mess.

In the morning, Paul confronts me the second I step foot downstairs. "Where are you going?" he asks. He's wearing his uniform, but I don't know if he's even working today. The guy would sleep in it if he could.

"The gym," I tell him.

"He thinks he's Muhammad Ali," pimply Allen calls out in a nasally voice as he sits on his ass in the family room. The kid hardly moves off the couch and his diet mainly consists of sugar and processed foods.

"Yeah," PJ chimes in.

I don't even respond, because I don't need to get into it with them. Especially in front of Paul. "Where's my mom?"

"Out," Paul says. "Come into the kitchen, Ryan. I need to talk to you." I hear the thud of his shoes on the hardwood floor as he walks into the kitchen.

I follow him into the kitchen and lean against the counter.

"Sit down," he orders. I can tell this little meeting isn't going to be fun. "I got you a summer job," Paul says. "At the Johnsons' farm. You'll be working in the fields and cleaning up after their cattle."

"I'm not working at the Johnsons' farm," I tell him.

"Yeah, you are. I already confirmed it," Paul says as he pushes his glasses up the bridge of his nose. "Five days a week, five in the morning till two in the afternoon."

Is he kidding me? Paul got Allen an internship at his uncle's law firm and PJ is going to be working at the police station with him. He gets me a job shoveling shit all summer. "Somehow you think you can just boss me around and I'll be okay with it," I tell him. "I'm not."

"I'm the boss of this entire town, you ungrateful *bastard*."

Time to drop the bomb. "I'm going to Mexico to train."

"For what? Bein' a loser? No," Paul drawls in his exaggerated Texas accent. "This is my house, and as long as you're livin' in it you do what I say."

"I won't be living in it this summer," I tell him.

"Ryan, stop pretending like boxing is going to get you somewhere. It's time to face reality."

Boxing is the only thing I got, but telling him that won't do any good. "I need to do it, to see where it'll take me."

Paul sneers. "It'll take you to the trailer park where you came from. Do you know where your father is, Ryan?" He braces both hands on the table and leans toward me. "He's in jail, Ryan. For *life*. You want to know what he's in for?"

I shake my head. "No."

"Well, I'm gonna tell you. He killed someone, shot him in a bar fight."

I really didn't need to know that.

"You're just like him," he spits out. "Your grades are shit and you won't get into college. You're gonna get some girl pregnant and leave her stranded like your dad did to your mother. Or you'll get married but get your head bashed in from boxing, leaving your wife and kids to take care of your ass."

His words bring back memories of one of my mom's boyfriends who used me as his personal punching bag when I was little.

My hands ball into fists and my entire body goes numb. Luckily the front door creaks open and I hear my mom's voice. She's home.

I leave Paul standing in the kitchen and meet her at the door. "Mom," I say. "I can't do this anymore. Did you know Paul set up a job for me to shovel crap this summer?"

She's clutching a brown bag with alcohol in it. "I have a pounding headache, Ryan." She groans. "Give me an hour, then we'll talk."

"You don't have a headache, Mom. You've got a hangover."

She tries to shoo me away with her hand. I'm used to it, so it doesn't affect me anymore. I remember when I was ten and came to her bed to tell her my stomach hurt and I felt sick. She told me I'd feel better if I went to school. I did, only to puke in the middle of Ms. Strasser's classroom. That just made me more of an outcast.

"I'm going to live in Mexico this summer and train at a gym there," I blurt out.

"Whatever," she says. "Do what you want."

She walks into the kitchen, signaling our conversation is over. I rush to my room and quickly shove a bunch of clothes into a duffel along with every last dime I've saved over the years.

This is my last hope in trying to prove that I'm not a loser like my father.

Failure is not an option.

EIGHT

Dalila

It's been a week since I've been back from Texas, officially dubbed the weirdest night of my life. Soona and Demi freaked out when they found out I was almost drugged and that Pablo's friend knocked the drink out of my hand. I loved the concert and the feeling of being reckless and free, but I wish I hadn't been so oblivious to Skyler's creepy motives. I should have been more observant so I didn't have to rely on some guy to save me.

Now I'm back home in Mexico in my same, boring routine.

The sweet smell of Mamá's homemade *chorizo* wakes me up. I look at my cell and realize it's only six o'clock. With my pajamas still on, I stumble into the kitchen. *Chorizo* is cooking on the stove while Mamá is rolling *albóndigas* into little balls. A hefty amount of random ingredients on the kitchen counter is a clue that she'll be cooking all day.

Mamá likes to cook, but this is not normal.

I sit at the kitchen island and take in the huge spread. "What's all this food for?"

"Cooking for your *familia* is important, Dalila," Mamá replies.

"You don't cook like this every day. Something's going on."

"When my husband's stomach is full," she says, "his stress goes down."

"Stress?" I had woken up in the middle of the night and seen Papá's light on in his study, but I hadn't thought anything of it. He rarely talks about his work or his clients, so as usual I'm clueless. "Is everything okay?"

"Everything is fine, *mija*." She expertly shreds some *pollo* for *sopa* and tosses it in a big pot. "He's taken on a new client and is preparing for a deposition."

"New client?" I pick up some *masa* and water to help make tortillas. "Is it someone famous?"

Mamá closes the door to the kitchen and says in a low voice, "It's a high-profile case."

"Who is it? Does it have to do with that heated discussion he had with Don Cruz?"

She doesn't answer. "Dalila, you just worry about being a role model to your sisters. Did you hear back from the university yet? You know you must score high on tests in order to get into medical school. If you slip even a little, your chances won't be good."

The stress of my parents' high expectations makes my stomach tie in knots. "I know. I'll make you proud."

She looks satisfied as she hands me a cup of water. "Of course you will."

I wash my hands in our large sink and the blue dishwashing liquid reminds me of Ryan's eyes.

Ugh, I don't want to think of him.

Ever since I came back, little memories of that night in Texas flash through my brain. I can't seem to shake the image of us kissing as I fall asleep each night. What was I thinking, making him kiss me so intimately? It was an impulse and I regret it.

Mamá hands me a tray of *chorizo con huevos*. "Bring this to your father. Maybe you can get him to eat."

"Yes, Mamá."

I find Papá in his office talking on the phone to someone. His dark hair is graying and his wrinkles are more deeply set than I can remember. As soon as I step into the room, he tells the person on the other end of the line that he'll call them back.

I place the tray on his desk. "Mamá said you need to eat. She's worried about you."

He smiles warmly. "No need to be worried, *cariño*. Everything is *perfecto*."

"I seem to remember you telling me that nothing in life is perfect, Papá." I sit on the edge of his desk and glance at the name on the file in front of him. Santiago Vega. My body stiffens. I read online that Santiago Vega, a businessman with suspected ties to the cartels, was arrested. My brain has a hard time wrapping around the fact that Papá has a file with his name on it. "Please tell me you're not representing Santiago Vega."

"I can't do that."

"Why would you work to help a criminal connected to *Las Calaveras* cartel?"

"You know I can't discuss my clients, *mija*." He takes off his glasses and rubs his forehead as if this conversation is giving him a headache. "I understand you're going to some boxing gym with Rico Cruz. You sure you want to go? I can call and cancel for you."

I know he changed the subject on purpose, but it doesn't make me feel any better.

"Of course I want to go with Rico, Papá. It'll be fun. Don't worry about me."

He kisses the top of my head. "I worry about all of my girls."

"I know. And we love you for it." I kiss him on his cheek and leave him to his work, not expressing the fact that I worry about him, too. Especially if he's going to represent a guy like Santiago Vega.

In the hallway ten minutes later, out of the corner of my eye I see Coco tiptoeing around the main corridor. My little twin sisters are mischievous and when Lola isn't watching they can definitely get themselves into a heap of trouble.

"Coco, what are you doing?" I call out.

She tries to hide her face. "*Nada*."

I grab her hand and lead her into my bedroom when I notice her face looks like it's been painted on. "Why are you wearing makeup?"

"To look pretty."

I kneel down and take her hand in mine. "Coco, you don't need makeup. You're naturally pretty with your big brown eyes and that sweet, bright smile. Where did you find makeup?"

She swings her arms back and forth. "It's a secret."

I raise a brow. "Where's Galena?"

Coco bats her mascara-clumped eyelashes. "She *might* be in our bedroom."

"Mamá won't be happy if you took her makeup without her permission."

"Umm . . . it *might* be your makeup, Dalila." Her big eyes go wide while her chubby little hands tug at her skirt. "But I didn't do it."

"Uh-huh. I'll give you and Galena sixty seconds to bring it all back."

She runs out of the room as I start counting. The patter of her bare feet on the ceramic tile echoes through the house.

While I wait for my sisters to come back with their stolen stash, my cell buzzes. It's Rico, informing me that he's five minutes away from my house. He's taking me to the gym to show off his fighting skills, but to be honest it's a way for me to just let some steam off.

I need to get out more. Even though we live on a huge estate, I feel claustrophobic here.

As I get dressed in shorts and a tank, Galena sets an armload of my makeup on my dresser. "This was in our room."

"Really?" I ask. "How did it get there?"

She shrugs. Her little accomplice, who's standing beside her, also shrugs.

I urge the girls to sit on the edge of my bed and I squat down so we're face-to-face. "I don't mind you playing with my makeup, but next time you need to ask. Or let me do it and we can have a makeup party." I reach out and ruffle the hair on top of their heads. "I won't tell Mamá about this," I say and relief floods their eyes. "But no more sneaking into my room and taking my things. You got it?"

Coco nods wildly.

"We got it," Galena agrees.

"We're sorry, Dalila," Coco chimes in.

"One more thing. You two are both unique and beautiful. You don't need makeup to feel pretty. Now go wash off your faces before Mamá or Lola sees you and makes you take another shower."

With that, they slink out of my room as if they're on a secret mission to hide from anyone who's going to make them shower again.

Rushing downstairs, I dash into the kitchen. Lola is frying the fresh tortillas I started to make this morning. The smell makes my mouth water. "Where's Mamá?"

"On the backyard balcony," she says.

I step onto the balcony and find her looking across at the fields behind our house. Her brow is furrowed and she looks worried. "Mamá, I'm going out with Rico."

She nods. "Your father told me."

"Is everything okay?"

"Of course. Just . . . be careful."

"I will."

I don't know why she's acting so distant, but since Lucas died there are times she retreats into herself. Sometimes it lasts for weeks and Papá says it's best to leave her alone instead of trying to comfort her.

"I'm here if you need me," I say softly.

"I know."

Back inside, I check myself in the hallway mirror. I don't have any makeup on and my hair is up in a ponytail. It's not like I have to dress up to hang out with an old friend to go boxing.

A few minutes later I find Rico sitting on one of the benches in the foyer waiting for me. "You ready?" he asks as he eyes me appreciatively.

He's wearing tight jeans and a button-down designer shirt, and his hair is perfectly spiked up as if he's going to a modeling photo shoot. He looks totally unprepared to be working out in a boxing ring, but that's typical Rico. Fashion before practicality.

"Umm . . . did you bring workout clothes?" I ask him. "We *are* going to a boxing club, aren't we?"

The side of his mouth quirks up. "Of course. I *always* dress like this when I go out."

I could never seriously date a guy who cares more about his appearance than I do. While I just threw something on, Rico probably planned out exactly what he'd wear the minute we made plans to do this.

In the car Rico turns on the radio and stares straight ahead. When we reach the main road and leave La Joya de Sandoval behind us, he rests his arm on the back of my headrest. The gesture is a bit too cozy and I wonder if he's still dating that girl he was seeing last year. I'm almost afraid to ask because he'll think I'm hitting on him.

"I've got to make a stop in Nuevo Laredo to drop something off at my cousin's place," he says as if it's no big deal. "It'll be a nice drive. His place is empty, so we can hang there before I take you to Sevilla."

At first I think he's playing a joke on me, but no. He's completely serious. "Rico, I'm not going with you to Nuevo Laredo."

He looks at me sideways. "Don't tell me you're not up for a little adventure."

What have I gotten myself into? "The only adventure I want is a boxing lesson in Sevilla, Rico." I hold my cell phone in my lap, knowing that I can call Papá to come get me if I need to ditch Rico. "I thought we were going straight to the gym."

"Plans changed. Don't worry your pretty little head, *chica*. It's just a quick side trip."

He turns off the main road, heading for the highway leading to Nuevo Laredo.

"Rico, take me to the gym," I say. "I'm not comfortable going to Nuevo Laredo."

"I'll protect you," he says, opening the middle console and revealing a pistol as if that's all the protection we need. "Believe me, nobody will mess with us."

What happened to the guy I once knew? We used to play card games and hide in the fields in the back of my house. Now Rico's into showing off his money and guns. I gesture to the pistol. "Is that supposed to make me feel better?"

He chuckles. "Kind of. What, having an *hombre* fight for you isn't your idea of a good date?"

His words remind me of Ryan, who didn't need a gun. He had his fists.

"I hate guns." I shake my head, hoping that he'll get the hint that I'm serious. "If you want to go to Nuevo Laredo, take me home."

He sighs loudly, then turns the car around and heads back to the main road. "Okay, you win. You used to be more adventurous."

"I'm adventurous."

A flash of humor crosses his face. "What was the last crazy thing you did?"

"I . . . crossed the border and went to a punk concert. My parents had no clue I went. Is that crazy enough for you?"

He nods. "That's on the low end of crazy. I can take you to some wild places if you're ever up for it."

"The Panche festival is coming up. I'm going with a couple of friends who can definitely get adventurous. You should meet up with us."

He nods. "Sounds like a plan."

I peer out the window at the bright sun dancing on the ceramic rooftops of the small houses we're passing. They remind me of the house my *abuela* lives in. It's small but feels so cozy. At least from what I remember. I haven't seen her in years.

The car is quiet when I decide to bring up what's been on my mind since his parents were at my house. "Do you know anything about Santiago Vega?"

He stills. "No," he answers tentatively. "Why?"

"I don't know. I was watching the news and saw that he'd been arrested. I think my dad might be representing him and I thought maybe you'd know something about him."

He shrugs. "I don't know anything."

But I get the feeling he does and he just won't share it with me.

Ten minutes later we reach the gym. It's situated in Sevilla, a small town in the mountains hidden from civilization. We pass one small *mercado* on the way, the only store for miles. The town is small and a few people are mingling outside, but it's mostly barren. Rico seems like a guy who's not afraid of anything. Or a guy who thinks a gun can solve all conflicts. I think he suffers from too much confidence.

"You sure it's safe here?" I ask Rico.

He shoves the pistol into a gym bag. "*Sí.*"

"Then why do you have a gun?"

"Because I don't want to leave it in the car for it to get stolen. It's all good. Come on." He leads me across the dirt parking lot to a big warehouse. "Hey, *cariño*. Are you ready to prove to me how tough you are?"

"Definitely. And if you call me *cariño* again, I'm gonna knock you out."

"Ha." He wags his brows. "If I go down, you're going down with me."

NINE

Ryan

Crossing the border into Mexico in my rusty old Mustang was easy. The border patrol dude at the checkpoint asked for my passport but hardly glanced at it. As usual, the border cops let people out of the US without much of a problem. I better not lose my passport while I'm in Mexico, though, because entering the US is another issue altogether.

I drive my car through Mexico feeling like I've abandoned everything I've ever known. I've never driven this far into the country before. At first the buildings and roads look just like what we have back in Texas.

As I drive farther, things start to change.

I look out the window and see people with carts selling eggs and buckets of fruit on the side of the road. One guy wearing overalls and a cowboy hat is selling avocados as big as a grapefruit. I guess I shouldn't be surprised considering that Mexico is the avocado capital of the world.

The weather is the same as in Texas. Heat permeates through my windshield from the brutally hot sun, a stinging reminder that my air conditioning has been out since I bought the thing. I suddenly long for the cold Chicago winters. It's too damn hot here and I feel like I'm gonna melt. Staring out the window, I watch in fascination at the lone tumbleweeds rolling over the land like little runaway straw bowling balls.

I follow the detailed directions Mateo gave me and end up at a bar called Mamacita's. I look down at the directions, then at the bar. Yep, this is the place.

Stepping out into the hot sun, I take in the town. It's got everything, from small grocery stores to *taquerias* and shops.

As I cross the threshold into Mamacita's, all eyes turn to me. My entire body is on alert as I scan the clientele. The place resembles an old-time saloon you'd see in the movies, complete with rugged guys playing cards and others getting plastered at the bar. It doesn't escape my attention that a handful of them are wearing pistols, but I've gotten used to that since I moved to Texas. In Chicago, you don't see guns unless it's on a cop or you're unfortunate enough to find yourself smack-dab in the middle of a shoot-out.

"Hey, Ryan. Come over here!" Mateo calls out from the corner of the bar. He's sitting with a few other guys who are glaring at me as if I'm some narc. "Glad you came." He checks his watch. "You're early. I like that."

"Where's Camacho?" I ask him.

"Whoa, slow down." Mateo waves over a female bartender. "What do you want to drink, Ryan?"

"I'm good."

"Sit down," he says with a grin. "Relax awhile."

"Listen, man. I'm not here to relax; I'm here to train." I gesture to the half-empty bottle of beer in front of him. "If you want to give me directions to the gym, I'll go myself."

He sits back in his chair and crosses his arms. "You, my friend, probably have the biggest *cojones* out of everyone I know." He nods to a beefy guy sitting across from him. "Including Chago over here."

"Why?" the guy named Chago asks.

"This guy challenged me to a boxing match," he explains. "And won. That's more than any one of you could do." Nobody disagrees. "So now I'm taking him to Sevilla for a chance to train with Camacho." Mateo downs the rest of his beer before slamming the empty bottle on the table. "Let's go, Hess. I'm a little plastered, so I'll let you drive."

In my car, Mateo rocks out to some kind of Mexican rap music as he directs me on which way to go.

"You sure you know where we're goin'?" I ask as he motions for me to turn off on a dirt road leading to the mountains.

"*Sí, amigo.*"

"You know I don't speak Spanish."

Mateo shrugs. "You've got to learn at some point. You're in Mexico now. Pay someone to give you lessons."

"With what money?" I think of the two hundred and sixty

dollars I have in my pocket, my entire life savings after I shelled out money for a cheap-ass cell phone. "I'm almost broke. If I don't get a fight soon, I'll be out on the streets damn quick."

"I already told you. You want to be the best fighter and make *dinero*, you're not gonna do it training in the US," Mateo says. "You want to be the best, you train with the best. Even if Camacho doesn't train you, stick with me and I'll find someone here in Mexico who'll take you to the top."

"Why are you helping me?" I ask. "You don't owe me shit, Mateo."

"The truth?"

I nod.

"Because you beat me at my own game. Not many people can do that." He looks out the window and gets serious. "And because I heard your stepfather's a dick and you might need someone to look out for you. Like a brother."

"You've been checkin' up on me?"

He takes his sunglasses off his shirt and puts them on. "Yep."

We keep driving. After a while, the towns are spread apart and we're passing smaller towns with few if any resources. Seeing these poor towns makes me think back to when we were on public assistance for a while. Mom didn't work and we got by on cheap crap food.

But it was food.

And it was free.

To my mom I was someone she had to deal with and feed, not someone she wanted. When I was eight she started leaving me alone so she could go party all night. In junior high, there were times she wouldn't come home the entire weekend, leaving me to fend for myself. I'd watch TV, blaring it so I wouldn't have to hear any scary noises outside our trailer.

"Shit," Mateo blurts out.

I glance in my rearview mirror. A police car is behind us with its lights on and the officer is motioning for me to pull off the road. We aren't near any towns and few cars have passed us as we drive, so I wonder if this is legit.

Mateo says, "It's cool, Ry. Let me do all the talkin'."

I slow to a stop and see two officers step out of the squad car. One is heading for my side. I keep my hands on the wheel as the officer approaches, and grip the wheel tighter when I notice he has a hand on the butt of his gun.

Damn, this is not good.

When he takes his gun and holds it at his side, I mumble under my breath, "I think he's crooked, man."

"You think?" Mateo says sarcastically. "Dude, they're all crooked."

"If he asks me to get out of the car and pulls a gun on me, I'm gonna disarm him before he realizes what's happening."

Mateo holds his hands up. "Whoa, don't get all vigilante on me, Hess. Trust me. We're fine. More than fine."

"*Hola, amigo*," the officer says.

"*Mi amigo no habla español*," Mateo responds. "*El viento está cambiando de dirección oficial, y estamos en el lado correcto.*"

I have no clue what Mateo is saying, but I can tell the officer is backing down the more Mateo talks.

The officer says, "*Dile a tu amigo que quiero dinero en efectivo.*"

Mateo taps me on the shoulder. "Give him a hundred bucks, Hess."

I blink twice. "A hundred bucks? Are you fucking kidding me?" I mumble.

Mateo shakes his head. "Nope. Sorry, man. They want a hundred to let us go."

"But I didn't do anything wrong."

"Consider it an entry fee into *Los Reyes del Norte*'s territory."

I quickly realize that it doesn't matter if I did anything wrong. Some cops straddle both sides of the law here. I reluctantly pull out my wallet and hand the cop a hundred, leaving me with only one-sixty left to my name.

The officer nods. "*Pásale, pero ten cuidado,*" he says, then taps the hood of my car twice before walking to the police cruiser.

Mateo leans back in the passenger seat as if it's a cushy recliner in his living room. "We're good."

"Good? Dude, I'm out a hundred bucks. I'm not good. What did you say to him?"

"I just told them you're a boxer from the US who's training here for the summer."

"And who's *Los Reyes del Norte* and how is this their territory?"

"You ask too many questions, Hess."

I'm on a roll and am not stopping now. "Is *Los Reyes del Norte* some kind of gang?"

"Yeah. A new movement of young guys calling themselves the

Kings of the North and they're recruiting like crazy. They're so powerful if you don't do what they want they'll fuck you up." He shakes his head. "You gotta learn how things work around here, Hess. You're a white boy with Texas plates in the middle of Mexico. That makes you a target. Besides, white boys from the US have a reputation for carrying cash."

"Not anymore I don't. If Camacho won't take what I've got after I pay for a place to stay, I'm screwed."

"I got your back," he assures me.

We pass a bunch of big ranches set between the mountains. Some of them have guards at the entrances, another stark reminder that parts of Mexico can be full of rich people with power and poor people struggling to survive. I guess it's kind of like Texas, or even Chicago, where people on one block live in million-dollar brownstones and on the next block live in housing projects.

"We're almost there," Mateo announces a half hour later as he directs me through a small town with one store and a bunch of old stucco buildings with colorful Mexican architecture.

"The houses here are cool," I tell him.

"Yeah." Mateo gestures to a couple of old men sitting on chairs outside their little houses. Mateo waves as we pass, and they immediately recognize him and wave back. "The guys who live here either work in the fields or retire here because nothing happens. Sevilla is kind of an oasis in the middle of the mountains. It's under nobody's control . . . for now."

"How'd you find it?"

"My *abuelo*, my grandfather, lived here when he was younger. See that building over there?" he asks, pointing to a warehouse with a couple of cars parked outside. "That's the gym."

After parking I grab my duffel from my trunk, ready to start my life here. I'll stay and train until I can move up and make some money fighting before heading back to Texas. The more I learn, the better chance I'll have of getting fights.

I need to stay focused, because I'm not going back to Texas the same way I came here. A loser.

The boxing club is dark and smells like old, stale sweat. The familiar sounds of fists hitting bags and the grunt of guys pushing themselves to their limit permeate the air. I scan the place, attempting to assess each fighter's punch and stance. Most of them are staring at the white boy who once again finds himself the minority. It's no different on the Texas border, where there's a strong Hispanic community.

There's one ring in the middle of the gym where a tall dude is coaching some short guy with skinny legs. "Hit my chest," he's saying. "As hard as you can."

I hold back laughter because this dude has no fucking clue how to train. *Hit my chest as hard as you can?* Is he kidding? While the short dude has protective headgear on, the tall dude has no mitts or gloves and looks like an amateur himself.

"Dude, seriously?" I say to Mateo. The other guys at this place look like they're hard-core fighters. The two in the center ring are a fucking joke.

Mateo shakes his head and leans in close. "Don't ask," he says so nobody else can hear. He doesn't need to worry; the acoustics in this place suck. "Wait here. I'm gonna go find Ocho, the manager."

While he disappears out a side door, I watch as the short kid in the ring tries to throw punches. At one point, he falls to the ground. I can't help but laugh.

The kid glares at me. "What's your problem, *gringo?*" he growls at me, frustrated, as he grabs the ropes to pull himself up.

"The problem is you hit like a girl," I tell him.

"*Eso es porque soy una idiota.*"

He yanks off his headgear and focuses on me.

Damn.

The dude is a girl. And not just any girl. It's Dalila.

Her dark eyes are piercing through mine and she blinks a few times in surprise. There's no doubt in my mind that she remembers me from the concert. I'm trying not to focus on the sheen of sweat that's covering her flawless, perfectly tanned skin.

Her hair is a mess, though. I guess at one point it was in a neat ponytail, but now it's falling down her face with the hairband still holding on to a small clump that refuses to be set free.

"Who the hell are you?" her pseudo-trainer asks.

One thing I know about dealing with fighters, especially ones with overgrown egos, is that you hold back information. Be a mystery, so they're always wondering what you've got up your sleeve. It gives you a little advantage, in and out of the ring.

"I'm nobody, man," I tell him.

"Obviously." He says something in Spanish, some kind of insult, but I don't give a shit. He can insult me all he wants. Maybe this guy is Lucas, the dude she was missing the night I met her.

My skin is as thick as leather. Actually more like bulletproof glass.

Dalila brushes the wayward strands away from her face as she turns from me. She's doing a good job of pretending she has no clue who I am.

While I wait for Mateo to come back, I step closer to the ring to watch the poseur resume "training" her. She's got a determined look on her face as if she's trying to prove something.

"You've got to keep your elbows in," I call out to her.

They stop and look at me.

"Don't you have somewhere else to be?" her pseudo-trainer-slash-boyfriend asks me. "Like building a wall or somethin' like that."

I put my hands up. "Just thought she'd want some pointers from someone who knows what they're talkin' about."

"What did you say?" He stands next to Dalila as if he's claiming her as his. I don't tell him that I'm not looking for any distractions, especially from a bossy girl with major control issues.

I shake my head. "Nothin'. I didn't say anything."

The dude points at me. "Keep it that way."

While I don't mind getting into it with someone, I need to rein it in. I'd like nothing better than to fight this blowhard, but not now. Especially when I see a glimpse of a nine millimeter sticking out of an open bag on the floor.

I'm not looking to get myself shot, at least not on my first night in Mexico.

I step away from the ring and head for Mateo, who just came

back with some old dude by his side.

"This is Ocho; he runs the place. He says Camacho hasn't been here in a few days, but will probably show up at some point."

"What the hell am I supposed to do until then?"

"Listen, I talked to Ocho and explained your situation. I got him to agree to rent one of the back rooms to you. You can live here and take showers in the locker room while you train. He wants a hundred fifty for the month. Up front."

"A hundred fifty?" That'll leave me with ten bucks left over. "I don't know, man."

"It includes access to the gym, twenty-four hours a day. What do you want me to tell him? He don't speak a word of English."

Oh, hell.

In a matter of hours, I went from having hundreds in my pocket to a measly ten bucks.

"I don't have a choice. I'll take it." I don't even know how I'll be able to secure a trainer here for a measly ten bucks. What if Camacho never shows up? This sucks.

"Hey, *Mr. America!*" Dalila calls out.

I stop and turn back to find her leaning over the ropes as she motions me back to the ring. Her sultry lips turn into an inviting grin, making me feel like I'm about to be lured into a trap. "You think you're so good at fighting?" she asks. "Why don't you show me what you got?"

TEN

Dalila

I don't know what it is about Ryan that made me want to call him back. Maybe it was the utter shock at seeing him again. Maybe it's something about his confidence and carefree attitude. He didn't show any emotion when it was obvious Rico was getting annoyed with him. It's like he doesn't care what people think of him.

How can he be so disconnected?

"I don't fight girls," Ryan says matter-of-factly.

Rico is standing beside me now, glaring at him. "You want to go a round with me?" Rico blurts out. "I'm ready whenever you are."

Mr. America shakes his head. "I don't fight amateurs."

"Who you callin' an amateur?" Rico is about to jump down from the ring, but I grab his arm and hold him back.

"Don't," I tell him. "He's just trying to get under your skin."

I can't help but notice Ryan holding back a grin. He's amused instead of scared, which boggles my mind. What guy wouldn't be intimidated by Rico Cruz?

Ryan says something to the guy next to him, who I remember being a bodyguard at one of Demi's parties. His name is Mateo Rodriguez. I can tell by the serious look on Ryan's face they're discussing something pretty intense.

"Listen to me, *gringo*," Rico says. "I don't know who you are or what the hell you're doing here, but this is a Mexican gym. Go back to your country and find your own gym."

"He's cool, Rico," Mateo says. "He's with me."

"I don't care who brought him. Get him out of here."

Ryan picks up a duffel and tosses it over his shoulder. "I'm not going anywhere, so you might as well get used to me." He walks up to the ring and boldly holds out a hand for Rico to shake. "My name's Ryan Hess."

Rico slaps Ryan's hand away. "This is fucked-up."

Ryan's eyes shift to me and my entire body tingles. "You want to see me fight, Dalila? Hang around here long enough and I'll show you what I've got."

When he says my name Rico's eyes go wide. "You know him?"

Umm. "Not really. I briefly met him when I went to Texas last week." If Rico blabs to my parents, I'll be grounded for life. I shoot Ryan a level stare as a hint not to reveal anything else.

"Don't lie, Dalila. We know each other well. *Very* well." Ryan's eyes pierce mine and I feel a tingling sensation all the way down to my toes. "Right, Dalila?"

I refuse to be taunted by him. "I hardly remember meeting you."

"Uh-huh." He starts walking away from the ring. "I seem to remember you kissing me. I might even have a selfie of the magic moment."

He didn't go there! Rico's nostrils are flaring. I grab the ropes hard, wishing it were Ryan's big, fat neck. "I kissed you because I had no other choice!" I yell after him. "And there isn't a selfie."

"No other choice? He forced you? You come back here and I'll fuck you up, *Ryan Hess!*" Rico yells.

Ryan walks cooly out the side door as if he can't be bothered with Rico's threats.

Rico suddenly jumps out of the ring and I panic. "Where are you going?"

"*Ahorita regresó.*"

He disappears through the door Ryan just walked through. "Rico, don't go after him!" I call out, but it's no use. "He didn't force me to kiss him. I wanted to. I mean—"

I'm getting myself into more trouble. Rico is about to challenge Ryan in a misguided attempt to defend my honor. It's so stupid and wrong. I need to stop him!

Rico's confidence is egocentric and stems from being born privileged. Ryan's confidence comes from somewhere else . . . as if he's had to fight for the right to act tough or it's a cover-up so people don't dig into whatever pain he's feeling on the inside.

I shake my head and silently scold myself. Maybe I'm confusing confidence with stupidity.

I glance at the other boxers at the gym. None of them are looking at me because they're too focused. Unlike Rico.

Annoyed at my friend for not listening to my pleas, I head outside to find Rico in Ryan's face. He's telling him to go back to the US where he belongs and never look at me again.

With a set jaw and his hands balled into fists at his side, I can tell Ryan is just biding his time, waiting for the right moment to strike. This is not good.

Walking toward them, I accidentally kick a soda can and stumble. The can makes a rattling noise as it rolls across the ground. I can feel Ryan's gaze on me as I look up . . .

"Fight me," Rico orders.

Ryan turns his attention back to Rico and shakes his head. "Dude, I'm not gonna fight you."

"You scared?"

Ryan walks away. "Sure, that's it. I'm scared. Now go back to your girlfriend before someone else comes along and pays attention to her."

"Don't turn away from me, *gringo*," Rico calls out. "Or you'll regret it."

"Rico, stop trying to fight him!" I yell.

When Rico looks at me like I just betrayed him, I quickly turn around and head for the car. I'm not going to wait around while he continues to threaten Ryan.

Five minutes later Rico appears. As he settles into the front seat, I can't even look at him. "You shouldn't have confronted him," I blurt out.

He grabs the steering wheel so tightly his fingers practically turn white. "Why are you mad at me? I was defending your honor."

"I don't want you to defend my honor, Rico. Did you fight him?"

"No." With a small chuckle, Rico starts the car. "But I'll fight him one day, whether it's in the ring or out of it. I promise you that."

The car tires spin when we drive off, another show-off move. The entire drive I sit silently, not believing that Ryan barged into my life again.

But he did.

"How was your date with Rico?" Mamá asks me when I get home.

"Eventful."

"*Bueno.* I'm glad you had a good time."

I don't tell her that what happened today wasn't fun. When I go to bed in the evening and replay the day's events in my head, a set of very blue eyes invades my thoughts.

Why is Ryan Hess in Mexico? Will I ever see him again?

Fate says yes.

My emotions scream no.

Every year our town puts on a summer festival. Since I was a little girl I've looked forward to the music, dancing, and food. It's great seeing everyone in town dressed up and enjoying themselves. I've been getting ready all morning, waiting for Soona and Demi to call me and let me know when to pick them up so we can join in the celebration.

"Why don't you ask Rico to drive you?" Mamá asks after I ask for her car keys. "It's dangerous to go on your own."

"Nothing's going to happen," I tell her. "It's a festival, not a cartel showdown."

"Sometimes one can turn into the other, Dalila." She snaps her bright red manicured fingers. "Just like that."

"We'll be fine. I promise."

At the festival, I get a rush of adrenaline just from being out of the house. There are red and yellow paper lanterns hanging from the lampposts. Jugglers and clowns in colorful costumes line the streets ready to entertain the kids. Vendors selling their food in kiosks are scattered around the festival. I breathe in the scent of freshly baked tortillas and my mouth waters.

I want to feel free to roam around the festival with my friends but every five minutes I get a text from my parents asking if I'm safe. What do they think, that someone is going to pop out of the crowd and kidnap us?

"Let's get our portraits drawn," Demi says, pointing to an artist selling charcoal drawings of people. She tugs my arm, guiding me to the artist, but my mind isn't on the drawings. I find myself scanning the crowd for someone specific.

Mr. America.

From what it sounded like, Ryan is living in Mexico. Or at the very least he was planning on being here for a while. My thoughts turn to the way he dismissed Rico, as if he couldn't be bothered being threatened by him.

The only plan Ryan lives by is his own. He's completely unpredictable and someone I would never want in my life.

While Demi admires the charcoal portraits and considers getting one, I turn my attention to Soona. She's showing off the outfit she got in Colombia when she traveled there with her parents on vacation last year. It's a stark white top that shows off her midriff and high-waisted blue shorts with white buttons running down the sides. She looks like a cute sailor. Demi opted for skinny jeans with a red skintight top, while I chose my new pink off-the-shoulder sundress I got the last time I was in a boutique in Mexico City.

"We can get our portraits drawn later. Right now I need some *machaca*," I tell my friends, unable to wait to taste the homemade tasty beef stuffed inside a burrito.

Demi and I buy *machaca* from a vendor while Soona chomps down on tasty hot *tamales*.

The celebration marks the anniversary of the founding of Panche. The streets are filled with mariachi singers and expert dancers wearing frilly traditional dresses. My friends and I dance with strangers and have a good time, reveling in the joyous festivities.

I scan the crowd once again, searching for Ryan. I know it's stupid, but my mind keeps wandering to thoughts of him. If I went to the boxing club again, would he be there? I don't even like the guy, so I don't even know why I care.

While my friends walk over to a guy doing a funny puppet show in front of a crowd, I catch sight of Rico and his friends on the other side of the street.

"¡*Señorita!*" a little boy around nine or ten years old calls out to me as I pass him. He's sitting on the curb wearing ripped, dirty clothes and my heart swells with sympathy. "*¿Me puede ayudar con algún cambio?*" he asks me in a soft, vulnerable voice while he holds out his hand, palm up. "*Tengo hambre pero no tengo dinero.*"

I kneel down to his level. "*¿Cómo te llamas?*" I ask, wanting to know his name so I can remember it tonight when I pray for the safety and security of the children of my country. Yes, there are vast differences in social class in Mexico but I hope one day to help bridge that gap so it's not so wide.

"Sergio," he says.

I ask Sergio if he has a home. He swallows, then shakes his head and tells me he stays on the streets most nights.

As I reach into my purse to give him money for food, I look down at the little, innocent, dirty face in front of me. Sergio's eyes show a sadness that tears into my soul. I'm not stupid enough to think there aren't thieves or pickpockets in town, but I can tell when a kid is in need.

Sergio's face lights up when I hand him some *pesos* for food . . . and more to spare. He immediately runs like a miniature rocket to the tamale stand a few feet away.

Rico is suddenly at my side. "You need to be more careful about who you interact with, Doña Sandoval. I have no problem telling your father that you interact with *pordioseros*."

"You, my friend, shouldn't tattle on people."

Rico shrugs. "You're right. So, *my friend*, why haven't you returned my texts and calls?"

I look up at his impeccably styled hair, which shines in the sun. "We didn't exactly end things on a good note the other day."

"I know. I'm sorry, okay? That guy triggered me and I lost it." He takes my elbow and leads me aside. "I promise not to be a jerk again."

I give Rico a small smile. "Okay. But if you fight or threaten anyone, I'm done."

His face softens. "Your dad raised a really independent girl."

Pride rushes to the surface. "Yep."

His friends stand next to him. One of them is laughing loudly and the other has bloodshot eyes. They've definitely been drinking.

"Who's this?" Demi asks in a flirty voice as she focuses on the guys with no small amount of interest. I admit they're an impressive bunch, as if they all jumped out of a Mexican prep school TV ad.

Soona, on the other hand, isn't impressed. She hasn't said anything, but I've caught her texting that Pablo guy she met at the concert. Ryan's friend.

"Guys, this is Rico Cruz. Our dads grew up together."

Rico nods at the girls, flashing his bright white teeth and friendly grin. "You didn't tell me your friends were beautiful, Dalila."

"I didn't?" I joke, trying to lighten the mood. "Well, they are."

Demi holds out her hand for Rico to shake. "I'm Demi," she says.

Soona twirls her long, highlighted hair around her finger as I say, "And this is Soona."

Rico points to one of his friends. "This is David and Marcus."

Rico and his friends hang with us the rest of the time, bringing us food while we sit at the park and listen to the various bands taking turns playing music very different from Shadows of Darkness. It's traditional and I get lost in the moment, wondering if this is what it was like when my parents were younger.

When the sun sets and darkness envelops us, Rico leans in and says, "We're planning on going to an underground club. Join us."

"What kind of club?" I ask.

"If we told you then we'd have to kill you," one of his friends says, then laughs.

"It'll be fun," Rico chimes in. "I promise."

Demi's face lights up. "I'm in," she says. "I've never been to an underground club."

"Sounds scary," Soona says as she bites on a nail. "I've heard underground clubs can be dangerous."

Rico's friend Marcus laughs. "We'll protect you. We know people who know people."

Rico drapes his arm around us. "What he means is that we have a lot of friends meeting us there. It'll be like one big party."

"If we hate it we can leave," I tell Soona, then stand and wipe the dust off my legs. "Let's go!"

ELEVEN

Ryan

I'm a loner, sitting in my tiny little hole of a room at the back of the gym on a Saturday night. The last six dollars I have after buying some food are lying on the floor next to my makeshift bed that consists of old gym mats I found in one of the closets.

I'm surrounded by four white walls in a room with one little window that doesn't do a lick of good. It's so damn hot in Sevilla and the air doesn't move, making me feel like I'm in an isolated jail cell. I found a fan in one of the hall closets yesterday, so at least the thing dries my sweat off at night. I wonder what Dalila would do if she came into my room. She'd probably scrunch up her nose and tell me to get lost.

I've been thinking about her a lot. Hell, images of her keep crossing my mind when I'm too hot to sleep. That dude Rico seemed more suited for a golf outing than a boxing gym. They're a perfect couple. The bossy girl and the blowhard.

But that doesn't mean I don't remember how she kissed me. Remembering that crazy night is the only entertainment I have.

My life here sucks, but at least I have food for the next week. Lucky for me, food is dirt cheap in Mexico and I've managed to stock up. I don't even know why I'm still here. Well, besides the fact that I'm almost out of gas and don't have anywhere else to go.

I've been here a week and haven't seen the legendary Juan Camacho. It wouldn't matter, anyway. I don't have squat to pay the dude. I've sparred with a few guys from the gym since I've been here and would love get an opportunity to show Camacho what I've got.

I glance at the cheap-ass pay-as-you-go phone I got, almost willing it to ring. It's useless because I don't get any calls. My mom hasn't called to see how I'm doing, even though I left her my number. All my life I've wanted her to tell me how much she values my existence, but it's just a fantasy. The reality is I'm the mistake that led to her being a poor young single mom disowned by her parents and desperate to find a guy who'd stick around.

My existence ruined lots of things for her.

I used to wonder what life would have been like if my parents had stayed together. I imagined Christmases with a huge tree decorated with colorful lights and shiny tinsel. We'd send out goofy holiday cards with a picture of our family wearing ugly sweaters. In the spring my dad would be my Little League coach and my mom would sit in the stands and cheer me on the loudest. I'd pretend she embarrassed me, but I'd secretly love it. I wouldn't have cared if we lived in a big house or an old shed. We'd be a family. And we'd be happy just because we were together.

I pick up my phone and stare at the empty screen. I've probably got less than a month until my minutes expire, so I figure I'll call my mom. I don't know where I'll go once that manager Ocho kicks me out of here. I don't think my mom cares where I am just as long as she's left with a bottle of booze.

Listening to each ring gives me anxiety. Will she answer or will she glance at her cell and ignore it because I'm calling? A million thoughts are rushing through my mind right now.

"Hello?" my mom's familiar voice answers.

I swallow hard. "Hey, Mom. It's Ry. I, um, just wanted to let you know I made it to Mexico. I'm, um, living in a boxing gym."

"Enough lies, Ryan."

My heart sinks. There's no concern laced in her voice. Only resentment. "What are you talkin' about?"

"Paul heard you were running drugs across the border," she says, her voice full of contempt. "He said he has informants keeping an eye on you."

Paul would say anything to make me look like a thug. "I'm not running drugs, Ma."

"Paul knows—"

"Paul doesn't know shit about me or what I'm doin'," I blurt out harshly. "I told you I was going to Mexico to train."

"Train to fight? Or train to smuggle drugs?" Her tone tells me how much she disrespects me. It's almost as if she wants me to fail.

"To fight."

I hear her chug something and then I recognize the sound of a glass set down on a counter. "I don't know what's real and what's not with you anymore."

I used to lie all the time when I was younger, but she caught me too many times. I stopped lying the first time she told me I was turning into my father. If it was possible, after that she started resenting me even more. She ignored me, stopped making me meals . . . hell, she even stopped taking me to doctor's appointments.

"I guess I'll just talk to you later, Ma."

"Take care of yourself, Ryan. Don't get yourself into trouble like you did back in Chicago."

Nobody else is gonna take care of me, I want to say, but I hold my tongue. "Uh-huh," I say, then before the line goes dead I mumble, "I'm not my dad."

I toss my phone aside, hating myself for calling her. It didn't do anything besides rile me up. Knowing that Paul was talking shit about me to my mom makes me sick. I would defend myself more, but what good would that do?

There's nothing else to do but go into the gym right now. It's empty at this hour, so I can practice my skills and kill time.

Wearing a T-shirt and sweats, I walk into the empty gym. At the speed bag I work on my technique. Then I jump rope until I'm warmed up enough to start punching the weight bag.

In the back of my mind I wonder if this is all worth it. All the time and effort I put into fighting is worthless if I don't get a trainer. I should probably give up, but damn it feels good to train. It's like my body wants to work harder and faster, daring me to push myself to the limit.

Daring me to make something out of my life.

I punch the bag over and over again. I don't stop, even when my arms get tired. It's like the bag is my life and I fucking hate it so much. It feels good to beat the shit out of it.

"Give that thing a break!" I whip around, startled. It's Mateo, standing at the front door wearing jeans and a button-down shirt. He's obviously not here to work out. "Didn't anyone ever tell you to take a day off, Hess?"

"No." I punch the bag again.

He spots me while I keep hitting the bag.

"Get dressed and come out with me tonight."

I jab again. "No thanks."

He peeks his head around the bag. "Come on, man. You've been stuck here for a week. It's time you venture out of this place. It's Saturday night. Live a little."

"I'm good," I say, picking up a jump rope from one of the hooks on the wall. "Actually, I'd be better if Camacho was here. I could use a trainer. Not that I can afford him, or even a crappy trainer for that matter."

"Speaking of Camacho . . . have you seen him?" he asks as he straddles a workout bench.

I stop jumping. "Nope. I thought you were gonna introduce me to him."

He nods. "I can't introduce you to him if he doesn't show up. He could show up tomorrow for all I know. He's kind of a recluse and comes here when he feels like it. I feel bad I haven't kept up my end of our bargain, so do me a favor and come out with me tonight. You'll be straight up *loco* if you don't get out of here soon."

I hesitate. He's right. I've been holed up here the past week. The heat is starting to get to me and I need to stop thinking so much. I guess it wouldn't hurt to go out.

"Fine. I'll go with you."

Mateo, with his short hair and a gleam in his eye, claps his hands. The sound echoes through the empty gym. "*¡Fantástico!*" He practically jumps off the bench. "Be ready in five minutes."

After a quick shower, I stare at myself in the small foggy mirror above the sink. I need a haircut and a shave. Paul would fucking hate the way I look. He'd say his house wasn't a homeless shelter, so I shouldn't look like a homeless dude.

I meet Mateo out front. He's driving an SUV this time. I've seen him drive three different vehicles since we got here. While he doesn't have money for his own transportation, the dude sure does have a lot of friends and family in town who let him drive their cars.

"Nice ride," I tell him as I slide into the leather seat.

He glides his hands over the leather steering wheel. "It's my uncle's. He owns a construction company in Matamoros and lets me borrow his cars sometimes."

On the ride, Mateo confides in me that both of his parents along with his two sisters died in a car accident a few years back. "When my uncle told me about the accident, I freaked out at first. I felt so fucking alone. Sure, extended family was there for me. But it's not like having your core family, you know."

I look out the window at the shadows on the darkened hillside. "I wouldn't know. I've never really had a family. It was always just my alcoholic mom and me."

"Well, we all have our shit to deal with." Mateo shrugs. "When you sit on the pity pot for too long, you tend to get numb. I refuse to feel sorry for myself. I'm twenty-four and not going to let life bring me down. The only way is up for me, even if it means taking odd jobs to pay the bills."

"I feel you."

He laughs a high-pitched staccato laugh that's unmistakably his. "We're just two *pendejos* trying to make it," he says. "I recently started a job as a part-time bodyguard. It's boring work, but it's cash in my pocket and connections I can use later if I need them. Nothin' comes easy."

I sit back and feel a sense of relief that I can chill tonight. I'm not going to think about my home life or boxing or that girl who's been invading my thoughts.

"Where are we goin'?" I ask when Mateo pulls into an empty parking spot in the middle of a town with bright lights outlining its streets like a runway guiding people to its doors.

"It's an underground club."

Underground? I'm not sure I like the sound of that. "What do they do at this club?" I ask.

"You'll find out soon enough. Come on," he says.

There's a big dude at the door who looks like a poster child for the overuse of steroids. In lethal doses. As soon as he sees Mateo he moves aside to let us in.

"I guess you've been here before," I mumble as we step inside and walk down a flight of stairs.

"Too many times to count."

After we make our way through a hallway filled with people, we end up in a huge, dimly lit room with music blaring. In the center of the room is a square cage where two guys are fighting. One dude is kicking the other guy's ass pretty good.

I look around. People are crowded around the bar. The fight is like an afterthought—just entertainment for the people inside this insane club.

I grab Mateo's shoulder. "What *is* this place?"

"It's called makin' money." Mateo turns to the dude collecting money in the corner of the room. "The guy standing in the cage at the end of the night gets a cut."

"Of what?"

"The pot." He pats me on the back. "You said you needed money, right?"

I look at the guys duking it out in the center of the cage. This isn't boxing. Or MMA. It's no-rules dirty fighting. This isn't what I came to Mexico to do.

"I'm out, Mateo. This ain't me."

He grabs my shoulder. "You can't be out. I've already bet money on you. It's a round-robin, and you're up soon."

What the hell! "You signed me up to fight?"

Mateo pats me on the back. "I'm telling you, bro, it'll be easy cash. I told you I'd take care of you."

"It's a *fucking cage*, man. I'm not some sort of animal."

"We're all animals, Ryan. Listen, you're a *gringo* in a bar full of *Mexicanos*. You're going to bring in big money. If you win, you'll have enough to pay Camacho if he agrees to train you. You came to Mexico to go pro and make a name for yourself. This is your first obstacle. Show everyone you're not a joke. You came to fight, kick ass, and make cold hard cash. Think about it."

But I can't think right now . . . because all of a sudden I scan the place and *she* is on the other side of the room. Dalila. A blaze of desire rocks my core, which agitates the hell out of me.

I know why I'm here. Mateo set me up and in the end I'm gonna fight so I don't let him down. But why does Dalila keep showing up in my life?

"I'll be right back," I tell Mateo.

"Where are you goin'?" he calls out, but I'm already weaving through the crowd.

I'm going to confront her again. Because annoying the shit out of her is the only light in my darkness.

TWELVE

Dalila

Rico and his friends lead us to an underground fighting ring. A scared Soona is clutching my elbow, but Demi is totally excited to party like everyone here.

"This is so cool!" Demi says, grasping a drink from one of Rico's friends.

I take it out of her hand and hand it back to the guy. "Remember what happened to me in Texas? Don't let it happen to you."

"Wow," Demi says. "That night really had an impact on you."

"I'm more aware now," I admit to her. I wince as one of the guys in the ring starts fighting as if it's a fight to the death. "What's cool about this?"

Rico takes a gulp of his beer. "Those fighters can make a ton of money, Dalila." He gestures to the betting cage. "I bet on Esteban Rivera and expect to make a killing tonight. He's undefeated."

I don't tell Rico that I'm not a fan of betting, especially on underground fights like this. Boxing is one thing. It's a religion to my father. But this . . .

I glance at the guys in the cage. I can see a splattering of blood on the mats as the cage opens and the winner of this round is declared. It's a huge guy with oversize muscles and a scary grimace on a grizzly face that reminds me of a bear.

Rico claps. "That's my boy."

Soona glances at the cage. "I don't like this place," she whispers in my ear.

"Just ignore the fight," I tell her. "Everyone else is dancing and having a good time."

Soona turns away from the cage. "That guy who just won *es enorme*. I don't think anyone can beat him. Why don't they just call it off and give him first place?"

One of Rico's friends comes over and leans in close to tell him something. "I'll be right back," Rico says, motioning to his friends to follow his lead. He heads to the other side of the club.

Demi, who's been flirting with Rico's friend Marcus all night, starts jumping up and down to the music. "This place is awesome! We should come here more often, Dalila! It's like a dungeon of heaven."

"That doesn't make sense," I tell her.

Soona nods. "Dalila's right. A dungeon can't be heaven. And heaven better not be a dungeon."

Demi flips her head back and holds her arms out wide. "Don't you two get it? Nothing makes sense here, and that's the beauty of it!"

I'm probably going to be grounded the rest of my life for coming to this *heavenly dungeon*.

"If you wanted to see what skills I got, you're going to get a glimpse of them very soon," someone with an extremely American accent calls out behind me.

Ryan Hess, otherwise known as Mr. America.

I whip around so fast it takes me a second before I can focus. Just staring into those bright blue eyes makes my body shiver with excitement. "Ryan, wh . . . what are you doing here?"

"I've been askin' myself that same thing." He gestures to the cage. "Lots of action tonight, huh?"

I glance at the now-empty cage and then back at Ryan. "You like watching fights?"

His eyes sparkle with a hint of mischief and something else I can't identify as he leans in close. "I like winning fights."

When he leans back and the sides of his mouth quirk up the slightest bit, I cross my arms. "You have a big ego, Mr. America."

"Sometimes."

"You can't win every fight," I tell him, thinking of the giant who just won the last fight. "Some guys will always be better than you."

He seems to contemplate my words for a second, then shakes his head. "Nah. If I thought about losing, I'd never win."

"So all you think about is winning?"

He shrugs. "Most of the time."

"Well, it's a good thing you're not fighting tonight, then." I gesture to the cage. "Because you couldn't win against that beast who just won the last fight. He'd tear you apart, and mess up that clean shirt you're wearing in the process."

He looks down. "You think he'd mess up my shirt?"

I nod. "Definitely."

"Well, damn." I'm completely unprepared when he pulls his shirt up over his head. His defined muscles shouldn't impress me, but I can't stop staring. Masculinity and that ever-present slew of confidence flows from every pore of his powerful body. "Well, then, you'll have to keep my shirt for me until I get out of the ring. We wouldn't want it to get messed up now, would we?"

His shirt is draped over my hand now. "You're *not* going to fight tonight," I tell him. I don't even know why I care. But I do. Big ego or not, I know how hungry guys are to fight Americans and show them that Mexicans are just as good if not better than our neighbors to the north. "That guy who won the last fight is a monster. I'm not even sure he's human."

"The thing about me, *Miss Mexico*," he says, "is that I'm not afraid of anything. Human or not."

"It's pronounced Meh-hi-co," I call out, but he's already weaving through the crowd on his way to the cage.

And I'm still standing here with his shirt in my hand.

"Um . . . what is Ryan doing here?" Soona asks me.

Demi wags her brows. "Did you see the six-pack on him?"

"I wasn't paying attention to his six-pack."

Demi looks down at my hand. "Oh, really? Is that why you were drooling as you stared at his retreating back? And is that why you're clutching his shirt as if it's your personal property?"

I shove the shirt at her. "Here, you hold it."

She steps back. "No way, *chica*. He gave it to you. You're the chosen one."

"Does it smell good?" Soona asks shyly.

I shake my head. "Ew. I'm not gonna smell it."

Soona holds her hands up as if she's surrendering. "I'm not crazy. I just read something in a magazine about some guys having a certain scent that attracts girls."

"Ryan attracts girls because of his looks . . . and body." Demi scans the crowd. "And those eyes. Did you take a gander at his *ojos*?"

"I didn't notice them," I tell her.

"Sure you did, just like every other girl in this place," she teases. "Or maybe you were too busy wondering what those full lips are capable of."

I pull my shoulders back and stand up straight. "I don't know what you're talking about."

As I scan the room for Ryan, I spot Rico walking over to us and my spirits drop.

"Oh no, Rico's coming. What do I do with this?" I say, holding out Ryan's shirt.

I hand it to Demi.

She hands it to Soona, who hands it back to me.

I quickly shove the shirt into my purse hoping Rico doesn't notice.

"The next fight's starting," he says, taking a swig of beer. "Esteban will fight the winner of the final round."

Ryan and his opponent are escorted into the cage. He looks just as tough and intimidating as he did when I first saw him at the gym, unwilling or unable to be frightened by anyone. His opponent looks like he's out for blood. All eyes are focused on the cage as the opponents face each other—Ryan versus a local fighter, ready to pound on the American as if it's war.

"No way! It's that *gringo* from the gym I was telling you about," Rico says to one of his friends.

While Rico explains to his friends how he knows the white guy in the cage, I can't seem to shake this feeling of dread off of me.

"*Güey*, I know that guy," Rico's friend says. "His old man's a crooked cop connected to Vega."

"How do you know?" Rico asks. I listen intently for the answer.

"I know all the crooked cops," he says. "They're all on the payroll. I've seen this guy fight before at some dive in Texas. He's good."

Rico narrows his eyes. "I don't give a shit how good he is or who he's connected to. Even if he wins this one, which I doubt, there's no way he can beat Esteban."

When the crowd roars, I stop thinking and focus all my attention to the fight in the middle of the bar.

Ryan's friend Mateo is standing close to the cage, urging Ryan on.

It isn't long before both guys are pummeling each other. The music is pounding so hard the floor is shaking. Or maybe that's my nerves. As much as I don't like guys with oversize egos like Ryan, I don't want to see him hurt.

But that isn't happening. Ryan is obviously more skilled than the other guy. When he lands a good hit, the other guy stumbles back and the crowd boos.

I watch as Ryan relaxes his stance and stops in the middle of the cage, standing completely still.

Oh no.

He's going to let his opponent get in a free shot. A courtesy hit. When the guy gets in a good punch and Ryan's lip starts bleeding, I turn away. I can't watch.

This is a cage fight. Why would Ryan let the guy get in any punches when he's obviously a better fighter? Who cares about decency and saving face in a dirty fight?

The boy with the big ego actually wants his opponent to lose with dignity. Demi is right. This place doesn't make sense.

I try to ignore the fight and focus on the music and having fun with my friends, but it's hard. Some of the guys in the crowd are shaking hands with Rico and his friends like they're celebrities. When a few guys with gang tattoos chat with them, the hair on the back of my neck stands up.

I don't know if Rico is just a rich kid with lots of connections, or if it goes deeper than that. Ever since Rico's family came to dinner, my parents have been on edge.

As if I don't have enough to worry about, Ryan is fighting another opponent. I don't want to care, and yet there's something about him that draws me to him. Throughout the night I keep glancing at the cage while trying to forget that Ryan is locked inside it.

Finally, it's the main event. Rico is standing next to me now, watching with anticipation. "I've got big money on this final round," he explains.

I don't want to watch Ryan fight the giant. While Ryan may be strong and muscular, Esteban's bugged-out eyes and bulging veins make me think he must be on some kind of steroids or drugs.

When the crowd starts chanting "Esteban! Esteban!" my gaze focuses on Ryan. His body is battered from the previous fights and I can see blood slowly dripping from a cut on his cheek. He doesn't seem fazed that the crowd is rooting for his opponent. He's stone-faced, unwilling to be emotional or intimidated just because the majority of people are against him.

I'm tense and hold my breath in an attempt to calm my nerves.

This is the main event.

Ryan glances at me as the ref walks into the cage and suddenly my face feels all hot and my chest feels tight. I find myself shaking my head as a signal to Ryan to stop this before it starts. *Don't do this.* This isn't boxing. It feels like a revenge fight. Instead of taking my subtle hint and stepping out of the cage, Ryan winks at me, then turns to face his opponent.

The air in the place is suddenly charged, the chants getting louder.

"I want to leave," I tell Rico.

He looks at me like I'm crazy. "No way. We can't leave now. The fight is about to start." He turns his attention to the cage.

I grab Soona's and Demi's hands. "Let's go," I tell them.

"Now?" Demi asks.

"Yes."

I don't want to see the bloodshed.

THIRTEEN

Ryan

Every part of my body aches.

Hell, it even hurts to breathe.

Last night I fought for what seemed like hours. Guy after guy stepped into the cage with me, hoping to knock me out. First were the preliminary rounds, which I won easily. I even let a few of the guys get some solid punches in so it'd be a good show.

Then came the final round with that Esteban dude. He growled a few times. I don't think anyone had the balls to tell him humans don't growl. It didn't matter, though. I don't back down. Esteban got in some pretty good shots. I haven't been challenged that much in a long time, not even with Mateo. But Esteban was too slow, too aggressive, and lacked any strategy.

I stunned him with my jabs. And when he let his guard down, I was there to take advantage of it. It was clear from the shocked look on his face that Esteban had never faced a challenger who wasn't afraid of him. Especially a *gringo*.

When I caught Dalila glance at me with a disgusted expression on her face, it just spurred me on more. I wanted to show off, to show her I wasn't a loser.

It didn't matter, though.

She missed the final fight.

I saw her walk out of the club with her friends, leaving her boyfriend behind. In that split second with my attention averted, my opponent landed a sucker punch to my ribs. It was a painful wake-up call that the girl who's invaded my thoughts didn't give a shit whether I lived or died in the ring.

Or cage, as it were.

I was winning until some random idiot in the crowd thought it'd be a good idea to use the ceiling as a shooting target. The ref stopped the fight as the crowd of people started pouring out of the club. We were left there waiting in the cage until someone let us out. The management said they couldn't declare a winner. They handed me fifty pesos for fighting as a consolation prize.

Fifty measly pesos.

I'm lying on the mat in my little makeshift bedroom in Sevilla. Mateo drove me here after the fight, apologizing the entire time for failing to get me a big payout. He was proud of me like a big brother. I couldn't get him to shut up as he recapped the fight in the voice of an announcer going through a highlight reel.

A knock at my door makes me wince. I know it's Mateo coming to check on me. He said he'd come by today and make sure I was alive. He also warned me I'd be sore and stiff, and he was right. I should make myself move or get dressed, but I don't want to.

"Go home, Mateo!" I call out to him.

"It isn't Mateo," a girl's voice comes from the other side of the door. "It's Dalila."

"Dalila?"

"*Sí.*"

I manage to get out of bed long enough to open the door. Standing in front of me is the bossy girl who hates heroes. This time her dark, shiny hair is perfectly straight instead of that natural curl she wore last night. I wonder if her hair is as silky to the touch as it looks. Too bad I'll probably never find out.

The girl has proved to be a distraction, but that doesn't mean I'm not attracted to her. Flirting with her might not be smart, but it feels good.

The sound of Dalila sucking in a horrified breath makes me take my eyes off her hair. "You look like death," she says.

"Matches how I feel, I guess," I mumble.

"You shouldn't have fought last night. It's not good to get your head punched so many times in one night. You could have a concussion."

"I've never been one to make smart decisions," I tell her. "Why start now?"

She doesn't smile or laugh. Instead, she stares at me as if I'm some sort of alien. I'm used to stares from people. Time is ticking by. I don't know what to say, and I have no clue why she's here.

"I, um, wanted to bring you back your shirt." She pulls my shirt out of her fancy leather purse with shiny metal buckles on it. "I figured you'd need it."

I take it from her. "Thanks."

"You can put it on," she says, eyeing my bare chest riddled with bruises.

"I'm good," I say, holding the shirt in my hand. I'm confused though. "You came all the way over here to give me my shirt back?" I ask, wondering if she has an ulterior motive.

She shrugs. "I guess." It doesn't escape my notice that her eyes are focused on my bare chest.

I toss the shirt on my bed. I might not have much, but I work hard at being fit. Going shirtless doesn't bother me one bit. And if it rattles her even the slightest amount, there's no way I'm going to miss that opportunity. Better her than me.

She clears her throat as her eyes travel from my chest to the cut on my lip. "You need to clean that," she says, gesturing to my face. "You could get an infection."

I don't tell her that at this point I don't give a crap if I get an infection. Or die.

"Thanks for bringin' back my shirt."

I start to close the door, but she shimmies her way inside. "Have you talked to your family back home?" she asks.

"Why?"

"People talk." She stands in front of me with her hands folded in front of her. "Do you know anything about the shooting last night? Like who started it?"

"Nope." I ask her, "Why all the questions?"

She stands there staring at me with those dark brown eyes that remind me of melted milk chocolate. "It just seems weird that you showed up when *Las Calaveras* and *Los Reyes del Norte* cartels are in some kind of power struggle. Then last night I find out you're related to a crooked cop . . ."

Wait one second. "Back up. Who told you he was crooked?"

"I can't tell you."

"Well, if you think I've been sent here to be some sort of spy or something like that, think again." A chuckle escapes my mouth. "I don't even like my stepfather enough to have a full conversation with him."

"Do you know if he's working with the cartels? Does he know a guy named Santiago Vega?"

So that's why she's here. She doesn't give a shit about giving me back my shirt. All she wants is to pry information out of me. I'd bet the fifty pesos I made last night that her rich boyfriend or father sent her here as a spy to find out what I know.

"I don't know if he's working with the cartels. And honestly I don't care. Tell your boyfriend I'm just here to fight, not get caught up with some cartel or be a damn spy. I don't know who Santiago Vega is, either. If that's all you wanted—"

"That's not . . ." She takes a deep breath, her chest moving up and down like she's doing some sort of calming exercise. Her entire demeanor changes and she pastes on a friendly smile. "I'm sorry. Let's change the subject. Have you eaten today?"

"Does it matter?"

"Of course it matters. I can see the bruises on your body and the blood on your face. You need nourishment to heal. Stay here. I'll be right back."

She's taking this fake caring thing way too far. "I don't take orders. From anyone."

"Cut the ego trip for five minutes, Mr. America."

"My name's Ryan," I call out.

She leaves the room and all I want to do is tell her not to come back. It's not about ego. The only person I trust here is Mateo, even if he did set me up to fight last night. He did it to help me make money because he knew I was broke. His intentions were good even if the outcome was a big fat failure.

I'm still standing in the middle of my room when Dalila comes back. She's carrying a wet rag in one hand and something wrapped in foil in the other.

"Sit down," she orders.

I could argue. I've been taking care of myself since I was eight and don't need anyone else. Especially someone who's only here to get information out of me.

"I'm fine," I tell her.

She eyes my bruised body. "I'll help you."

Fuck that. I shake my head. "Playing nurse to me isn't going to make me change my story. I'm here to train with Juan Camacho and make money. That's it. So you can just go back to whoever sent you here and tell them I know nothing."

"Shut up, Ryan," she interrupts as she steps so close to me I can smell her sweet perfume that reminds me of wildflowers. "I'm here because there's something about you that intrigues me. I don't know why. I hardly know you and to be honest you've got a crappy attitude. Now if you want me to stay and help you . . ." She points to the mat on the floor. "Sit down."

Her brutally honest words coming out of that perfect heart-shaped mouth rock me. While my head tells me to push her away, there's something comforting about her being here. The truth is that I don't want her to leave.

"Fine," I say, then sit on the mat and wait for her to tend to my wounds.

When she kneels beside me, I briefly wonder what it would be like to have a girl like Dalila in my life. She's probably used to being treated like a princess. I can tell from her expensive jewelry, the designer clothes, and the way she holds her head high as if she doesn't carry heavy burdens in life.

Her hand reaches up and she starts wiping the side of my lip with the cloth. Her touch is gentle and warm, reminding me of what her lips felt like when she kissed me at the concert. "Tell me about your life, Mr. America."

She's trying to get information out of me again. If I had my guard down, I'd probably fall for it. "There's nothin' to tell."

She sits back on her heels. "Everyone has a story."

"Mine's a pretty shitty one."

"Do you have any brothers or sisters?" she asks as she leans forward and examines my brow.

"No." At least none that I know of. My stepbrothers don't count.

She smells so damn good I could breathe in her scent forever. And when she bends over to tend to the cut on my cheek, her cleavage makes my groin twitch. If she's trying to distract me, it's working.

"Tell me about your parents."

I take her wrist and hold it still. I can feel her pulse quicken in my grip. "I don't want to talk about me."

I need her to back off because I'm not about to be manipulated by a girl who has the ability to make me lose my senses.

"I'll talk about myself, then." She looks at my hand still holding her wrist. I slowly let go and let her continue nursing me as I concentrate on a spot on the back wall. It's better than focusing on the way she's staring intently at me. "I have three younger sisters," she says in a soft, feminine voice that fills the room. "Two of them are twins, and they're always getting in trouble. Margarita is only thirteen but she wants to be older. She's boy crazy and has a crush on a different boy every week. My mom is an amazing gardener. She's obsessed with flowers and is the best cook I know. She's old-school, so I can't really share everything with her. My parents want me to go to medical school to become a heart surgeon." Her hand falls to her side and she looks down as if she's too vulnerable to look at me right now. "So that's my plan."

"What about your father? What does he do?"

I sense her hesitating the slightest bit before she says, "He's a lawyer. Now it's your turn to tell me the truth about your stepfather."

"How do you know English so well?"

She moves her attention to the cuts on my hands. "My father made it his business to hire the best English teachers in Mexico."

"Is he connected to the cartels? Or maybe that boyfriend of yours?"

"What? No!" She straightens her shoulders and looks regal and proud. "I don't know anyone with connections to the cartels," she says in a frosty tone.

I hold my hands up. "All right, calm down. No need to get all freaked out on me."

"I don't freak out."

"Good. I'm just here for the chance to train with Juan Camacho."

There's silence for a while. When she sits back on her heels again she says, "There's no way Juan Camacho will train you. He doesn't train anybody. He hardly leaves his house."

"I guess that makes me a fool, huh?"

She shrugs. "I guess so. But miracles do happen, so you never know."

"Miracles don't happen in my world. I'd owe a big fat favor to anyone who could get Camacho to train me. I'm running out of hope fast."

"What happens if Camacho never shows up? Will you go back to the US?"

"I don't know." Just the thought of crawling back to Paul and my mom depresses the hell out of me. I'll continue to be the loser they always knew I was and become a professional shit shoveler after high school. The thought is beyond depressing. "Thanks for dropping off my shirt. I need you to stop playing nurse and leave."

"Why?"

"Because you're trying to get info out of me and I just don't have any," I say. "I'm not here to make friends, especially with a bossy girl who's as manipulative as she is pretty."

Her mouth opens wide and she sucks in a breath. "I'm not manipulative. I need to find out who you are, besides a boxer with a killer left hook."

I look down at the bloodstained rag still in her hand. "I'm a boxer looking for a trainer. Nothin' more."

She stands and tosses the rag on the floor next to me. "Uh-huh," she says in a sarcastic tone.

"You don't believe me?"

"No." She starts heading for the door. "And one day soon I'm going to find out if you're lying to me."

"And if I am what are you going to do about it?" I challenge. "Kill me?"

"I guess you're just going to have to find that out when the time comes," she teases before letting herself out. "See you later, Mr. America."

FOURTEEN

Dalila

My papá is a lawyer who might represent people who don't follow the laws one hundred percent, but he isn't involved in cartel business. He can't be.

Last night we heard gunshots coming from inside the club as we stood outside figuring out how to get home. And as the club cleared out, I heard El Fuego's name thrown around more than once in the crowd. He's the leader of *Los Reyes del Norte*. Rico found me and quickly ushered me and my friends into a car, telling us *Los Reyes del Norte* was responsible for the shooting. El Fuego's men.

It all confuses me.

Ryan told me the only reason he's in Mexico is to train with the great Juan Camacho. I don't know anyone who would change their life and move to another country on the slight chance of meeting someone who hardly shows his face anymore. It seems so suspect and I need to get him to open up to me.

When Ryan vowed to owe someone a big favor if they got Camacho to train him, a lightbulb went off in my head.

What Ryan doesn't know is that my father knows Juan Camacho. Papá worked with him many years ago. I remember the first time I saw The Great Camacho. He was sitting in the courtyard talking to my father when I walked in on their conversation. At the time I was frozen and couldn't talk. Juan Camacho is a boxing legend. I was just a little girl and Juan talked to me like I was an important person, not just his lawyer's daughter. Every time he came over, he'd tell me a story about his life. I was mesmerized by his life and his success. I haven't seen him in years, but I know he'd still remember me.

When my father comes home, I pull him aside.

"What's wrong, *mija?*"

"Nothing, Papá. I just . . ." I don't know how to bring it up, but I figure I might as well just blurt it out. "I was wondering if you still talk to Juan Camacho."

He raises a brow. "Why?"

"Um . . . I have a friend who wants an autograph."

Suddenly my face gets hot. Even though I've done it on occasion, I don't like lying to my parents. I also hate the feeling that Papá is hiding something important from me. He's a strong man and I look up to him so much. I don't want him disappointed in me or pushing me away when all I want is for him to look at me with respect and pride.

"Tell your friend he doesn't give autographs. Not anymore." He crosses his arms. "Does this have anything to do with the fight you attended last night? I heard there was a shooting. I don't want you to go there again."

"I won't. I promise." I look at him curiously. "You'd never be involved in anything illegal, would you?"

"What are you talking about?"

"I heard Don Cruz ask you for information the other night. You argued with him."

He sighs, then walks up to me with a concerned look on his face. "Dalila, focus on getting into medical school and stop worrying so much about what me and the rest of the world are doing."

It's my nature to be curious. Ryan thought I went to the gym trying to get information out of him. He was right. I was trying to find out what he knows about the connection between his stepfather and Santiago Vega.

What if I got Juan Camacho to meet with him? Would Ryan open up and tell me what he knows about his stepfather and his connection to the cartels or Vega?

I wait until nighttime after everyone is asleep before I tiptoe into my father's office. Finding Juan Camacho won't be easy, but my father must have a way to get in touch with his old friend.

Papá's files are locked. I know he's got secret compartments around the house where he keeps confidential information. His office is dark, and I whack my toe on one of his office chairs. Ouch! I didn't want to turn on the light from my cell phone, but I have no choice. His office is like a maze.

I sit in his big leather chair and pray he forgot to lock his file drawers. I try each one with no luck. The cabinets behind his desk are also locked.

As I reach under his desk for a hidden key, I hear footsteps in the hallway. I freeze.

If someone catches me I'm in trouble. Shutting off my cell phone light, I quickly duck under the desk and hope nobody sees me. But who's in the hallway?

The stories of our neighbors' homes being robbed cross my mind. I know I'm being paranoid. At least I hope I am.

The footsteps come closer.

And closer.

I can tell someone is right outside the office door. If my family is in danger, I know where our guns are. I wouldn't hesitate to hurt someone if they were threatening my family.

And yet, the thought makes my hands shake uncontrollably. I think of myself as tough, but right now panic stabs at my insides. My heart is beating fast as I hold my breath and wait for more footsteps. Then I hear Lola's unmistakable cough outside the door. I let out a thankful breath as her footsteps get faint.

I'm safe and alone, locked in Papá's office. I turn my cell phone light on and catch a glimpse of an envelope with my grandmother's name on the return address sticking out of the little garbage can under his desk. I pick it up and find a ripped-up check made out to my grandmother and a letter inside.

Tears come to my eyes as my *abuelita* tries to convince my father to remember where he came from. In the letter she pleads for him to fight for the good people. Until then, she'll refuse to come to La Joya de Sandoval.

Does she know if he's working with a cartel?

In the letter she writes that she's getting old and desperately wants to see her grandchildren but won't do it under the circumstances. I tuck the letter and ripped check back into the envelope and shove it in my pocket with a vow to see my *abuelita* soon to get the answers I need.

Keeping my movements slow and careful, I continue my search for the hidden key to my dad's files. Time is ticking and I keep looking, but I can't find a key.

I let out a frustrated sigh as I sit back in my father's big leather office chair. Where would my dad's client information be? I stare blankly at the computer on his desk.

Papá is always on his computer typing up briefs, preparing testimony, and sending out emails. Careful not to make noise, I turn on his computer. The cursor blinks, waiting for me to type in the password.

It takes me a couple of tries before I get it. It's his nickname for my mother. *Sirenita*, little mermaid.

And I'm in.

As I scan his files, I recognize names of his clients as famous celebrities and businessmen. No information on Santiago Vega.

I keep scrolling down to find Juan Camacho's contact information.

Finally I find Juan's name on a list of clients. It has an address and phone number. I quickly scribble the numbers down and feel a sense of relief.

As I tiptoe back to my room, I'm grateful that the house is completely quiet. In the morning I'm going to contact Juan Camacho.

And get information out of Mr. America, who might just have one of the puzzle pieces I need.

FIFTEEN

Ryan

I'm sweating my ass off in the gym. Not because of the scorching heat in Mexico, which is brutal, but because I ran four miles this morning before attacking the punching bags at the gym.

The problem is that Dalila, with her silky hair and questioning eyes, is etched into my mind.

Damn.

I'm not one to get stuck on a chick, especially one with ulterior motives. Hell, for all I know her boyfriend's got a hit out on me. Not that I care. At this point I've got a couple of weeks before I'm kicked out on my ass and then it won't matter if I'm dead or not.

"If you relax your shoulders, you'll have an easier time focusing on your target." A voice echoes through the gym.

I turn to find none other than Juan Camacho, the greatest Mexican boxer of all time, walking toward me. He's got a head full of gray hair and he moves slow but I bet he could still kick ass in a fight.

"I. Uh. Wow, um . . ." I'm too stunned to speak coherently.

"Go on," he says. "I hear you're a good fighter. Show me what you got."

I don't move. I saw videos online of when he knocked out Cody Sanchez in the first round of the championship back in the seventies. And when he fought Hunter McGehee, known as the biggest threat to his winning streak, he surprised everyone with a huge upset. McGehee was supposed to give Camacho a run for his money, but that didn't happen. McGehee stopped fighting after Camacho knocked him out in the third round.

"You're here," I say dumbly. "Wow. I'm Ryan Hess."

He nods. "I know."

My mind is a blur. I realize I'm pretty much frozen, and I tell myself to snap out of it.

"Hit the bag, but make sure your shoulders are relaxed and square," he says.

I work on the bag until Camacho tells me to stop. When he puts on target mitts and orders me into the ring, I jump in without hesitating. I want to show him this isn't just a hobby for me. Boxing defines my life. It makes me feel worthy of living.

I know that sounds stupid. But when you're told all your life that you're a worthless loser, you search for something to validate your existence.

I show off every skill I have. I jab fast and furiously in a perfect rhythm that feels like music.

After an hour Juan puts the mitts down. "You've got skills," he says. "But you're overly eager and you're in your head too much."

"Yes, sir. I'll work on it."

Mateo and a couple of other guys walk into the club. Even Mateo, who's been trying to get Camacho to come watch me fight, widens his eyes as he stares at the legend.

They all greet Camacho with a mixture of eagerness and awe. I'm still feeling like a little kid who just met his hero.

Camacho stays for a while, watching us spar while giving pointers.

But it's over all too soon. Before he leaves, he shakes our hands and starts walking out of the club. It occurs to me that I might never see the guy again. I know it's a long shot, but I rush to the parking lot.

He's walking to his car but stops when I stand in his path.

"I need a trainer," I blurt out as the hot Mexican sun beats down on my back.

He pulls out his car keys from his pocket. "I don't train anyone. Not anymore."

Before he gets into his car, I call out. "Wait!" He looks at me with impatience written on his face. "I came to Mexico with nothing but a few bucks in my pocket. Just a dream to meet you and the hope that you'll teach me what you learned. I've watched videos of you boxing. The way you moved, the way you played with your opponent . . . it was like a warrior's dance. I wanted to be you when I grew up, someone that people admire." I swallow the lump that's forming in my throat. "Someone who wasn't just defined as an unwanted bastard."

Camacho stares at me as my words sink in, then pats me on the back. "You're a good fighter, Ryan. But I heard you were fighting in the underground cages. That kind of fighting is dirty. It won't teach you strategy or discipline." He gestures to the bruises on my face. "It'll just teach you to beat the crap out of your opponent until they're lying flat on their back."

"Isn't that what it's all about?" I ask.

He shakes his head. "No. That's not what it's all about."

I watch as he slides into his car.

I can't let him leave, not now when his help could mean the difference between a life worth living and one that isn't worth a peso. "I'll pay you whatever you want, Mr. Camacho."

He cocks a brow. "You just said you're broke."

"I made fifty pesos last night. I'll give you everything I have."

"Fifty pesos, huh?" His upper lip twitches in amusement. "I'll tell you what, Ryan. I'll come by a couple days a week to train you. You do what I say, eat what I say, and sleep when I tell you to. Then I'll get you a legitimate fight, and we'll see if you really have what it takes. *¿Entiendes?*"

I nod. "Yes, sir."

He closes the door to his car but rolls down the window. "One more thing. Get a tan and learn some Spanish. You stick out like a piñata in the White House."

As he drives off I feel like I've just won the lottery.

Juan Camacho just agreed to train me.

It's too unreal. Not able to contain myself, I let out a triumphant yell that can probably be heard in the next town over.

Back in the gym, I share the news with Mateo. "Thanks for everything, man," I say, grateful he was able to get Camacho into the gym.

"Dude, you did it all. *You* did it!" he says as we do a bro handshake. "I knew if he just saw you in the ring he'd train you."

"What about you?" I ask him. "Don't you want him to train you?"

"I wish, but I've got so much shit goin' on I don't have time to commit to anythin' right now."

"You giving up boxing?"

"Nah," he says. "Just taking a mini break for the summer. I'll be closely watchin' you from the sidelines though, Hess. I've got your back, remember?"

I want to call my mom and tell her the news. It's stupid, I know, but I'd like to hear that she's proud of me for what I've managed to accomplish. Although to be honest, I haven't accomplished anything but winning fifty pesos and Juan Camacho's promise to train me a couple days a week. It'll sound pretty weak to someone who doesn't know anything about boxing.

For the next two days I focus on working out and sparring with anyone who walks into the gym. Some guys refuse to spar with me because I'm a *gringo*. The fact that I don't have any championships or real fights behind me makes me a noob.

But when Camacho comes in, I earn a little street cred.

Most of the guys hardly talk, so the language barrier isn't an issue.

I'm not so lucky when Camacho is training me.

"*Mantén las rodillas dobladas*," he says. "*O perderás tu equilibrio.*"

I look at him with a deadpan expression on my face. "I have no clue what you just said," I tell him.

He points to his knees. "*Rodillas.* Knees. Bend your knees, Ryan."

When I do what he says, he nods in approval. "*Muy bien.*"

At the end of our session he lays down the rules. "Sleep by ten, wake by six, and run for an hour. Eat four eggs for breakfast with spinach and tortillas. Girls are a distraction, so no girls."

"Of course. No girls."

Camacho shakes a crooked, arthritic finger at me. "And no cage fighting. You fight outside of the gym, I'm done. *¿Comprendes?*"

"I won't let you down."

"You better not."

After Camacho leaves, Mateo enters the gym wearing a suit and tie.

"You getting married?" I ask him. "Who's the lucky girl?"

"There's no wedding." He puts his foot up on a chair and poses as if he's on the cover of GQ magazine. "What do you think? I look good, right? I've got bodyguard duty for some rich girl's birthday tonight. Pays two hundred bucks."

"Bucks or pesos?"

"We're talkin' cold hard American dollars."

I'm so hard up for money that two hundred bucks for one night's work sounds like a fucking fortune.

"I'd ask you to come, but I'm gonna take a wild guess that you don't have a suit. Besides, all the security and bodyguard positions are filled."

"It's cool," I tell him. "I'll just hang in the gym tonight."

Mateo shakes his head. "I already told you. Too much time in the gym'll make you go *loco*, Ryan."

"Yeah, well I don't have much of a choice. My car is almost out of gas, I've got less than ten pesos left to my name . . . and I've got a fight coming up."

"Life could be worse, *mi amigo*."

"You don't see me complaining."

"Well, let me know when you're fighting," he says. "I'll be rooting for you, even if I'll be the only one rooting for the anonymous white dude."

It's nice having a friend like Mateo who doesn't give a shit about where I come from. He'll root for me no matter what, which is more than I can say for my blood relatives.

He starts bragging about some girl he met last night when he gets a text. "Damn. This guy Arturo canceled tonight and they're looking for another bodyguard." He looks up at me. "Someone in charge saw us together at the cage fight the other night. He wants me to ask if you're interested in filling in for Arturo. He'll lend you a suit. Two hundred bucks to stand around while some rich princess gets showered with gifts."

I don't even have to think about it. "I'm all in."

SIXTEEN

Dalila

I love parties, except when they're my own. I hate being the center of attention. I want to jump out the window and escape, but I know my mamá is looking forward to hosting my birthday party. Every family member will be here along with neighbors and friends.

To calm my nerves, I put in my earbuds and listen to Shadows of Darkness. Instead of thinking about Lucas, now every song somehow reminds me of Ryan. It's completely annoying. When the song "Too Tough to Fall" comes on, I think about Ryan not backing down when Rico confronted him and when he was in the cage at the underground club. As I close my eyes and listen to "Heartbreak," the lyrics trigger questions about Ryan's love life. I wonder if Ryan's left a trail of heartbroken girls back in the US like that redheaded girl Mikayla from the concert.

I yank my earbuds out in frustration.

Margarita, Coco, and Galena are already downstairs. My sisters love parties. They also love being the center of attention, which is fine with me.

"What did you decide to wear?" Lola asks me as she sets a water pitcher on my nightstand.

I shrug. "Maybe the white dress."

"What about the red one your mamá bought for you?" She grabs it out of my closet. It's a beautiful fitted dress that still has the tags on it.

I look at the dress Lola is holding. What if it was bought with illegal money my papá made from representing clients like Santiago Vega?

I need to stop thinking about it. Papá is a lawyer, that's it. A powerful lawyer. He helps people who might not live their lives within the law, but that doesn't mean he's involved in any illegal activity. He's not connected to drug lords, even if his clients are.

That thought doesn't make me feel any better.

"Lola, I need you!" Coco yells from the hallway. Lola places the dress on my bed with an apology and quickly leaves my room to tend to my sister.

Soft music starts playing and I can hear people starting to arrive, their voices carrying throughout the courtyard into our rooms. The courtyard is brightly decorated with colorful lights. Tables with enough food to feed an entire town are placed around the house.

I hold the red dress up to my body in the mirror. It's soft and beautiful and feels like silk against my skin. As I slip into it, I push away all negative thoughts.

After putting makeup on and getting texts from my friends asking where I am and accusing me of wanting to make a grand entrance, I'm ready to celebrate my eighteenth birthday.

"*Mija*, you look gorgeous," Papá tells me as he walks into my room.

Mamá is standing beside him, wearing a long white dress fit for a queen. Her hair is in a perfect updo and her bright red lips accentuate the beauty of her flawless honey-brown skin. She opens her arms wide and pulls me into an embrace as she wishes me a happy birthday.

Papá holds out a little box wrapped with silver paper and a big blue bow.

"It's your present," Mamá chimes in.

"Open it," Papá says.

After carefully unwrapping the box, I open it and suck in a breath. Inside the box is a stunning necklace with a big ruby heart surrounded entirely with diamonds.

"It's too much," I whisper as I finger the sparking jewels.

"Nothing is too good for you, *mija*," Papá says.

Mamá takes the necklace out of the box and secures it around my neck. "It shines as much as your spirit and is as beautiful as you are, Dalila. Inside and out. We can't wait until you graduate from medical school." She smiles warmly. "You're the perfect daughter."

"She's right. You make us proud to be your parents every day," Papá says.

Mamá leaves the room after being summoned by Margarita. Something about being low on tortillas.

I grab Papá's elbow before he can walk out of my room. "Papá, can we talk for a second?"

"Sure, *mija*. But only for a second. We have guests to attend to."

"Why did you hire bodyguards tonight?"

"Because we have a lot of guests and I want to make sure everyone is safe," he tells me.

"Why wouldn't we be safe?"

He cocks a brow. "Why all the questions?"

Suddenly I don't even want to bring it up. Is it because I'm afraid of knowing the truth? "I heard something at the club the other night."

He places a comforting hand over mine. "What did you hear?"

I swallow and my heart starts racing. "Nothing. I just want to make sure you're okay. I know you've been under a lot of stress and now you've hired bodyguards for tonight. It all worries me."

"Whoa." My dad holds up his hands as if halting my concern. "Don't worry about me. It's my job to worry about you. I'm a lawyer, Dalila. My ultimate goal is to help my clients with their legal issues. Sometimes it's stressful." He kisses the top of my forehead. "Come downstairs. Everyone is waiting to wish you *feliz cumpleaños*."

"Okay," I say, but there's a nagging feeling inside me that he's holding back the truth of why he's been under a lot of pressure. My *abuela*'s letter is proof of that.

Fingering the jewels on my neck anxiously, I walk down to the party. A huge chorus of "*¡Feliz cumpleaños!*" erupts in our courtyard.

I want to retreat and hide from all the attention, but instead I do what's expected of me. I plaster a smile on my face and walk gracefully down the stairs to the waiting crowd, half of whom I've never seen before.

"I love the necklace!" Soona cries out as she envelops me in a big hug. "It's beautiful. Why have you been hiding that from me?"

"It's new," I tell her. "A birthday present."

I greet my cousins and get hugs from my aunts and uncles while classical music echoes through the speakers scattered throughout our courtyard. It's not Shadows of Darkness, but it makes me think of better times. As I weave my way through the crowd, I see my dad's business associates and clients. It's easy to spot them. They're wearing expensive suits, and their wives, girlfriends, and children are dripping with shiny jewels.

Passing the hallway mirror, I feel like one of them and it just makes me feel embarrassed. I wonder how many meals that little homeless boy Sergio could buy with all the jewelry here tonight.

After talking to a couple of my cousins and making small talk with my father's clients, I head to the food table.

"Did you miss me?" Rico asks, coming up behind me. I turn around to see him holding a beer. "I haven't seen you since the cage fights."

I manage a smile and dodge his question.

He sets his beer down on an empty table. "Show me the gardens. It'll be like the old days when we were kids."

I lead him through the house and walk out the back door. Nobody is out here except for one of the hired bodyguards for my celebration. I've always felt safe at home, even at night when I come out here to be alone. The inviting smell of the flowers is familiar and comforting, something I'll miss when I go away to the university in Mexico City.

Rico's following me, but he's concentrating on his phone and hasn't even stopped to notice the impressive yellow-and-white frangipani. I close my eyes as I breathe in their fragrance and my stress level immediately lowers.

When I open my eyes, Rico's face is inches from mine. Before I can pull back, he presses his lips to mine and wraps his arms around my waist, pulling me close. I'm not ready for this. Not now. Not with him.

I push him away, glad when our lips separate. "Rico, we're just friends," I tell him.

He looks too sure of himself as he closes the distance between us again. "I know you like me."

"As a friend."

He laughs. "Come on, Dalila. Last year you were upset when I was texting other girls. I'm not preoccupied with anyone now. You don't have to play games with me."

"I'm not playing games, Rico."

"Have you ever had a boyfriend?"

I don't tell him I've been too busy trying to make up for Lucas's death to have time to devote to someone else. "Not for a while."

"You've been too sheltered by your parents, stuck in this compound." His slightly arrogant attitude shines through with a mischievous smile. "Your dad will approve of us dating. Don't think so much, and let me be a distraction."

Rico presses his body to mine again, so close that I can feel how much of a distraction he wants to be.

"Let her go," a deep, commanding voice orders. A voice I've replayed in my head over and over since I met him at the Shadows of Darkness concert.

It's Ryan.

He's standing a few feet away from us wearing a suit that's meant for someone a few inches shorter and not as muscular. He's also got a walkie-talkie hooked on to his belt.

Rico's grip on me loosens. "What are *you* doing here?"

Ryan gestures to his walkie-talkie. "Isn't it obvious?"

"It's obvious you're the hired help, *pendejo*. Nothing more."

The insult doesn't seem to faze Ryan. He takes a step toward us. "*The hired help* is telling you to get your hands off her."

Rico stands tall. "I'm warning you. Leave us alone."

"If you touch her again without her permission," Ryan says, not backing down, "you'll wish you listened to me the first time I said it. I don't give people two warnings."

SEVENTEEN

Ryan

It's me against Rico. He's staring me down as if I'm likely to cower and back away. That's not gonna happen. It doesn't happen with my stepfather, Sheriff Paul Blackburn. It sure as hell isn't happening with this punk.

Mateo appears at my side. His eyes are wide as he witnesses the standoff. "Rico, your father is looking for you," he says. "He told me to find you."

Rico straightens his shirt, then steps away from Dalila. "You're lucky this time," he says, pointing to me. He starts to walk back into the house but stops when he's a few inches from my face. "She'll never look at you as more than a pathetic peasant. Keep your filthy paws off her." He leans in close so only I can hear. "Oh, and the next time you cock-block me like that, I'm gonna make sure you never get hired in Mexico again. By anyone."

After he disappears, Mateo gives me a questioning look. "Everythin' okay out here?" he asks, his eyebrows furrowed in confusion.

Dalila's eyes capture mine. I don't look away. "I'm fine," I tell him.

She glances at Mateo. "I'm fine, too," she says.

Mateo can't keep the amused smile off his face. "If you need anythin', you know where to find me."

So now Dalila and I are alone in the garden.

Hell, if I knew it was Dalila's birthday party I was hired for tonight, I wouldn't have come. The girl has been nothing but a distraction, the one thing preventing me from focusing on what I need to do. The fact that I was barely able to keep myself in control while confronting Rico is a sign that I need to keep my distance. This is a job, nothing more. But the feelings of protectiveness are all too personal.

"Just so you know, I still don't need a hero," she tells me with a little tilt to her chin. "Rico isn't a threat."

"He's bigger than you. And stronger." What does she think, that she could fight him off if he decided to assault her?

"I'm tougher than I look."

"I'll bet." Taking in the bright red dress that hugs the curves on her small frame, I try to hold in my laughter. "Next time you pick a boyfriend, you might want to pick someone . . ."

"Like you?" she says. "I don't think so. Besides, Rico Cruz isn't my boyfriend. Since I'm obviously fine, you can go back to your lookout now."

She storms off farther into the gardens, her red dress like a beacon weaving through the maze of brightly colored flowers and lush greenery. She's steering away from the party and isolating herself. I follow because I'm not about to let her out of my sight. I've got a job to protect this place, which includes Dalila. If protecting the princess means pissing her off, then that's what I'll have to do.

She glances back at me. "I want to be alone."

"Then go back inside the house."

She throws up her hands and looks at me as if I'm an idiot. "How do you expect me to be alone when there's like two hundred people back there?"

I state the obvious. "If you wanted to be alone, maybe you should have thought twice about inviting half of Mexico to your birthday party."

"I didn't have a choice about the party. My parents planned it."

"Be grateful you have parents who want to throw you parties," I throw back at her.

"You don't know anything, Ryan Hess." She looks off into the distance beyond the compound. "Sometimes I want to be free of this place. It's confining, like a prison sometimes, with someone watching over me every second of every day. I'm sheltered and yet I'm supposed to be happy. You have no clue what it's like to have your entire life planned out for you by other people."

"I'd do just about anything to have parents who care," I tell her. "And a place to call home. Maybe you're just a spoiled, privileged rich girl who'll never be happy with anything you have. Nothing will ever be enough. Not the fancy clothes or the beautiful house or people who get paid a lot of money to protect you."

She narrows her eyes at me, as I've obviously hit a nerve. "As long as we're analyzing each other, why don't I turn this around? Why do you take such pleasure in fighting, Ryan?"

"I'm sure you have a theory. I'd love to hear it."

"Obviously you need to feed your ego. You want people to look at you like you're superhuman."

"I don't have an ego," I tell her. I'm not about to share the sob story called my life. Not with her or anyone else. I step up to her and cross my arms. "I've been hired to protect this compound and I'm not about to be dismissed back to my station because some bossy girl insists she can fight off some jerk who might want to force himself on her. Sorry, but none of those things are happenin' on my watch."

Her nostrils flare as she breathes through them. "Nothing's going to happen to me."

"Right. Because I'm here."

"No. It's because I can take care of myself." The mighty princess puts her hands on her curvy hips.

I clear my throat. "Oh, really? Do you have a gun or any other weapon?"

"No." She tilts her chin in the air. "I don't need one."

"You think what Rico taught you back at the gym is gonna save you?" I laugh. "Because I'll tell you right now, he's an amateur."

"You don't think I've got skills?"

Time to give her a dose of reality. "I'm not denying you have skills, Dalila. Just not the skill to fight off someone who might want to put their hands where you don't want them. You might be smart, but you sure don't act like it sometimes."

"Why do you care about me?"

"I don't."

She steps closer. "But you do. You care so much you saved me from that guy at the concert, and let me kiss you . . . and you threatened Rico . . . because you care."

"I don't give a shit about anything but gettin' ahead in boxing."

"That's a lie." She reaches out for me. "You care about me, Ryan. Admit it."

My breath hitches as she steps so close I can feel the heat of her skin against mine. Without hesitation, she reaches up on her toes and her sexy, full lips meet mine. They're soft and wet and full of passion. I hate myself as I take hungry possession of her mouth. I'm shocked when her body relaxes and I want nothing more than to keep kissing her.

My lips are still on hers as my tongue instinctively darts out, taking this kiss to the next level.

Instead of turning her face away or laughing at my eagerness, her tongue darts out and meets mine. All bets are off as our tongues slide against each other's and our kiss deepens. Damn, why is my body reacting so much to this girl?

As she moans against my lips and whispers, "Ryan," I'm well aware I could be punched or kneed at any second, but at this point I'd deserve it. Hell, I deserve to be fired for letting this happen.

Without breaking our heated kiss, I gently cup her face in my hands. Her arms wrap around me.

When I finally pull back and end our kiss, Dalila is looking up at me with big brown eyes full of desire. "I proved my point," she says breathlessly. "I win this round."

EIGHTEEN

Dalila

After I tell him that I win this round, I grab the lapels of his jacket and urge him closer. "Kiss me again," I order. My heart is racing. I'm not usually this bold or assertive, but something comes over me. I don't want to let this moment pass.

We're in the back of the gardens close to the fields behind our house where nobody can see us.

I've kissed a few boys before, but never like this. My knees are weak and my entire body is tingling. This whole kiss started because I wanted to prove my point that he cared for me. I didn't plan to kiss him, but as soon as he looked down at me with those blazing blue eyes I couldn't resist.

"We shouldn't do this," he says.

I bite my bottom lip. "I know."

As he leans in and kisses me again with those strong lips and that sexy, experienced tongue, a loud *pop* pierces the air. Before I can even contemplate what's happening, Ryan pushes me to the ground and is on top of me. He's shielding me with his body.

"What's going on?" I ask in a panic, my entire body shaking.

"Get down! It's a shooter!" Ryan yells. "Don't move."

Another *pop* echoes in the distance, and I wince. I can't process this right now. This isn't happening.

Ryan radios for backup on his walkie-talkie and swiftly informs the other bodyguards there's a shooter in the field behind our house.

This isn't my life, not here at La Joya de Sandoval. At least it wasn't before my father started representing Santiago Vega. I grab the lapels of Ryan's jacket as tears stream down my face. "My family needs to be safe, Ryan. My family and friends are in the house. We need to warn them!"

"The bodyguards are handling it," Ryan explains. "I promise. Everyone inside is safe. Your father hired a lot of men to protect your home."

My mind is freaking out and quickly running through the worst-possible scenarios. "What if there's a shooter inside?"

Ryan gathers me into his arms and hugs me tightly, a gesture to comfort me. He can't guarantee there isn't a shooter inside. "I promise not to leave until you're safe. Okay?"

"I'm scared," I tell him, tears welling in my eyes. "Who is it? Who'd want to hurt us?"

"I don't know." He brushes stray strands of hair out of my face.

"I got you. Don't panic."

Ryan's friend Mateo is rushing toward us with a concerned look on his face. "The house is secure. Which direction were the shots coming from?"

"I don't know, man," Ryan says. "Somewhere in the field. Could've been any direction."

Another shot is fired.

"Shit," Mateo cries out, visibly disturbed, before jumping the wall and running into the line of fire. "I'm going after that *pendejo*."

"Why would he run toward the shooter, Ryan?" I ask, my voice trembling. "He's going to get killed."

Ryan doesn't answer. My entire body is frozen in fear as Ryan's body shields me. "I need to get you into the house. It's not safe here."

"I can't move," I tell him in a panicked voice. "I'm too scared."

Another *pop pop pop* fills the air and I suck in a horrified breath. "Mateo!"

"He knows what he's doing, Dalila. Hold on to me," Ryan urges as he swoops me into his arms and heads for the house. Another *pop*. And another.

I think we're safely in the house when I hear another *pop*. Ryan swears under his breath.

"What? What's wrong?" I ask as he rushes me through the line of bodyguards and into the house, where the guests are eerily quiet as the head bodyguard, Gerardo, tells them to stay calm.

"Nothing's wrong, Dalila." He sets me down and steps back. "Go sit with your family."

I look at the ground and realize it's not nothing. Fresh blood drops from Ryan's side onto the floor.

And I scream.

Gerardo rushes the bleeding Ryan into the back hallway away from guests.

"How bad is he hurt?" I blurt out, my lips trembling uncontrollably as I follow them.

My distressed Papá is behind us. "Put him in the bedroom on the first floor while I talk to the police. Dalila, stay with your sisters in the courtyard," he says in a frosty, clipped tone that makes me want to shrink into myself.

Papá turns to our guests, explaining that the shooter is being pursued by the hired security. I don't miss the tense look on his face as he focuses his gaze on Don Cruz and Rico as if they're somehow responsible for this dangerous turn of events.

"Why is this happening?" I frantically ask my father. "Who'd want to hurt us? Is Santiago Vega involved in this?" I follow him to the guest bedroom near the back of our house. I'm still agitated and nervous, which seems to mimic everyone in my house right now. "Are *Las Calaveras* involved?"

"Don't say that name in this house, Dalila."

"Why not?"

"Do as I ask. Go to the courtyard with your sisters," Papá commands. "We need to act as normal as possible. No more talk of cartels, ever."

"Normal? *Nothing* about this is normal," I cry out. I can't help but blame him, as if his connections with all of those new clients and colleagues attending my birthday party are the reason we're in danger.

The reason Ryan is hurt.

"Calm down," Papá says. "I'll take care of this."

His words register, but all I can think about is that Ryan doesn't have family here to take care of him. And now my family has become a target because of Papá's associations. A pang of anger enters my heart and settles there.

As I enter our guest room, I see Ryan sitting on the edge of the bed. There's a lump in my throat as I eye the bloodstained towel he's holding at his side.

Papá walks up to him. "Thank you for protecting my daughter."

"It's my job," Ryan says.

"Do you need to go to the hospital?" Papá says the words with no emotion, like this is a business meeting.

"No," Ryan replies. I notice he hasn't made eye contact with me since I walked into the room. "I'll be fine, Don Sandoval. It's a surface wound."

"Good." Papá glances at Ryan's bloodied side, then rubs his hands together as if the situation is under control. "I'll send in Lola and make sure she bandages you properly. Stay here tonight. I'll have you driven home in the morning."

"Thank you, sir, but I'll be fine," he says. "As soon as I clean up, I'll go back to my post. I've still got a job to do. Mateo went after the shooter and might be hurt."

My dad shakes his head. "You'll stay in this room and sleep here tonight. You're done for the night."

"Mateo is accounted for," Gerardo chimes in.

Ryan tosses the towel aside as if the wound will miraculously heal on its own. "Seriously, Don Sandoval. I can go out there and do my job—"

"Do what my father says, Ryan," I blurt out from the doorway. "Please."

"Dalila, you know me. I'm not a quitter," Ryan says.

Papá furrows his brow, obviously confused that Ryan and I already know each other. "Dalila, *te quiero afuera de este cuarto.*" When I open my mouth to protest being ordered out of the room, he stands stiffly and says, "*Ahorita.* Now."

NINETEEN

Ryan

Tonight definitely didn't turn out as planned. I thought I'd be doing a bogus bodyguard job for some rich Mexican girl. When it turned out to be Dalila's party, and I saw her in that sexy red dress that hugged her curves, I knew I was in trouble. When she kissed me it should have been a bonus, but instead it made me realize how much I want her.

The gunshot was a wake-up call in more ways than one.

After Dalila and her father left the guest room, the woman named Lola came in and dressed my wound. She handed me a pair of cotton jogging pants and a T-shirt to wear to replace my mangled suit. The bullet grazed my side, but it didn't do much damage. It bled a lot, though, all over Mateo's friend's white shirt. Now the shirt has a big bloodstain and a hole in it. The suit jacket didn't fare much better.

I didn't see the shooter, but I'm pretty sure he had an automatic weapon. Luckily, his aim was way off. If he'd been a good shot, I wouldn't be here to analyze what happened. I'd be dead.

I can hear the last guests leaving when Mateo appears in the doorway. "How're you holding up, bro?"

"I'm fine. The bullet just grazed me." I look down at the bandage on my side. "Looks worse than it is. I swear when you jumped over the wall I thought you'd be jumpin' to your death."

"Didn't I ever tell you I'm bulletproof?"

"Dude, nobody's bulletproof."

"Maybe it's luck then. Or I'm just luckier than you." He inspects my bandage. "They told me I couldn't check on you until my shift was over. Sorry about that."

"It's cool," I tell him. "I'll be fine in the morning."

"At least you can brag about surviving a gunshot wound." Leave it to Mateo to look at the bright side. "Gives you street cred. As a *gringo*, you gotta take whatever cred you can."

"I don't need street cred, Mateo."

"Ooh . . . I forgot. My boy's bein' trained by the one and only Juan Camacho." He holds up his hands mockingly. "No other street cred needed."

I gesture to the big sculpture in the shape of a cobra in the corner of the room. "You mocking me in front of the cobra?"

"What the fuck is that thing?" He saunters over to the silver sculpture and flicks the sharp gold fangs sticking out of the cobra's open jaws. "You think this shit is real gold? Man, these people have way too much *dinero*. Did you see that spread downstairs? You'd think it was the presidential inauguration with all that damn food. And that sniper who got a piece of you, shootin' up this place as if it's filled with diplomats and royalty?" He hesitates. "Or kingpins. I swear this life is unreal."

"Did they find the guy who shot me?" I ask.

"Don't know." He shrugs. "I didn't ask the dude in charge, and he didn't offer any info. I'm pretty sure Don Sandoval is connected to some cartel."

I was thinking the same thing. From the huge compound they live in to the massive amount of security tonight . . . my protective instincts perk up. "Who or what was being targeted?" Were they there to try to kidnap Dalila or just cause havoc?

"I have no fuckin' clue, man." He walks over to my jacket and shirt strewn across the back of a chair. He fingers the hole in the jacket and stares at it, amused. "Why are you so interested?"

I shrug. "I got shot, Mateo. I'm kind of involved now, you know."

He crosses his arms on his chest. "Maybe you're involved because you're hot for the birthday girl."

"No. It's definitely not that," I tell him. "My focus is on boxing, not girls."

"Uh-huh," he says, unconvinced. "Who wouldn't like to date above their means for a night, or longer?"

I shake my head. I'm not going to end up like my dad. "Not me."

"Well, I would. But I'm not you." He picks up the suit from the chair and tells me he'll figure out how to get it back to his friend.

"You think Gerardo will notice the hole and bloodstain when I give it back to him?" he asks.

"If he's got half a brain he will."

"Here," he says as he tosses an envelope onto the bed. "Two hundred cold hard American dollars."

"How much do you think your friend will want to replace the damaged suit?" I wave the envelope, fanning myself. "If you say two hundred, I'm gonna kill you."

"I'll cover it," Mateo says. "It was my fault you took this job in the first place."

"I can't let you do that."

Mateo holds a hand up. "What are friends for if not to bail each other out. Right? Besides, if I pay my friend off for you, you owe me one."

"All right, man. Thanks a lot."

"Good luck tonight," he says as he pulls his cell out of his pocket and takes a selfie with me in the background. "I'll bet my left nut that sleepin' on an expensive mattress will make you crave the good life, especially if the rich chick finds her way into it."

"Not gonna happen."

He raises a brow. "I'll bet you two hundred dollars it will."

"I'm not takin' that bet."

He laughs heartily. "Well, I'll catch you on the poor side of town, *amigo*." He pushes down on the mattress, feeling its softness. "Makes me wish I was the one with the bullet hole in my side." With a flick of his wrist he waves and walks out of the room.

After he's gone, I lie on the bed and stare up at the ceiling. For the first time in what seems like forever, my body sinks into a mattress that isn't made out of gym mats.

It's late, but I can't sleep. I keep tossing and turning while attempting to forget the stinging pain in my side. When I close my eyes, all I can see is a Mexican beauty in a red dress . . . with her lips on mine. I slowly relax and at some point fall asleep.

It's hours later when I wake up and, for a second, forget where I am. The stinging in my side is a reminder of what happened and that I'm in Dalila's house. The events of the party flash before me. Kissing Dalila. The shooter. Wondering if Dalila's father is truly some kind of drug lord. Hell, for all I know he's being targeted by some rival cartel because of his connections.

What the hell am I doing coming up with stupid, random thoughts that don't make sense? It just underscores the fact that I don't have a clue how things work in Mexico.

My stomach grumbles and I realize I haven't eaten anything. After she bandaged me up, Lola told me to grab something from the kitchen if I got hungry.

It's two o'clock in the morning. I think about what Mateo said— that there was a shit ton of food at the party. Suddenly I feel hungry enough to take a big chunk out of those leftovers, so I head out of the room in search of some fancy grub.

The house is eerily quiet. The only sounds are the humming of the portable air conditioners and fans throughout the house.

When I reach the kitchen, I expect to be alone. It's dark and I figure everyone is asleep, but I stop in my tracks as I see a silhouette by the refrigerator.

It's Dalila, holding open the refrigerator door with the light shining on her silky nightgown.

Damn.

She looks more angelic now with her flowing nightgown and her hair settling over her shoulders and running down her back. I should alert her that I'm here, but just watching her is mesmerizing. I'm not usually speechless, but when it comes to this one girl I'm at a loss for words.

She pulls out a glass pitcher and closes the fridge.

I clear my throat, alerting her to my presence.

She gives a little shriek before I walk into the glow cast by the dim nightlight on the counter. Her hand goes to her heart as she lets out a sigh of relief. "You're still here?"

"Yep. Your old man didn't really give me a choice."

Her eyes dart to the bandage. "Are you okay? Are you in pain?"

"I'll let you know after boxing practice later today."

"You at least have to take a few days off, Ryan," she says. "You're injured."

"No days off for me. Besides, it'll heal quick. The bullet just grazed the skin." I gesture to the clock above the microwave, my movements seeming stiff and unnatural. What is it about this girl that makes me nervous? *She's just a girl you kissed, nothing more*, I try to tell myself. "It's late. Why are you up?"

She sighs. "I couldn't sleep. I'm so freaked out by what happened tonight. I know the police said they'd do extra patrols around our house, but I have a feeling of dread deep in the pit of my stomach that tonight was just the beginning."

"Of what?"

"I don't know." She shakes her head as if shaking off negative thoughts. "I don't want to talk about it. Papá said Lola took care of your wound. I would have come by to see you, but my father was watching me and insisted I leave you alone."

"Smart man," I mumble.

She tilts her head to the side in an innocent gesture. "Why would you say that?"

"Because I'm not good for you. And you're not good for me." I pop a grape from the fruit bowl into my mouth, trying to make light of the conversation. "If there were somethin' going on between us, it'd be a bad thing."

I take in the sight of her nightgown clinging to her body. I have the urge to pull her close and this time kiss her without any distractions.

What am I thinking? The only reason she kissed me in the first place was to make a point, not because she really wanted to make out. I need to stop thinking about that kiss. To stop myself from digging a deeper hole or acting like a complete moron, I open the fridge and peruse its contents. Boxing. Boxing is my only focus, the one thing I'm good at. Anything else puts me dangerously close to following in my father's footsteps.

"Are you hungry?" Dalila asks, coming up behind me.

I try to ignore the heated electricity in the air between us. "Very."

Think about the food, Ryan. Not Dalila.

There's a lot of food staring back at me, but I can't focus. I absently start pulling out random platters.

"Here, let me help you. At least it'll get my mind off things."
She starts arranging unrecognizable food on a plate. "Some of this
needs to be heated."

"I'll eat it cold," I say, abruptly pulling the plate from her. "I'm
not picky."

She snatches it back. "You can't eat this food cold. Trust me."

"Chicken is good cold," I tell her.

"Not stewed chicken."

"Are you ever gonna stop bein' bossy?"

"No. Are you ever going to stop being a hero?"

"I've never been a hero, Dalila."

"Right," she says. "You only took a bullet for me. No big deal."

Giving up, I sit on one of the stools and watch as she expertly
heats up a hefty portion of leftovers. After she places hot food in
front of me she says in a soft, apologetic voice, "I'm sorry I kissed
you in the gardens. It was stupid and really immature."

I stab a piece of stewed chicken with a fork. "You don't see me
complainin', do you?"

"It took you away from your job. I distracted you and then you
got shot."

I wag the now-empty fork in her direction. "I can't argue with
you there. You are a distraction."

"Why did you do it?"

I take a bite of a *tamale* and my mouth waters for more. "Do
what?"

"Put your life in danger? You could have died."

"Yeah, and who would care?" Hell, I don't even think my mom

would shed a tear if I disappeared forever. On second thought, maybe one or two tears when she sobered up, but that'd be it. Paul would throw a party celebrating my departure from this earth.

I'm aware that I'm shoving the food in my mouth like a pig, but it's so damn good. The flavors are so sweet and spicy, I could eat it every day. And the chicken dish has just the right amount of heat.

"Slow down," Dalila says with a look of shock as she watches me shovel the food in.

"I can't. It's so damn good." I point at the *tamales*. "Whoever made those is a genius."

"I'll tell Lola to make you more."

Her words linger in the cool night air.

Time to be honest with her, because we can't pretend this is something it's not. "We're never going to see each other after tonight, Dalila. I've got to stay focused and you've got to realize that it's not me who's caught up in some kind of cartel power struggle. It's your family who's caught the attention of somethin' bigger than you're willing to admit."

"I don't know what to think anymore," she says in a soft, wistful voice. She swipes at her eyes a couple of times and I realize she's trying not to cry. "I've got to go."

Before I can call her back, she's disappeared into the dark house.

I'm in trouble, because I'd like nothing more than to take Dalila Sandoval in my arms and comfort her until the sun comes up.

TWENTY

Dalila

He said we'd never see each other again. Oh, how his words stung, but I kept up a brave face. Before he could say anything else that would make tears run down my face, I rushed out of the kitchen.

When I reach my bedroom I close the door and put a hand over my beating heart. The way I'm feeling isn't normal. Being near Ryan makes me happy and sad and nervous and excited all at once. I don't know what Ryan thinks of me. He probably thinks I'm a mess.

He'd be right.

I can't even call Soona or Demi because they're sleeping. And they wouldn't understand what I'm going through, mainly because I can't even explain it to myself. The shooting tonight really made my entire life turn upside down. I always considered myself independent, able to be alone and take care of myself.

Until tonight.

Calm yourself, Dalila. Ryan Hess is just a boy. A really lean and muscular boy who can make a girl want to cling to him for safety and security and . . .

He made it clear he doesn't want to see me again. There's nothing between us at all.

I plop down on my bed, bury my face into my pillow, and groan. Why do I feel like I can trust Ryan more than my own family? I believe him when he says he knows nothing about the connection between his stepfather and Santiago Vega. I used to look at my parents and see two perfect people. But they're not perfect, and they refuse to trust me with the reality of the danger they're putting our family through.

My parents seem like strangers to me now, holding back critical information to try to keep me safe from the truth.

As I turn over and try to sleep, fears of that shooter in the distance keep clogging up my head. Suddenly fear grips my entire body and I start shaking uncontrollably. Ryan was shot tonight protecting me. What if I lost him before I really got to know him?

I'm sweaty, my heart is aching, and I can't stop worrying that something terrible is about to happen. It's almost three in the morning now. I sit up in bed and hope the fear will subside, but it doesn't.

Five minutes go by. Every creak and sound startles me as if something evil is around the corner.

Without thinking, I rush downstairs to the guest bedroom. Ryan is awake. He's lying in bed with one arm behind his head.

"Hi," I say sheepishly as I lean against the door.

"Hi," he says back. "What's up?"

"I can't sleep," I tell him, my voice trembling.

He sits up, concern etched into his chiseled face. "Is everything okay?"

I nod.

Then I shake my head. "I'm kind of freaking out about what happened this afternoon. I mean, I should be okay with it. I know my dad hired a lot of people to help protect this place so we're safe. But . . ." I hesitate. I don't want to put crazy ideas in his head about my father. "I know we're never going to see each other again. But, Ryan, will you hold me tonight?"

My eyes are locked on his.

"Come here," he says. Ryan moves over and lifts the covers. I walk to the bed with tentative steps and slide in, reveling in the sheets warm from his body heat. "Thank you," I say, laying my head on his pillow. "I know you're hurt. I don't want you to be uncomfortable with your wound."

"I don't even feel it anymore," he says in a deep, calm voice.

It's dark in the room and silent except for the hum of the ceiling fan.

"Do you have a girlfriend?" I find myself blurting out, then immediately regret it. I don't want him thinking that I came here to hook up with him.

"No."

"When was the last time you dated someone?"

He chuckles. "I'm in a bed with a girl and she's asking me about other girls I've dated. That's never happened before."

"I need you to distract me from my racing mind, Ryan." I lean on my elbow and look at him. I can't imagine any girl not being attracted to him. "Have you ever been in love?" I ask, holding my breath for the answer.

"There's no such thing as love."

"Yes there is."

"Physical reactions to someone isn't love. It's lust. Lust eventually fades." He sighs. "My parents were supposedly crazy in love when they met. They even got their names tattooed on each other's wrists. That fake love lasted for six months. Love is just something people come up with to try to understand these physical feelings that eventually fade, but they don't know it yet."

"You're so cynical."

"I have every reason to be. I don't get attached. I know what I'm good at, and boxing is it. Boxing is the only thing I love."

My heart sinks a little. "Maybe one day you'll fall in love with an actual person. Then you can come back and tell me how wrong you were."

"Don't count on it."

We lie in silence for a long time.

"I'm really glad you're here, Ryan."

"I'm glad I'm here too."

I put my head on his shoulder and look up at him. "Can I tell you something?"

"Sure."

"Just being near you makes me feel safe. I know I sound needy, but it's true. And I don't need you to be my hero or to say anything romantic or weird back to me. I know this isn't more than you comforting me because I'm scared. That's it. And if you want to tell me to leave, I'll understand. I've seen where you sleep. Gym mats are not as comfortable as this bed, so if you want the bed all to yourself—"

"Dalila?" he says with a sigh.

"Yeah?"

He takes his arm and wraps it around me. "Shut up and go to sleep."

My entire body relaxes. I don't know what'll happen in the future, but I'm content right here and now. In Ryan's arms.

He pulls me in close, and just as I'm about to fall into a deep sleep, I feel him kiss the top of my head and whisper, "Sweet dreams, princess."

In the morning I open my eyes and find myself back in my room. I quickly sit up and notice a bright red sunflower on the pillow next to me. Ryan must have put it there.

I vaguely remember being picked up from the guest room and brought here, but I thought I was dreaming. In reality Ryan must have carried me into my room sometime in the middle of the night while I was sleeping. In my sleepy state I remember him laying me on my bed and telling me something, but I have no recollection of what he said.

I take the red flower and hold it gently in my hands, knowing that last night was just the beginning.

I'm going to see Ryan Hess again, because I'm not letting him go.

TWENTY-ONE

Ryan

I could have held Dalila Sandoval all night. Hell, I could have held her for weeks. But I know that eventually I'd have to let her go.

It's too bad I live in reality.

Sleeping next to Dalila was a reminder that you can't order the life you want—you're dealt a certain hand, and you have to live with it. Last night she snuggled into my chest and made me feel like I was her savior. I'm no savior. When she realizes I'm just a bastard with nothing besides a talent for boxing, she'll look at me with contempt instead of adoration. I'll never be a doctor like she's going to be. I'll never be a lawyer like her dad or a college-graduate professional. She deserves a guy who's smart and has a future.

The only chance I'll have at a decent future is in the boxing ring.

That's not to say I didn't eat it up. Last night when she held me close she made me feel like I could conquer the world if I wanted to.

I stare at the boxing ring in front of me. If I'm going to be worth something, this is where it'll be. In the ring.

"You ready to work hard?" Camacho says as he prepares the training lesson for today.

"*Sí, señor.*"

"*Veo que estás aprendiendo español. Que bien.*"

"To be honest, I have no clue what you said. My Spanish still sucks."

"What happens if you're in the middle of a remote Mexican town where nobody speaks English?" he asks me.

"I've managed to survive eighteen years. I figure I can get by."

When I take my shirt off Camacho eyes the bloodied bandage on my side. "What's that?"

"Nothin'. *Nada,*" I tell him, remembering another Spanish word.

"Doesn't look like *nada* to me. Were you in a fight?"

"If you mean with a bullet, then yes."

Instead of being shocked, he shakes his head in disappointment. "You got shot?"

"Grazed is a better description." Then, because I don't know the word for grazed in Spanish, I try my hardest to come up with it. "*Grazado? Grazie?*"

"*Rozar.*"

"Sure, that one. But I'm fine, really."

"Want to tell me what happened?"

"I got hired as a bodyguard last night, which means my job was

163

to put myself in between a shooter and the people I was paid to protect. There was a shooter, there were people, and I came between the two. It's as simple as that."

He sighs. "I sure hope you got paid enough to put your life on the line, Ryan."

My life is probably worth less than the two hundred bucks I got paid last night, so I'm pretty sure I got the better end of the deal.

He makes me show him the wound. He examines it, then cleans it and agrees that it's not too bad.

"Take care of the cut," he orders as he wags an arthritic finger at me. "Or it'll get infected. Take it from an old man who's seen it all. Once infection sets in, you feel like you're rotting from the inside out."

"I'll keep it clean," I promise as he bandages me back up. I take a swipe at one of the speed bags. "I'm ready to kick some butt today."

"*Bueno*. That's what I like to hear." He chuckles to himself. "You remind me of myself back in the day, *muchacho*. Just keep your mind clear and focused. No distractions. "

My mind wanders to Dalila. If she saw me train, she'd yell at me to get back in bed and rest. That's just the kind of person she is, taking on the problems of others and making sure they're okay. She'll be a great doctor one day.

Camacho hands me a jump rope. "It's old-school, but it works," he says.

He leans back in a metal chair and looks at his phone. I crane my neck and see him playing solitaire.

"Must be nice to sit back and relax," I say as I jump.

"Keep going," he says after ten minutes of me jumping rope.

My entire body is covered in a thin sheen of sweat. At this point I don't even try to wipe it off, because I know ten seconds later I'll be sweating even more. I don't see the Mexican guys here breaking half the sweat I do because they're so used to living in this heat.

"I did my time, Ryan. If you want this, it's your turn." He glances at me. "I'll warn you now that word gets out fast around here when you're muscle for hire."

"I got shot. I'm obviously not that great of a bodyguard. More like a bull's-eye."

He raises a brow. "When you're loyal and are more than willing to become a bull's-eye to protect someone else, you become a valuable commodity. The fact that you're a fearless fighter will only make you more desirable to cartels who'll want to recruit you."

"Cartels? I'm not stupid enough to get involved in that crap."

I think the subject is over until he blurts out, "Some of the smartest kids I know got caught up in it. They'll lure you with whatever your weakness is. If that's money, they'll throw it at you. If it's fear, they'll scare you until you're pissing your pants. If it's a girl, they'll find the prettiest angel you've ever seen to lure you in."

I will myself to push away thoughts of Dalila looking up at me last night, as if I was somehow going to make everything okay. It's impossible to forget how good her warm body felt nestled against mine. But I came to Mexico to further my boxing career. I have one goal, and I'm not going to focus on anything else.

They'll get the prettiest angel you've ever seen to lure you in. Camacho's words stick in my head.

Maybe she's one of them and is suckering me into falling for her.

It doesn't matter anyway. It's not like I'll see her again. I made it clear that we needed to cut all contact.

"I've got someone coming here to spar with you tomorrow," Camacho says as we walk to the weights so he can spot me while I lift. "You've got good technique, but I need to see how you box with a real opponent."

The sweat is dripping off every part of my body, but I don't care. Camacho is teaching me how to move properly, how to jab without opening up and making my body vulnerable.

"Why are you helpin' me?" I ask him.

"Because everyone deserves a break in life. You never had one, so I guess I'm it."

I don't know if it makes me feel good that Mateo shared my life story with Camacho, or embarrassed. "Do you think I'm good enough?"

He shrugs. "You've got talent, but if you choke when you're between the ropes, then no. But remember: even if you win, there will always be another guy to come knock you down off your pedestal."

My confidence kicks in. "But what if I never lose?"

"Then you become a legend." He motions for me to come close and he puts a hand on my shoulder.

"I'll be a legend like you."

He chuckles. "I'm a has-been, Ryan. If I was younger and fighting these guys today, I don't know if I'd be the one slinging the belt over my shoulder. Times have changed. Guys are tougher, meaner, faster."

I sit on the edge of the weight bench. "So it'll be my goal to be tougher, meaner, and faster."

"It's more than that." He looks down at me. "Always remember to protect the integrity of the sport. It's a story, Ryan, between you and your opponent. It has a beginning, middle, and end. And it's full of dance moves. Remember that." He gestures to my feet. "And you definitely need dance practice."

"You don't think I can dance?"

He looks me up and down. "You're a *gringo*. That's enough to tell me your footwork isn't good enough. You move like a *burro*."

I give my best impression of a Michael Jackson spin, making Camacho shake his head in amusement. "I can dance. Don't underestimate me because of the color of my skin."

Camacho crosses his arms on his chest and nods. "I won't," he says. "But hopefully your opponents will."

Every word Camacho says sinks in. I want to learn everything I can from him.

"Come on," he says when we're done for the day.

"Where are we goin'?"

"My place," he says without turning back.

It doesn't take long to get to Camacho's apartment building, in the middle of a town with a few stores flanking it. We park on the street and he leads me to his small, one-bedroom apartment. A woman greets us with a warm smile. Camacho starts talking to her in Spanish, then she waves to me and walks out.

"Was that your daughter?" I ask him. I take in the worn couch and old, random paintings of landscapes and boxers nailed on the wall. In most of them I recognize Camacho when he was younger.

"No, that wasn't my daughter," he says as he shuffles to the small kitchen and fills up a kettle with water. "That was the caretaker. She helps out a couple of days a week."

A caretaker? "I didn't know you needed a caretaker."

"I don't." He motions for me to follow him into the bedroom off to the side. Propped up against a flood of pillows is an older woman. "This is Valeria, my wife."

The minute his wife lays eyes on him, she smiles wide and holds out stiff, shaky arms. There's a little drool running down the side of her mouth and her greeting is slow, like that of a child learning to speak for the first time.

"She was disabled after a car accident on her way to my last fight," he explains. "She lost oxygen to her brain." He sits on the edge of the bed and gently takes her hand in his. "This is Ryan Hess," he tells her. "The boxer I told you about."

I don't know how much she understands as she stares at me with a curious expression on her face.

"You've talked about me?"

"Don't get your head full of ideas. Sometimes I'm bored." He kisses her forehead, then leads me back to the kitchen.

"Where are your championship belts?" I ask, expecting them to be proudly displayed on the wall.

"I don't need to have a reminder of the past." He points to his head. "The memories are in here. It was a long time ago, Ryan. Nobody remembers me anymore."

"You're wrong! I used to watch tapes of your fights. I used to mimic your stealth moves. Remember the fight with Manuel Reyes? Oh, man, you were on fire." Camacho's mouth turns into a smile when I mimic his jabs.

"That was a long time ago, Ryan."

"I'm sorry about what happened to your wife. Is that why you disappeared after your last fight?"

He nods. "She was the love of my life, Ryan. Still is. Many times she left me to go live with her parents so I could stay focused, because she knew that's what I needed. Before the accident she was an independent wife. Maybe I had a few more fights left in me, but she needed me, so I left the sport." He sets down cucumbers and tomatoes on the table. "Here." He hands me a knife. "Make yourself useful."

While I cut the vegetables and he starts to cook dinner, I wonder what his life would have been like if Valeria hadn't been in the accident. "Do you miss it?"

"Every day. When you're a true boxer, the sport consumes you. You think about boxing, everything you eat is to fuel yourself for a fight, you dream about boxing." He looks me straight in the eye. "But at the end of the day, boxing won't be there to smile at you when you walk in the door."

TWENTY-TWO

Dalila

I've tried ignoring the fact that everything has changed since the shooting, but I can't do it anymore. Papá's newly hired bodyguards patrolling our house at all hours of the day and night make me feel claustrophobic. This constant feeling of dread isn't going away and instead gets more intense every day.

Since my birthday party I feel like we're all in a fog. My parents are so distant they might as well be living in another country. I feel so alone. Once again I tried to press Papá for answers and he shut me out.

Yesterday investigators came to our house. They were in Papá's office for what seemed like forever. When they came out, one of them was holding a briefcase that he hadn't walked in with. Was there bribe money inside?

What has my father gotten himself involved with?

The news on the TV didn't make me feel any better.

While the reporter admitted that drug violence has been on the decline, he said new concerns have developed. *Los Reyes del Norte* cartel, the newest cartel wreaking havoc across the country, was waging war on *Las Calaveras* for power and territory. The leader of *Los Reyes del Norte*, El Fuego, was said to be paying off some police and government officials to look the other way. They said he was smart, resourceful, and knew how the law worked.

Papá is smart, resourceful, and knows Mexican law like the back of his hand. Did he pay off the investigators yesterday with a briefcase full of cash? Could he possibly be the mystery man they call El Fuego?

Sitting back waiting for answers isn't going to happen anymore. If nobody will tell me what's going on, I need to find out for myself. One person knows something. It's time I stop trying to be the good girl and let the rebel in me come out.

I tell my parents I'm sleeping at Demi's house and they order that bodyguard Gerardo to take me. After Gerardo drops me off, Demi lets me borrow her car. I lied to my family on purpose. I should be full of remorse, but I'm not. I'm a girl on a mission and I'm not letting anything get in my way. For once I have a plan that isn't orchestrated by someone else.

I'm going to find answers on my own. There's just one problem. I can't go without protection. I need my own bodyguard.

And there's only one person who can fill that role.

I drive through the small towns that lead to the boxing gym and my heart beats fast in anticipation and fear. I haven't seen Ryan since he was at my house the day of my birthday, but that doesn't mean he hasn't been close to my thoughts. I wonder if he's at least thought about me a little.

Or more than a little.

It's dark now and Sevilla is a desolate town. It isn't in a shady area, but I'm hyperaware that I could be in danger if a cartel member is tailing me.

When I reach the gym, I grab my bag out of the car and head to the front door. It's locked.

The place is dark and being here alone is starting to creep me out. It looks deserted except for the lone Mustang with Texas license plates parked in the lot. I know Ryan is here.

Damn.

Standing out here all alone is probably not the best idea I've ever had, but I'm not turning back now.

Maybe there's another door in the back. I peek around the corner using my cell phone light to guide me. There's a door about twenty feet away. I reach for the handle but before I can turn it, I hear someone clear their throat.

I gasp in fear and almost fall backward.

"Didn't anyone ever tell you trespassing is a crime?" Ryan's husky voice echoes through the air.

I let out a relieved sigh and shine my light into the darkness. Ryan is sitting about ten feet away from me on an old, rusty metal chair. He's all alone.

I walk toward him and can't help the feeling of elation that washes over me. "I came here to ask you a favor. What are you doing outside in the dark?"

"It's not dark." He points to the sky. "Those are stars."

"I know what they are, Ryan. I just didn't know you were into astronomy."

"I'm not. I needed to think. Lookin' at the stars helps. They're the only light I need."

"What do you need to think about?"

"Life. Boxing. Strategy on life . . . and boxing," he says with a chuckle.

So he's not thinking about me. A pang of sadness pulses in my chest. When I'm in his presence, my body feels all tingly and my heart races. I'm drawn to him and get a renewed sense of energy when he's near. It's apparently one-sided and he doesn't feel the same way about me. He's been my hero when I didn't think I wanted one, but now, when I need a hero, I'm too nervous to ask.

"How's your wound?" I stutter.

"Nonexistent at this point. Or maybe it's so infected it's numb." When I open my eyes wide with worry he holds up a hand. "I'm just kiddin'. It's all healed."

There's another chair next to him. He gestures for me to sit on it, so I walk over and plop myself down. I'm trying not to think that someone could be lurking in the darkness, ready to hurt me in an attempt to get revenge on my father.

"Did you come up with anything?" I ask. "On life strategy, I mean? Because I could use some advice on that."

"Nah," he says. "I don't have any answers."

I gaze up at the stars twinkling in the sky. "When I was a little kid I thought each star was a Martian sending signals to earth." I glance at Ryan. The angles of his face are outlined in the moonlight, making him look older. "It's stupid."

"I used to think I would be the first person to live on Mars." He shrugs. "I'd volunteer to escape my crap life on earth. Talk about stupid. I'm not even goin' to college. Who'd want some dumbass living on Mars? I'd probably do something idiotic and accidentally blow the planet up."

"Speaking of idiotic, once I slept on my arm and when I woke up it was numb," I tell him. "I lifted it over my head to try and get the blood flowing and it hit me in the face. I thought my arm was paralyzed forever."

"You think that's bad?" he says. "I got an erection during the swim unit freshman year. One of the girls noticed and screamed it out to the entire class. I asked my mom to write me a note explaining I had a condition that prevented me from swimming the rest of the year. She didn't, and the kids nicknamed me Hardy for the rest of the school year."

I look at him sideways and try not to laugh. "I have to admit that's pretty bad."

He nods. "Yep."

"If it makes you feel any better, when I was seven someone called our house and told me that I'd won a new television. All I needed was to give them my credit card information for the shipping cost. I obviously didn't have a credit card, so I went into my father's wallet when he wasn't looking and stole his card. It was a scam, obviously. We never got the TV and I never told my dad it was me who was responsible for his identity theft."

He grins. "When my mom was dating this guy I didn't like, I took his phone number and had a teenage neighbor of mine, Trixie, lend me her phone. When my mom was out for the night with the jerk, I used the girl's phone to text the guy all this sexual stuff hoping my mom would see it. She did, and she dumped him the next day. She cried for three weeks straight. Even though the guy was a jerk, I felt like shit about what I did."

"I hadn't seen my grandmother in a really long time and she was sick." I take a deep breath. "Actually, she was dying. So I decided to ask this boy to drive me the two hours to her house so I could see her one last time and say good-bye."

"Did you go?" he asks.

"I don't know yet." I clear my throat in anticipation of the words that are about to come out of my mouth. "You haven't told me if you'll escort me, so I can't tell you what happens."

He sits up. "You want *me* to escort you?"

I nod. "*Sí*. It's two hours from here. I promise I'll pay you for your time, and we can drive back tomorrow, so we'll be gone for less than a day." I sound desperate, but that's how I feel at this point.

"Have your parents take you."

I wish I'd thought of an answer to that beforehand. "They're busy," I blurt out. "And if they find out I've gone alone they'll seriously make my life miserable. They're old-school and think a girl shouldn't travel by herself." I shrug. "They think I'll get kidnapped if people find out my father is representing Santiago Vega, especially after that sniper thing happened. I told them I was going with a bodyguard and they said it was fine." Lies lies lies. They're flying out of my mouth as if I was born to be a liar.

He shakes his head. "Sorry, I can't help you."

"Why not?"

"Because I have to stay focused. I'm bein' trained by Camacho and I can't screw it up."

I can't have him say no. He's the only one who can help me.

"I need your help, Ryan. Think of it as a vacation. Going to my *abuela*'s house will be like going to Mars. It's far away, and it's an adventure. I know you like adventures!" I squeeze my eyes shut as I add, "And I know you're a nice guy and would want to help me see my dying *abuela*." I reach out and place my hand on top of his. "She doesn't have much time left. And I don't trust anyone else to take me but you. The fact is, Ryan, I don't want anyone else there with me. I know we've only known each other for a small amount of time, but the truth is I need you."

The lies I've been spouting suddenly turn into a moment of truth.

I do need him.

More than I ever thought I'd need someone.

I don't want to scare him off by revealing my true feelings.

He leans forward with his elbows resting on his knees and sighs. "I can't do this."

A sinking feeling settles in my stomach and lingers there. "Do what?"

"This. Us. You and me, it won't work. I mean, could I have a one-night fling with you? Sure." He turns and looks right at me. "Is that what you want?"

"No. I want more."

"I've been dead inside for so long this is unfamiliar territory. There's something going on between us, but Camacho says I need to stay focused. He took a chance on me to help me fulfill my dream of becoming a pro boxer. Letting him down isn't an option. I owe so much to Mateo for hookin' me up, I can't let him down either. I owe him."

I can't hold it in any longer. "Ryan, Mateo didn't send Juan Camacho to you. I did."

His brows furrow in confusion. "What?"

"I called Camacho and told him to give you a chance. *I* asked him to train you if he thought you were good enough. You told me you'd owe a big favor to anyone who got Camacho to come see you."

"*You* did it?" he asks slowly as his brain processes the news. He leans back and groans, as if I just took the wind out of his sails. "Wow. I really am an idiot."

"No. I'm the idiot," I tell him. "Because I came here tonight and figured you'd want to help me without having to call in the favor you owe me."

"How do you know Camacho?"

"He's an old friend of my dad's. He used to come to my house a lot. Maybe I got Camacho here, but you made him believe in your talent and agree to train you."

"Now you expect me to pay you back by escorting you to your grandmother's house?"

"Yes. As my bodyguard."

"I can't."

"Fine. Go back on your word, Ryan. I held up my end of the bargain. If you can't hold up your end—"

"We didn't have a bargain, Dalila."

"You said you'd owe someone who got Camacho to look at you. I guess your word doesn't mean much. If having honor isn't your thing . . ." My voice trails off.

I start walking back to the car, but Ryan runs up to me and blocks my path. "Give me a minute to explain, will you?" He runs a frustrated hand through his hair. "Listen, I meant what I said, but I can't get attached to you. I feel like I'm already gettin' in too deep. You need to understand who I am."

"I know who you are. You're the guy who wants to escape to Mars, regrets making his mom cry, and gets erections in swim class," I tell him.

He nods. "Exactly. I'm simple. And poor. No complexity here."

"I sent Camacho to see you because I care about you," I say sheepishly. "I got you what you wanted." I avoid his eyes as I tear up. "Don't deny me my grandmother. It's not safe for me to go alone. I need you there. I need you there to protect me. I need you to be my hero."

Ryan presses his palms to his eyes. "Fine, I'll do it. I'll take you to see your dying grandmother. No payment needed," he says. "Havin' Camacho train me is payment enough."

"You're talking like this is a business deal instead of a favor for someone you like as more than a friend."

"It is a business deal. Listen, as much as I'd want to be more than just a bodyguard escorting you to your grandmother's, I can't. Not now. We go, you say your good-byes, and we head back."

"Fine," I say. At this point I'm afraid he'll change his mind if I don't take him up on his offer. "I'll sleep here so we can leave first thing in the morning."

He stops in his tracks. "Sleep here?"

"You don't expect me to drive all the way back to Panche now, do you?"

"I guess not. Be aware that I don't have one of those soft beds with fluffy pillows like you're used to."

"That's fine," I tell him. "I can rough it."

The side of his mouth quirks up. "Uh-huh," he mumbles under his breath.

This is going to be one interesting night. Ryan thinks he's going to stay distant, but I'm not going to let him.

TWENTY-THREE

Ryan

I can't believe I agreed to be Dalila's escort. What the hell was I thinking? It's not like I don't want to go with her. I just don't know if I can be physically close to her without falling into something dangerous. As I lead Dalila inside the gym, I wonder how tangled up I am in her world of deception and power.

I just have to resist the pull she has on me. I have to keep my distance, literally and figuratively.

As we pass the boxing ring on the way to my room, she stops. "I think it's really cool that you're a boxer," she says.

"Most girls I know hate boxing," I tell her. "They think it's brutal. You go in the ring and fight other guys and get sweaty and gross. Even after you shower, you can't wash off the cuts or bruises."

"Speaking of showers," she says. She twirls her hair around her finger. "I think I need one."

I cock an eyebrow. "You need a shower?"

"Yeah. Why? What's the problem? It's the end of the day and I feel gross."

"There's no problem. Come on," I say, leading her to the lone bathroom in the place. "I'll stand guard to make sure nobody bothers you, although we're the only two people here. Nobody else trains this late." I haven't even seen the manager dude, Ocho, for a few days. "But just in case, I'll stand outside the door."

"Thanks," she says, slipping past me as she enters the bathroom with her purple bag in tow.

I stand guard, leaning against the doorjamb. If I were another guy, I'd have made a move on her already. Hell, maybe in the past I would have been that guy. Then I hear the shower turn on.

My mind isn't as chivalrous as I'd like it to be, because suddenly visions of her naked body being sprayed by the showerhead enter my brain. Images of her soaping her breasts and stomach and lower. If I were in there with her, I'd offer to . . .

Oh, hell.

Now my body is reacting, willing and ready to be called into action.

There won't be any action, I tell myself. There would be consequences.

Like expectations that I could never meet.

Like commitments that I could never keep.

Like feelings I would refuse to feel.

This is torture.

I groan and bang the back of my head against the wall. This is not what I signed up for. I'm a boxer, here in this shithole in Mexico to train. I'm not here to fantasize about some entitled, beautiful girl who wants to guilt me into escorting her to her ailing grandmother's house.

"You okay?" Dalila's sweet feminine voice, which suddenly reminds me of thick honey, lands on my ears. I swallow hard as she appears wearing a small towel from the gym. A towel! Is she kidding me? Does she realize that I'm an eighteen-year-old guy?

Sure she does. She knows exactly what she's doing. Manipulation, plain as day, is what's going on here.

"Put your clothes on," I say in a monotone voice, unwilling to give her any satisfaction.

It's ironic. Usually I'm the one shirtless and *she's* trying to convince *me* to cover up. Oh, how the tables have turned. But I won't let her win. Nope. My will is as strong as steel. I'm not my dad, being selfish for a piece of ass. My will is stronger than his.

Dalila starts walking to the back room with that damn skimpy towel around her body and her girly bag slung over her shoulder.

"*Obviously* I'm going to put clothes on, Ryan," she says in a sexy, flirty tone. "I just have to dry off first."

The princess is playing with me.

I might have had a few too many hits to the head, but not too many to know that I'm being manipulated.

In my room I gesture to the gym mats on the floor. "It's not much of a bed, not like what your parents have in their guest bedroom."

She eyes my shitty bed but doesn't give any indication that she's repulsed. "It's fine."

My room is dark except for the square of light coming from the little window that teases me with a small breeze every now and then. Suddenly I feel like an inadequate dolt who can't even offer her a decent bed to sleep on. No matter her motives, the girl doesn't deserve to sleep on gym mats.

She kneels down and pulls out a small piece of clothing from her bag.

"I don't own a blanket," I blurt out.

She glances back at me before standing up, the movement edging the towel down a few inches. The tops of her full breasts are now in full view. "That's okay. I don't need a blanket. Can you turn around while I slip into pajamas?"

I'm standing here like a dumbass trying to act like a girl *slips* into pajamas in my room every day. She's testing me, and I'm failing. My body is suddenly on fire and sweat drips down my forehead, but for once it's not from the Mexican heat.

"I'll be back," I tell her. "Lock the door until I come back. Don't open it unless you know it's me."

I head for the door, the entire time looking away so I don't get a glimpse of whatever she *slipped* into.

"Where are you going?"

"To take a shower," I say in a gruff voice. "A *very* cold one."

TWENTY-FOUR

Dalila

Okay, so maybe I took it too far.

I wanted to make Ryan realize he has feelings and an attraction to me that he can't ignore. I want to break through that wall of his, and if driving him crazy by flirting is the way to do it, I have no problem taking that chance. He's the only one I can trust and rely on, and that scares me.

He's desperate to ditch me, but I can't let that happen. When I'm with him, I don't feel alone and isolated. I feel a tiny bit sorry for him. The way he rushed out of the room a few minutes ago was a telling sign that he's not as immune to me as he'd like to be. My plan is working.

I should feel guilty that I brought a short, almost sheer

nightgown with me. When I slipped into it, every inch of my skin was sensitive to the fabric. My entire body is aware and alert as I wait for Ryan to come back.

I stand in the middle of his room practicing sexy poses. I feel like such a dork, standing here waiting for him. What if he doesn't come back tonight? It's almost two in the morning. He's used to sleeping on mats. What if he decided to sleep in the middle of the boxing ring instead of in the room with me?

I'll just wait. He said he was taking a shower, but it's been like thirty minutes since he left.

Sighing in frustration, I plop myself down on his makeshift bed and lean my back against the wall. I'm relieved I haven't gotten any texts from my parents. At least that's good news. I play some stupid game app on my phone and wait for him to come back.

Time ticks by.

I keep waiting, but he doesn't appear.

Discouraged, I toss my phone beside me and, unlocking the door, make a path down the darkened corridor to the bathroom. I step inside the bathroom and focus on Ryan's silhouette behind the curtain.

"What's taking you so long?" I blurt out. "I mean, how clean can one person get?"

Ryan pushes the curtain aside, revealing most of his perfectly sculpted body. "I told you to stay in . . . in . . ." He hesitates as his gaze roams over my skimpy, sheer nightgown that covers every imperfection of mine so he can only see the flawless parts. ". . . in . . . um, I mean, I told you to stay in my room and lock the door."

I step closer to him. "I wanted to talk to you."

He shakes his head. "No way. I can't talk with you when I'm in the shower and you're wearin' that."

"What's wrong with what I'm wearing?" I ask innocently, even though I'm acting anything *but* innocent right now.

"It's too perfect." He swears under his breath. "Can't we talk about whatever it is tomorrow, when we're on the road? Not here, when all I want to do is . . ."

I shake my head slowly and step even closer. An errant spray from the showerhead soaks the front of my sheer baby-doll nightgown and I feel mischievous and powerful. "I'd rather talk right here and right now, Mr. America."

His eyes boldly rake over me and my entire body tingles with excitement. When his eyes rest on my mouth, my tongue darts out to lick my lips.

"Damn you. You're going to be the death of me," he growls, then with a swift movement his arm goes around my waist and urges me into the shower with him.

His breathing gets labored as the water drenches my nightgown, making it completely see-through. I'm trying not to think about the fact that I'm practically naked here and I want him to look at me.

"You wanted to talk right here and now," he says, his strong hands still on my waist. His sky-blue eyes right now have a hunger in them I've never seen before. It's empowering knowing that I'm having such an effect on him. "So talk," he says, then swallows hard as his eyes focus on the sheer fabric clinging to my breasts.

Suddenly I'm self-conscious and nervous. I'm trying hard not to look down and admire his naked body.

But I do.

And he's glorious.

"Talk," he orders again as if it's not a request.

But now I'm speechless.

I'm exposed.

And he's very, very aroused.

I clear my throat, pretending not to be affected. "I, um, was wondering . . ." I swallow, then squeeze my eyes shut because I want to take another peek but that would be losing the small ounce of dignity I have left. I step out of the shower and turn off the light so we're cloaked in darkness, then step back into the shower with renewed vigor. My only guide is the tiny glow from the hallway light. "Ryan, I'm not tired."

"Then why'd you turn off the light?"

"To set the mood."

"For what?"

Okay, here goes. I take a deep, calming breath. "I don't know why or even how you walked into my life, but you did and now I can't get you out of my mind." I can feel my face getting hot as I add, "If tonight is the last time we'll be alone together, I don't want to waste it." I tentatively reach out and touch him. "Do you?"

With gentle fingers, he cups the back of my neck. "I can't resist you," he whispers as his fingers deftly slip the strap of my nightgown off my shoulder. My breath hitches as he leans down and gently licks my wet skin, the sensation sending shock waves through my veins.

As his tongue is replaced by his mouth, he places soft, sensual kisses on the hollow of my neck. Oh, my. This is nothing like I imagined. Nothing like the books or movies or stories my friends told me. I grab his shoulders because I'm suddenly deliriously dizzy and my knees go weak. This isn't supposed to be how it happens. I'm supposed to take control and be the strong warrior woman. I'm supposed to make him fall in love with me so he won't leave.

But I'm not in control.

While I'm trying to make him fall under my spell, I'm falling into his.

His hot, wet tongue graces my earlobe and then his lips place tiny, light kisses on my mouth. A fire burns within me that I've never experienced before. I couldn't describe what I'm feeling right now even if I tried. It's like my entire body is experiencing an overload of sensations all at once. This feeling is like a drug and I want more.

With the last ounce of control I have left, I pull back just the slightest bit. Water is dripping on us and steam from the hot water is surrounding us in this darkness, making me feel like we're in our own little cocoon.

This feels so right, it can't be wrong.

My trembling, tentative hands skim over the hard ridges of his chest. With a renewed sense of determination, I wrap my arms around his neck and press my body to his.

"Promise me this doesn't mean nothing," I whisper into his ear.

"It won't, but it can't mean everything," he says.

TWENTY-FIVE

Ryan

Living my life hasn't been easy. In fact, I've lived a pretty shitty existence.

Until last night.

I lie on my uncomfortable bed made of gym mats while the most amazing girl sleeps soundly curled against my chest. Last night I carried her from the shower to my room, where we both explored and experimented and drove each other insane until she said those words that stopped me from taking everything she was willing to gift me.

I think I'm falling in love with you.

We'd agreed to keep feelings to a minimum. At least that's what I meant when I told her that last night couldn't mean everything.

I'd have been okay with *like* or *lust* because those two emotions don't come with baggage.

But *love?*

I can't do that.

Love comes with commitment and expectations.

And while I care for Dalila even more than I want to admit, I can't give her more of myself than I already have.

I won't let myself destroy a girl like Dalila, which is why I stopped us from going all the way last night. I'd like to think I did the right thing, but even now as she lies naked with her long hair splayed across my chest I want her more than I've wanted anything in my life.

Including boxing.

She stirs and entwines her legs with mine. Something tells me that if I don't disconnect from her now, I might never be able to do it.

I gently rub her tanned, slender arm. "Dalila, wake up."

Instead of waking, she nuzzles her face deeper into the crook of my neck.

"Dalila," I say a little louder this time. With her so close it's hard to keep my body in check.

"Mmm," she replies in a groggy voice, which only seems to turn me on even more.

I don't have an agenda here, but what if she does? Trusting anyone isn't my strong point, especially when I've been warned that I should keep my distance from girls who have the power to make me question everything.

Fuck that.

I'm not letting anyone have power over me. I might owe her a favor to take her on a little trip to see her grandmother, but I'm in control of my emotions.

"Come on," I say in a gruff tone as I move out from under her embrace. "Time to go."

I quickly shrug into a T-shirt and jeans, ready to get out of here. Suddenly I'm claustrophobic with just the two of us in this small room.

As if it randomly got cold in the room, she sits up and shivers. Her hair is mussed and she looks tired and beautiful. And she's fully exposed. Damn. Dalila Sandoval could make any guy grovel for her affection. Including me. But I can't . . . and won't.

I shove the last of my things into my bag and toss her another shirt of mine. Seeing her naked affects me more than I'm willing to admit. "Here, put this on. Let's get on the road."

"I'm hardly awake yet," she mumbles as she slips the shirt over her head.

"Well, wake up. We leave in less than five minutes."

I storm out of the room and enter the main gym. Mateo is here punching a speed bag, the staccato sound echoing off the walls. A few other guys are working out, oblivious to the fact that Dalila Sandoval is in the building and that she spent the night. I wish we would've left earlier, because I don't need anyone knowing who I'm spending time with or getting into my business.

"Hey, Hess!" Mateo calls out. "Wanna spar?"

"I can't," I tell him.

"Why not?"

"I'm goin' out of town today."

He stops hitting the bag. "Out of town? What about your training?"

"It'll have to wait until later tonight or tomorrow. A job came up."

"A job, huh?" As if on cue, Dalila appears still wearing my T-shirt. "Ah, I get it," Mateo says, staring at Dalila's back as she walks out. The door slams behind her, the sound reverberating through the gym. "I wish I had your job."

"No, you don't," I say. "That girl expects too much."

"In my experience all girls expect too much. You better run after her. If she gets away, another guy will be waitin' in the wings to snatch her up. Trust me on this, bro."

He's right. I rush out of the gym to find her struggling to start her car. It keeps turning over, then dies.

"What's wrong?"

With her teeth clenched, she turns her attention to me. "This stupid car."

I glance at the gas gauge. She's got more than a half of a tank, so there's no reason her car shouldn't turn over. "Pop the hood."

I'm not a huge car guy, but I might be able to tell if something is off with it.

"You got car trouble?" Mateo asks as he struts outside to join us. I swear the dude walks to an invisible beat he's listening to inside his head.

"Her car won't start. She's got gas," I explain. "But it won't turn over when she turns on the ignition. You know anything about cars, Mateo?"

He looks under the hood. "A little." It doesn't take him long to point to a tube that's completely melted. "Take a look at this," he says. "The tube is destroyed, bro."

"How long will it take to fix?"

Mateo shrugs. "I don't know. Maybe a couple of hours after ordering the part, but it'll probably take a day or two to get. I can ask one of the guys . . ."

"Oh no!" Dalila cries out. "It can't be melted. This isn't even my car."

"We can use my car," I offer, "but I don't have gas. I've got some cash left over, so if I can get to a gas station we can be on our way."

"That car isn't going to last a car trip in the middle of the brutal Mexico heat," Mateo tells me. "And depending on where you're going, it's not a good idea to be flashing Texas plates. I don't know where you need to go, Ryan, but feel free to take my uncle's truck," Mateo offers, pointing to a Chevy pickup. "He's out of town for the week and I can drive another one of his cars. It's no big deal."

"We won't be back until tonight," I tell him. "No way I'm takin' your uncle's truck for that long."

"He won't care. I'll call him if it'll make you feel better." He pulls out his phone and starts dialing his uncle. After talking to him, he holds out the keys. "He said to take the truck. He'll tell one of my cousins to pick me up here after I'm done working out. I'll pick up the truck in the morning. Have fun."

With long, purposeful strides, Dalila heads for the Chevy.

Mateo is trying to hold in laughter. "*Buena suerte*, Hess," he says with a knowing wink. "That means good luck."

I don't tell him I need all the luck I can get to keep my distance from her.

In the truck, Dalila directs me to the highway. I use her phone to call Camacho and tell him I need to take a day off. He's not happy about it. He said if I don't keep training while I'm away, he'll know I'm not committed and won't hesitate to give up on me. I have to get back soon, because I'm not forfeiting everything I came to Mexico to do.

After I hand her back her phone, I tell Dalila to call her parents and let them know our plans.

She drops her phone into the cup holder. "I texted them last night. They already know where I am." She looks at me sideways and I can tell something's up. "I just need to be home by dinner-time."

A little voice in the back of my head tells me there's more to the story. Her father seems like a super-strict dude. Why would he just let her spend the night with me? And why aren't her parents accompanying her to visit her dying grandmother?

"What if we're late getting back?" I ask her.

"Then my dad will ground me," she says matter-of-factly. "After he kills you."

The crazy thing is, I don't know if she's joking or not.

TWENTY-SIX

Dalila

We drive through Sevilla and head for Tulanco, where my *abuela* lives. "Tell me something good about your childhood," I ask, trying to get to know more about Ryan as I direct him on which way to go. "You've mentioned a bunch of bad stuff, but what about the good?"

He thinks for a minute. "This teacher back in Chicago, her name was Mrs. Berman. One day after school in first grade, she pulled out this little present wrapped in sparkly candy cane wrapping paper from under her desk." He chuckles at the memory. "I thought it was the coolest thing I'd ever seen. When she handed it to me, she told me Santa left it under her tree but he must have dropped it off at the wrong house because it had my name on the little tag attached to it."

"That's so sweet. What was it?"

"A little plastic superhero figurine kids used to bring to school. They'd always play with them, and I felt left out because I didn't have one." He smiles at the memory. "It was the Falcon, who lived in a rough neighborhood and for a while led a life of crime. He'd lost his mom and dad, so he was pretty bitter. In the end he fought injustice."

"Mrs. Berman really liked you."

He nods. "She was great. Once she found me hidin' in the janitor's closet after the kids made fun of my old, ripped jeans. The next day she came to school wearin' ripped jeans and told the kids she got them at the expensive boutique in town. You should've seen the kids' faces when she said she had to pay more money per rip. Nobody made fun of my jeans after that. Okay, your turn."

"My life has been pretty boring."

"Have you traveled a lot?"

I nod. "I've been to Rome, New York, and London." All of those cities look very different from my country. I look out the window at farms and small towns outlining the highway and think I could pick a Mexican town out of any other in the world. The sounds, sights, and smells of Mexico are familiar and comforting.

"I haven't been anywhere," he says. "Well, besides Mexico."

I hold my arm out the window and let the wind blow against my fingers. "Tell me your impression of my country."

"It's got its own flavor and attitude, like Chicago, where I used to live. I thought we had authentic Mexican food in Chicago, but it's nothin' like the tamales and tacos I've eaten here." He shrugs. "I haven't seen one ground beef taco since I've been here."

I raise a brow. "Ground beef taco? Seriously? That's not Mexican, Ryan. That's something you'd find in the US."

"People in Mexico also love music. I've seen more radios here than I have in my entire life. The guys play music while they're workin' out or hangin' out . . . or sittin' on the front stoops of their houses."

"We do love music, from classic to contemporary. It's in our veins."

"And punk," he adds. "You like punk music."

"I think I'm the only one in Mexico who likes American hardcore punk. Besides Demi, but she pretty much likes everything that's out of the norm."

"And what's this morbid fascination with skulls?" He points to a mural on the side of a building with colorful skulls painted in bright colors.

"It's not morbid, Ryan. Mexicans like to celebrate people's lives and decorate skulls to bring their spirits closer to us. We even have a special celebration called *Día de los Muertos*, the Day of the Dead. We decorate tombstones with painted skulls and bring our deceased family members their favorite food. I swear you can feel their presence."

"When I die, bring me some of Lola's tamales, please. I'll definitely come back from the dead for those."

I laugh. "Will do, Mr. America."

He settles into his seat. "There is *one* thing I hate about Mexico and the south."

"What's that?" I question.

"The heat."

I smile. "I don't notice it half the time. I guess I'm so used to it I don't even think about it."

"When I'm sweatin' just standing in the sun, I think about it. A lot. Or in my bedroom back at the gym, where there isn't a breeze to break up the monotony. Back in Chicago the summers are brutal, but the winter and snow break it up."

The entire three-hour-long car ride, we talk. While we share information about ourselves, I feel closer to him than ever before. There's not a single lull in conversation as I talk about my parents and sisters. He laughs when I tell him that I used to be afraid that someone was hiding under my bed at night. I had a huge fear that if I stepped off the bed, a hand would reach out and grab me.

He tells me about his mother and why they're not close. She's an alcoholic and drinks heavily to numb whatever pain she's going through, which leaves Ryan feeling neglected. I watch as his shoulders slump when he mentions her.

It's so easy to talk to him when he opens up. I wish he'd let down his guard more often, but I know his past rejection makes him closed most of the time. Does he feel closer to me now that I've shared stories about myself with him?

I reach out and put my hand close to his leg. Will he take it? Does he crave the physical contact between us like I do? I keep my hand there and look out the front window, acutely aware of my surroundings and the people and cars we pass on the highways.

He lifts his free hand and I wait for him to take hold of mine, but he doesn't. Instead, he reaches under my hair and starts caressing the back of my neck with his thumb. The gesture makes my senses spin. It feels so good. "I love your curly hair," he says, then winds his fingers through it.

"It's too unruly and frizzy," I say.

"Nah. It's perfect."

His words settle inside me like a personal gift I'll cherish forever.

I instruct Ryan to leave the highway and head toward Tulanco, the town where my *abuela* lives. "Don't expect her to live in some huge *rancho*," I tell Ryan.

"It's a small *rancho?*" he asks.

"More like no *rancho*. If you blink, you'll miss it."

When we pull up to my *abuelita's* house, I watch Ryan's expression turn from confusion to surprise. Her house is just a little one-bedroom ranch with a quaint garden outside. I remember this place from when I was a kid. Papá used to bring us here on weekends and I would help her plant flowers and herbs in her garden.

"There's no way your grandma lives here," Ryan says.

"Why would you say that?"

He looks at me as if I'm nuts. "Have you seen the mansion you live in, Dalila?"

"Maybe she likes living here," I tell him. "Not everyone wants to live like—"

"A princess," he finishes.

I playfully punch him in the stomach. "No. I mean live with modern conveniences."

"*Abuelita!*" I cry out when she appears at her front door and lets out a squeal of delight when she sees me.

My *abuelita* might be tiny and short, but she's tougher than any woman I know. She's wearing a flowing sundress that reminds me of a flag waving in the wind.

"*¡Bienvenidos, mija!*" she says as she runs up to me with a warm, loving smile and a hug so tight I wonder how so much strength can come out of such a little woman. Just seeing her soothes a piece of me that felt unsettled.

"*Él es uno de mis amigos*, Ryan," I tell her, gesturing to Ryan and explaining that he's a friend of mine.

Abuela Carmela opens her arms wide, then grabs hold of each side of Ryan's face and kisses both of his cheeks. "*Gracias por traer a mi nieta a visitarme*," she says, then kisses him on both cheeks again as a grand gesture of gratitude.

"She's thanking you for bringing me to her," I explain to Ryan as Abuela Carmela bounces back toward the house and motions for us to join her. "How's your Spanish?"

"About at a one-year-old's level," he says. "Or an infant. Why?"

"Because she doesn't know any English. Come on, let's go inside." It feels so good being here, like my soul is being healed from the inside out. Sometimes La Joya de Sandoval feels fake. My ancestors lived in this town for many generations and my roots feel deeper here than anywhere else.

Ryan holds back as he assesses Abuela Carmela's spry gait.

"What?" I ask. I point to the front door. "She wants us to follow her."

His jaw is clenched, his eyes slightly narrowed.

"She's not sick."

With a resounding sigh I say, "She's old."

"You fuckin' lied to me, Dalila. You said she was on her *deathbed* and you needed to say your last good-byes."

"Technically, you're right. But . . ."

He clutches my arm and pulls me to him, his eyes piercing mine as if they're searching for some kind of truth. "What else are you lyin' about, huh? Tell me."

"I didn't lie. I manipulated the truth."

"That's the same thing," he says in a curt tone.

I have to fix this, but I don't know how. If I reveal the truth, will he abandon me?

TWENTY-SEVEN

Ryan

I'm not going in Dalila's grandmother's house until I get answers. That woman might be old, but there's no way she's on her deathbed. I doubt she even has a cold, let alone some debilitating affliction about to kill her.

Dalila shrugs with embarrassment. "Well, she *is* old."

"You said she was *dying*," I say through gritted teeth. "You specifically said you wanted to come here to say good-bye."

"Fine, I admit it. I lied. When you said you'd owe a favor to the person who brought you Camacho, I called him. I was holding on to that favor for when I needed it." The words leave her lips, but I don't hear any amount of remorse. "I don't know why you're so mad." She holds her hands up in frustration.

"It's a big deal, Dalila." Last night fucked with my emotions and my focus. If she hadn't told me her grandmother was dying, I'd have told her to find someone else to act as her stupid bodyguard.

"I lied because I thought if I said I just wanted to come for a visit, you'd have said no, whether we'd made a deal or not."

I feel so fucking stupid. Camacho tried to warn me, but I was thinking with the wrong brain. I wanted to believe her sweet, lying lips so much that I became the fool I vowed never to be.

If she's willing to lie about her sick grandmother, she'll likely lie about anything.

"Tell me who you're workin' for," I say. "No fucking around this time."

She steps back, and her brows furrow in confusion. "What are you talking about?"

"*Who* are you workin' for? Just tell me."

Her grandmother appears in the doorway. The poor woman probably has no clue her granddaughter is a master manipulator.

"*Ahorita vamos, Abuelita,*" Dalila calls out to her, then grabs the sleeve of my shirt. "I'm not working for anybody, Ryan. I lied because . . ." She hesitates. "There's something going on with my dad. I think he might be involved in the cartel and Santiago Vega, but he and my mom have shut me out. I think my grandmother knows the truth and you became the one person without ties to my father who could take me."

I shake my head. I'm not about to be duped by her again, so anything that comes out of her mouth is going through a filter. "I don't believe you."

"Well, you're going to have to believe me because that's the truth."

"You could've just called her on the phone."

"She doesn't have a phone, Ryan. Everyone on earth doesn't necessarily have a phone, especially here in the middle of nowhere." Dalila gestures to our surroundings. I'm trying not to focus on the way my T-shirt flows around her body and instead focus on my anger. "Look around us. There are no telephone poles. If you think you can get a cell phone signal anywhere around here for miles, good luck with that."

"I don't know what to believe anymore," I mumble. I had one goal in my life.

One *fucking* goal.

Suddenly Dalila Sandoval comes along and I've become entangled in cartel bullshit.

"Believe this." She walks up to me with determination and looks me right in the eye. "I'm sorry I lied about my *abuela* being sick. I really am. But I need to protect my family or distance myself from them if they're involved in the cartel. I trust you with everything I have and everything I am. Last night wasn't any manipulation. It was just you and me, and it was real. Now that I've told you the truth, get over the fact that I manipulated you. I think it's about damn time you start to trust me. I don't have ulterior motives."

She whips herself around, and I watch her back as she struts into the small cement house.

So now I'm not just a fool, I'm a fool who's standing outside with the sun beating down on him in the middle of one-hundred-degree weather.

A very healthy Abuela Carmela is still standing at the doorway motioning for me to follow Dalila's lead. *"Hace mucho calor, entra a tomar un refresco."*

I give Abuela Carmela a small smile and enter her house. When I step inside, it's obvious the woman doesn't have many possessions. It kind of blows my mind that Dalila and her family live in a mansion with all the luxuries of life while her grandmother lives in this tiny house. She doesn't have a television, but she's got a bunch of books on her bookshelves. The woman must love to read.

I scan a wall full of pictures. Some are old black-and-white portraits of families and couples. Others are of Dalila and her family. I point to an old picture of a man holding a baby on a running track. "I bet this picture has an interesting story behind it," I say.

Abuela Carmela gently glides her hand over the picture with her small, thin fingers. I watch as her expression softens while she explains the picture to Dalila.

"She says the man is her father. He was an alternate runner on the Olympic team and he's holding my grandmother after a race he won," Dalila explains as she translates her grandmother's words. "I've never heard that story before. I guess I never stopped to pay attention to the pictures."

Dalila pats me on the back. "Maybe *you'll* be on the Olympic team one day, Ryan. For boxing."

That would be amazing, but I've got a long way to go. Hell, I'm probably too old to start training for the Olympic team. "Dreams don't always come true, no matter how hard you try."

"Miracles happen, or that word wouldn't exist. Never lose faith,

Ryan." With a big, encouraging smile Dalila plops herself down on one of the chairs in the kitchen. "Here," she says, holding out a mug to me. "Taste this."

I peek inside and see something that looks like tea. The steam wafts up my nose when I sniff it.

Her grandmother chuckles, then says something to her in Spanish.

"It's mint tea," Dalila explains. "Made with mint leaves from her garden."

Wow. I breathe in the fresh scent before I down the glass in one gulp. I hold up the mug and throw out one of the handful of words I know in Spanish to accurately describe the tea. "*Bueno.*"

"*Gracias,*" Dalila's grandmother says with a smile that reminds me of her granddaughter. The old lady takes Dalila's hand and my hand and holds them together.

"She thinks we're a couple," Dalila tells me, then looks at me with those bright chocolate eyes that shine with something I'm not ready to acknowledge.

I look down at our hands and a pang of sadness fills me.

Damn. *Ignore all feelings and emotions.*

I snatch my hand back and get down to business. "Tell her why you came here so we can get back before dinner."

As soon as I say it, Abuela Carmela starts pulling leftovers out of her refrigerator and freezer. She dismisses Dalila's protests that we're not here to eat. The woman starts talking so fast as she heats up the food, it's a wonder Dalila can even keep up. I'm in awe of how quickly the woman prepares the food. In no time at all she's got a huge spread in front of us.

I'm not here to disappoint the old lady.

I pick up a piece of meat from a plate that her grandmother set on the table and cut it with a sharp, jeweled knife she hands to me. "This looks old," I say, examining the green and shiny stones set in the wooden handle.

Dalila holds up the knife and asks her grandmother about it. "She says her great-grandfather made it after the war. She says he carved his initials in it and embedded green emeralds into it to represent a good harvest and red rubies to represent the blood and tears that go into the hard labor they did to make their lives easier. It's good luck to prepare food with it."

I examine the butt of the handle. The letters *PH* are carved into it. I wonder what it would be like to have a family heirloom, something that was cherished because of those who owned it before you. I have nothing from my ancestors to tie me to them.

"This knife is cool," I tell her. "I bet if it could talk it would tell some pretty good stories."

"Yeah." Dalila fingers the tip of the knife, but quickly jerks her hand away. "Ouch! That's sharp."

"Be careful," I say, then take the knife from her and stab some fried thing with meat inside. As I bite down the burst of flavors makes me wish I could bring some home with me.

Abuela Carmela keeps talking to me as if I can understand every word. "What's she sayin'?" I ask.

"Nothing."

I raise a brow.

"Fine," Dalila finally says. "She says you have kind eyes, and that must mean you have a kind soul."

I pop another fried meat thing in my mouth. "Sorry to break the news to you, but your *abuela* is blind."

"She's not blind."

"I don't have kind eyes. And my soul is pretty dark. Maybe you jinxed her when you said she was deathly ill. She's obviously ill-informed."

She aims a nugget at me. "Fate put us together. Did you ever think that I could fix that dark soul of yours?"

I catch the nugget and pop it into my mouth. "Fix it with what? Food?" The dark part of my soul knows I need to push her far away. "And it wasn't fate that brought us together. It was a punk rock concert. And now it's because you need answers about your family."

"You're right." Dalila's expression stills and grows serious. The mood changes instantly.

"*¿Pasa algo?*" Abuela Carmela asks.

With a deep breath, Dalila pulls out an open letter from her pocket and holds it out to her grandmother. The lady takes one look at it and her expression matches Dalila's. They talk back and forth in Spanish, so I have no clue what they're saying, but something she says upsets Dalila so much that she breaks down and chokes back tears.

"What's wrong?" I ask.

Dalila looks up at me as tears run down her cheeks. "She said my father has been involved in some shady business deals outside the courtroom. When she confronted him, he didn't deny it. My father is no better than his clients."

Full of emotion, Dalila pushes her chair away and runs outside.

I'm about to go after her when Abuela Carmela reaches out and touches my arm. She points to herself. She wants me to stay here while she talks to Dalila.

I look out the living room window and see Dalila sitting on the ground with her head bent in her hands. Her grandmother is rubbing her back, consoling her. A part of me wants to run out there, kneel in front of her, and tell her I'll be her hero to protect her from anything.

I can't deny it to myself any longer. I care deeply about Dalila. More than I should, and more than I ever wanted to.

TWENTY-EIGHT

Dalila

Everything is stressing me out and the truth of my father's involvement in illegal activity and the cartels is too real. Abuela Carmela is rubbing my back, telling me that everything will be okay.

But it won't.

She takes my hand in hers and tells me that she comes from a time when people worked hard in order to put food on the table, not to buy personal possessions. But it's not all about that. She mentioned that the people she saw Papá working for and associating with were against everything she believed in. Papá told her he was doing what he had to do and she should mind her own business. Abuela Carmela hasn't been back to La Joya de Sandoval since.

Ashamed for even putting my thoughts into words, I ask if she thinks Papá is connected to the new cartel *Los Reyes del Norte.*

"*Ojalá supiera,*" she says with sadness clouding her sweet face.

She doesn't know.

But I can tell she suspects he's getting more deeply involved.

"*Aveces es mejor ser ignorante, mija.*"

Sometimes it might be good to be ignorant, but I don't want to look away and pretend bad things aren't happening around me.

"Can we talk?"

I turn to see Ryan standing behind me and I quickly wipe away the tears falling down my face. "Sure."

Abuela Carmela walks back into the house, telling me to lean on Ryan if I need to. She leaves us alone to talk even though I don't feel like saying anything.

Ryan holds his hand out. I furrow my brow as I stare at it. "What do you want?"

"Take my hand," he says. When I do, I feel the warmth and strength in his touch as he helps me up. "Walk with me."

I wipe my tears with my free hand, hating that I feel so alone. "You should probably stay away from me, Ryan. Very far away from me."

"Well, that's not going to happen, Dalila. Just walk with me."

With my hand in his, he leads me away from Abuela Carmela's house. We walk for a few minutes, weaving our way through the hilly, grassy land with vines sticking up from the ground that always made me feel free and alive.

"I'm sorry you're upset," he finally says as he kicks a rock down the little cobblestone path leading to the shed.

The concerns I have about Papá are too real and too overwhelming.

He stops and turns to me. "We're in this together, you know."

"No, we're not. I'm alone in this. You said yourself that we can't be involved and your only focus is boxing."

"I thought I couldn't have both." He takes a deep breath. "You've got to understand that I've been numb for so long, Dalila. And all I wanted to do is prove that I'm good at something so my mother would love me and not regret the fact that I was born. But when I saw you out here cryin', something inside me woke up." He swallows hard. "What if I asked you to be my girlfriend?"

My stomach flutters. "Are you serious? What about boxing? I thought—"

"I can do both," he says in a determined voice. "Just . . . be honest with me. Always."

The problem is I do have secrets that I can't share with him. I've already told him so much. I'm worried he'll think I'm too much trouble if I reveal that I suspect my father isn't just affiliated with the cartel; he might actually have escalated to be the drug lord El Fuego. His association with Santiago Vega, and the investigators that came out of our house with that briefcase are clues that he's not innocent. And now my grandmother told me he's had some shady business deals.

I'm selfish when I say, "I want you to be open with me, Ryan." It pains me that I can't be as open with him.

"I will." He flashes me a little smile. "If I'm gonna be honest, your grandmother's little fried beef things are addicting. Add those to my gravesite on that Day of the Dead. I'm in training and shouldn't be eatin' anything fried."

"I need to be a good influence on you, or else Juan Camacho isn't going to be happy with me. No more fried food."

Suddenly I feel like I can figure out the puzzle that's become my life. If the Ryan piece fits, then I have one part of my life in order. I won't be alone.

At least for now.

Back in the house Abuela Carmela can tell the mood between Ryan and me has changed. It's lighter, as if a rain cloud has just been lifted.

After a few hours of visiting with her and sharing some of my life over the past few years, we have to cut our visit short even when she begs us to stay the night. I tell her I need to be home tonight, so she packs us a bunch of food and gives me a pep talk on staying strong.

Tears fill my eyes as I say good-bye, but I promise to visit her again soon.

"I hate crying," I tell Ryan as he pulls away from her house and we head home.

"I don't cry," Ryan says. "Not since I was in seventh grade."

"I'm a crier," I admit. "Not all the time, but when I'm stressed out. Crying releases part of the stress." I glance at him sideways. "You should try it sometime."

"Are you sayin' I'm stressed?"

I laugh. "Yes."

"Yeah, you're right," he says.

"What do you want to do with your life, Ryan? Besides boxing,"
I ask.

He rests his wrist on the top of the steering wheel. "I don't know.
I haven't really thought that far ahead." He hesitates and lets out a
big breath. "It's not like I've got a lot of options."

"What about college? That's always an option."

"I'm not smart enough for college. My grades in school suck."
He looks at me sideways. "Let me guess. You've got the whole ten-
year plan figured out. After graduation go to college. Get a job as
a surgeon. A few years after graduation, get married and have kids.
Am I close?"

"I don't have a ten-year plan," I tell him, then smile sheepishly.
"I'm going to be a heart surgeon, but to be honest it's not *my* dream."

"Whose is it?"

"My brother, Lucas."

"I didn't know you had brother."

"He died a few years ago. From a heart murmur." I pick at my
nail. "All my plans have been dictated to me by my parents, and I'm
too scared to protest because I don't want to see them in pain from
missing my brother so much."

"I thought Mexicans were supposed to celebrate the dead."

"I do," I tell him. "In my own way. I never told you that Lucas
and I used to sneak into my dad's car and listen to Shadows of
Darkness. He'd crank it up so loud my eardrums would ring for
days." I sigh. "I miss him."

"I think he'd want you to do what you want to do in life, not
what he wanted to do."

I shrug. "You're probably right."

"If you could do anythin', what would you choose to do?"

"I guess I'd like to help needy children like this little boy I met at the town festival. Giving him money for food made me feel really alive and present."

"You're an amazing girl, you know that?"

It's not long before we're on the main highway, but when we encounter a portion that's closed and we're instructed by some highway patrolman to use a side road, I'm on alert. The patrolmen aren't in uniform and they're not acting normal. When I see a guy with a shotgun and what looks like a truck full of drugs behind one of the patrol cars I tell Ryan we have to turn around and take the back roads.

Rumors about the war between *Las Calaveras* and *Los Reyes del Norte* are fresh in my mind.

"I don't like driving on the back roads for too long," I say, watching out for cars in front of and behind us for any more suspicious activity. I just want to get as far away from the roadblock as possible.

"I don't like it either," he says, his voice echoing my deep concern.

Ryan grips the wheel as he drives at a fast pace through the desolate rolling hills with farms and open land on each side.

"This isn't known to be a dangerous area," I inform him. Most places are safe, but you can't always tell the bad guys from the good guys.

"I won't let anything happen to you, Dalila."

After driving for another half hour on the dusty back roads, he lightly brushes his hand on my arm, making my skin feel refreshed and alive. It feels so right being here with him on this journey. I couldn't have done it without him.

Just when I think we're out of danger, the engine starts to rev and the truck slows down.

"What the hell?" he says, pressing on the gas.

"What's going on?" I ask in a panic.

Ryan pulls off the side of the road as the truck comes to a complete stop without him even pressing on the brake. "I have no clue. We still have a quarter of a tank of gas, and we haven't blown a tire. I think it's overheated."

"Overheated? Oh no. I have to get back home tonight, Ryan. It's not safe for us to be stranded here."

Especially when there's nobody around to help us.

TWENTY-NINE

Ryan

Just when I think my bad luck is behind me, something comes along to remind me that I can't escape from living under a black cloud.

I step out of the truck and examine the tires. They're perfectly fine. Popping the hood doesn't give me any more clues as to why the truck just stalled. The engine is definitely hot but not smoking.

Shit.

I check the fluid levels. They're fine. I check the wiring, wondering if the lines are melting in this hellish heat. They're all intact. The truck isn't old, so I don't know what the problem is. We're stranded in the middle of fucking nowhere.

"I guess it just overheated," I mumble as I sit back in the driver's seat, frustrated. "I'm not an automobile expert, but that's pretty much the only explanation."

Dalila sits up straight as if she's going to take control of the situation. "We need a plan."

"See if you can get cell reception," I tell her.

She lifts her cell in the air trying different locations, even holding her arm out the window. "None. Not even one bar."

"Let me try."

She hands me the phone and I walk down the road, keeping a close eye on our truck the entire time. This situation is putting me on edge. Staying in one place could make us a target for some vigilante who wants to start trouble. Mateo made me paranoid and Dalila's suspicion about her father makes her a target. It's better to be cautious than stupid.

No matter what I do or where I stand, Dalila's phone is completely out of range. It might as well be a brick at this point.

After a while I try starting the truck again. It's completely dead. I look at Dalila's furrowed brow and those full lips, which are now frowning. "Hey, it's okay. If we can't flag down a passing car to help, we can walk back to the highway and talk to one of the patrol officers who blocked the road. Maybe they can help."

"I don't want to do that," she says.

"What's going on, Dalila?"

She gives me a poor excuse for a smile. I don't buy it for one minute. "I'm just freaking out for no reason."

"Do you know somethin' I don't?" I ask, wondering if she's holding back crucial information.

"No. I just want to get back before dinner."

Oh, yeah. Her dad is expecting her home. "He knows we went to see your grandmother. He'll probably think we stayed there overnight."

She looks straight ahead at the long stretch of gravel road in front of us. "Right."

We sit in the truck waiting for a car to drive by so we can flag it down, but after two hours we still haven't seen anyone. I try starting the truck four more times with no luck. It feels like we're on a deserted island. We're tired and hot.

She leans her head on my shoulder as I wrap my arm around her. "We can't just stay here," I tell her. "They might have reopened the main road already, so nobody would be takin' the side roads. We might not see people for a while."

"What should we do?" she asks.

"I think we should walk back to the highway and try to flag someone down. If nobody comes at least we can see if we can get cell reception and call Mateo to come get us."

"Ryan, I have to be honest with you about something." She looks pale. "Those guys who blocked the road weren't in uniform. I'm not sure they were legit."

I'm seriously confused now. "How do you know?"

She lets out a big sigh. "I don't know. I just have a weird feeling about it."

"Why didn't you say anythin' earlier?"

"Because if they realized we were suspicious, we could have been a target. I didn't want you to go into protective mode and give them a reason to stop us." She rubs my arm. "They weren't after us, but I don't want to go back there."

"Come on," I say, stepping out of the truck.

"Where are we going?"

"To hide the truck behind those boulders over there," I say, pointing to a patch of huge boulders ahead of us. "Get in the driver's seat and put the truck into neutral. I'll push, you steer." I look at the sky and realize the sun will be going down soon. "We'll stay in the truck tonight, then head out tomorrow on foot. Keep your phone off so it doesn't lose battery."

She clears her throat. "Ryan, can I talk to you for a second?"

She didn't tell me about the suspicious guys at the road block. What is she about to tell me now?

"My dad doesn't know I'm with you." I look down at her as she twists her long, curly hair around her fingers and adds, "And he thinks I slept at Demi's house last night."

"He's expecting you home for dinner tonight, right?"

"Yeah," she admits in a pained voice.

"Oh, great. So basically your dad doesn't know where you are, he might actually be involved in a major cartel, and when he finds out you lied to him he's going to freak the hell out."

"That's probably a correct assumption."

I can either worry about it, or just take it easy and try to fix things tomorrow. "You want to try and hike it all tonight?" I ask her.

She looks shocked. "You're not mad?"

I shake my head. "What good would it do to be mad at this point? I can't change our situation now, can I?"

"No, but I'm sorry I didn't tell you sooner. If you knew he was against me going to see Abuela Carmela, I was afraid you wouldn't take me. Or that you'd make me call Papá and get permission from him to go, which I knew wasn't going to happen. He'd make his newly hired bodyguards make sure I never left the house."

"Come here," I say, pulling her into an embrace. I'm not going to get mad or upset with her. We're a team now. When she's down I need to help pick her back up. I'm not going to be in a relationship with her just to break her down when things get tough. "We can walk down the back roads until we find a house with a phone or someone to drive us to a town so we can call Mateo."

"Why are you being so nice about it? I lied to you."

"We're in this together, Dalila. I'm not about to abandon you unless you want me to."

"Wow." She hugs me tight. "That's the coolest thing anyone's ever said to me. It's getting dark. Let's just do what you said. We can pull the truck behind those rocks for the night so we're not seen, then head out in the morning."

"You sure you're okay with the plan?" The thought of her strict father not knowing where she's sleeping tonight isn't going to go over well. "I can leave you in the truck and go find help."

She shakes her head vigorously. "You're not leaving me. No way."

It isn't long before the truck is hidden behind huge boulders and we're sitting on the bed of the truck watching the sunset. The air is finally cooling off. There's a howl in the distance that reminds us we're smack-dab in the middle of deserted land.

"It's peaceful here," I tell her as she lays her head in my lap with her hair splayed across my jeans. "I could live here," I say, stroking a soft blue curl between my fingers. "I mean, without the threat of the cartels or drug lords."

"My country isn't all filled with drug lords and cartels."

"I know. The news in the US makes it seem like Mexico is a war zone."

"News reports on Chicago feel the same to us. They make it look like a war zone there."

"I guess the news just shows certain parts that make good stories," I say.

She holds me tighter. "Let's build a house right here, Ryan. We'll have a bunch of kids and live off the land."

"A bunch of kids?" I ask. "How many is a bunch?"

There's a mischievous grin on her face as she sits up and says, "At least six. Eight at the most."

I start to choke. "Eight? How about three? That sounds like a good, even number."

"Three is not an even number, Ryan. Eight is."

As long as we're in fantasy land, I might as well give in to her delusions. "Okay, we'll have eight kids. We'll even have enough land here to build Abuela Carmela a new house."

"Don't forget my three sisters. We'll build them houses, too. One for each of them."

I can imagine everything in our fantasy as if it could one day become a reality. I'd have to add one thing. "We'd have to build a house for my mom, too. After sendin' her to rehab she could come live with us."

"Maybe she'll change when she gets older," Dalila tells me. She moves to sit on my lap facing me. I can't believe I tried to pretend my attraction to her and my feelings for her don't exist. Her perky nose rubs up against mine. "Everyone can change, Ryan. Even your mom." She holds my head in her hands. "But if she doesn't come around, we'll have each other. And our ten kids. We'll create our own loving family."

I hold a hand up. "Whoa, slow down. Did you just say *ten* kids?"

Her smile widens. I love that smile. "Maybe."

"If we're having ten kids, I think we better start practicing right now." I cup the back of her head and kiss her tenderly. She grabs at my shirt and moans as her tongue reaches out to meet mine. I'm going to lose it before we even start.

Truth is, I can imagine spending the rest of my life with this crazy, amazing girl who holds too many secrets and keeps me on my toes. I don't know what to expect next, and I don't completely trust her.

And despite all that, I'm falling for her.

She breaks our kiss and, still straddling me, lifts my T-shirt that she's been wearing all day over her head. Her fingers go to the front hook of her sexy lace bra and she releases the material, making me feel like the luckiest guy on the planet. It falls down her shoulders revealing her full, perfect breasts. I swallow and my breathing gets ragged as her hands reach for my zipper.

"Ryan," she whispers into my ear. "Let's pretend tonight is the last night of our lives. *Okay?*"

Usually I don't play pretend.

But tonight I'm all in.

THIRTY

Dalila

We didn't sleep much for the second night in a row, but I don't care. It's nice to see Ryan's face in such a peaceful slumber. Last night I gave him everything I have—my heart, my soul, and my body.

I hold him tight against me, never wanting to let him go. I'm nervous about what'll happen when I get home. I know Papá will be beyond angry. I'll just have to make him listen to me and let him know that I needed to go see Abuela Carmela even though he forbade it.

I have more questions now than I did before, though.

I don't know where my father's loyalties lie. Is he like those highway officers, putting on a facade?

There are so many more good people in Mexico than bad. If we all rise up against the violence, we can fight it. I know some people are manipulated and forced to join gangs with the threat of their lives being taken away. Or worse, their families' lives. Would I join a gang to protect my sisters' lives? I don't know. I'd let someone kill me before I'd take another life. But if I had to kill someone to save Margarita's life . . . or the twins . . .

I can't even think about it.

Truth is, I'd die for my family. I look over at Ryan. I'd die for him, too.

But would I kill to protect them? Tears stain my eyes because so many unfortunate people in my country are faced with that very scenario. It's not a show on TV; it's reality. For some it's life or death. It's kill or be killed.

I shiver just thinking about it.

"You cold?" Ryan asks as he pulls me closer to him, his voice all deep and groggy from sleep.

"I'm okay." I kiss him and watch as his lips turn into a sleepy grin.

I lay my head on his chest and watch the sun starting to rise. I know we were just joking last night about living here, having kids and a future together. But I could see us being happy without the added stress of the outside world.

"What're you thinkin' about?"

"Nothing." I sink into the warmth of his palm. "Just wishing things were different."

A worried look crosses his face. "Last night?"

"No! Not that!" I remember the look of adoration on his face as we explored and loved each other. It was special and beautiful. I'll cherish the memory forever.

"I want you to know somethin', Dalila." He looks across the horizon. "I don't know what I did to deserve you, and maybe I'm a fool, but I don't even care. Whatever you ask of me, if it's in my power I'll do it."

"And whatever you ask of me, if it's in my power I'll do it."

The sun is coming up now. "We should head out," he says, sitting up. "Let me just lock the truck, get our bags, and then we can go. I'll try the car one more time and see if the engine cooled off enough to go or if it's completely dead. If it's dead, are you ready to do some major trekking today?"

Not really, but it's the only way we're going to get home and face my papá. From the ground I pick up a black rock that resembles a heart. "Here," I say, handing him the rock. "It's for good luck." He climbs into the truck.

"Pray for a miracle!" Ryan calls out from the front seat. He kisses the rock, then turns on the ignition. It hums perfectly as if nothing was ever wrong with it.

"No way!" I hug him through the window. "It works!"

His mouth is open in shock. "I can't believe it." He puts the heart-shaped rock in the glove compartment. "We're keeping that rock with us. It's definitely good luck!"

Running around to the passenger side, I hop in. "Let's go before it decides to overheat again."

"Yes, ma'am." Ryan puts the truck in gear and we drive off. It's not long before we reach the main highway again. I breathe a sigh of relief. This time we don't come across any barrier or patrolmen acting shady.

"Try your cell," Ryan says when we pass a cell tower. "Call your parents and tell them we're on the way."

I wince at the thought of Papá and Mamá mad at me. And the thought of confronting them with the information Abuela Carmela gave me. "I can't."

"You have to. They're for sure worried and need to know you're safe. They probably think you got killed or kidnapped. It's not cool."

I take a deep breath. "I know. You're right."

He takes my hand in his and rubs it gently. "Call them and listen to them scream at you and threaten to take away all your freedom for a little bit. Take it like a champ."

I'm feeling nauseous and don't want to take it like a champ. If the truck hadn't broken down last night, I would have been home and nobody would know I had visited Abuela Carmela.

It's the truck's fault, not mine.

Of course I'd like to think that's true, but it's not. It's my fault. And like Ryan said, I have to face the consequences. I turn on my phone. As I suspect, I have about a hundred texts and messages from my parents and Demi.

I call my parents first. Papá answers on the first ring. "Dalila!"

"It's me. I'm safe," I quickly say before anything else. "Our truck broke down last night in the mountains after visiting Abuela Carmela and—"

Papá goes off on a tirade, ordering me home right away and questioning who I'm with. I contemplate lying and telling him I'm alone or with Demi, but I decide to tell him the truth. When I reveal I spent the night in a truck in the mountains with Ryan, he orders me home immediately and hangs up.

"How did it go?" Ryan asks when I set the phone in my lap.

I don't answer. I want to cry. I am definitely not taking this like a champ.

"That good, huh?" He reaches out to hold my hand but I push him away.

"I think he might hurt you," I tell him, my voice quivering uncontrollably.

"I'll take it like a champ," he jokes.

"It's not funny." Just the thought of Ryan being hurt makes my stomach churn.

I'm eighteen and it's not like I'm a little kid anymore, but my life has always been dictated by my parents. The fake freedom I did have was whatever freedom they decided to give me. It's time I have a mind of my own.

We drive for hours. My entire body stiffens when I see the sign for Panche.

The truck, which is usually filled with our endless conversations, is suddenly eerily quiet as we drive up the road to La Joya de Sandoval. It's the first time I've actually been scared to go home.

Papá, Gerardo, and a half dozen other bodyguards are in front of the gate waiting for us.

"Don't get out of the truck, Ryan," I plead. "Please promise me you won't get out of the truck."

He turns to me with apology written all over his face. I know he's going to get out. I've never seen Papá violent, but I've never spent the night with a boy before.

I hop out of the truck hoping to stop Papá from going off on Ryan. "It's my fault," I tell him frantically. "I lied to Ryan and told him you said it was okay. Then our truck broke down and I told him it wasn't safe for—"

"*Entra a la casa, Dalila,*" Papá orders.

"But, Papá!"

He's not even looking at me. "Get in the house," he orders again.

He's changed in the matter of a few weeks. He went from a warm father to a harsh, unforgiving dictator.

Papá keeps a pointed gaze on Ryan, who's stepping out of the truck now. I know what's going to happen. Papá hasn't summoned his hired muscle here in full force to make sure Ryan gets a meal before he heads back to the gym.

They're here to scare him and, possibly, hurt him.

I can't let that happen. I vowed to myself that I would protect him. I'm not going to stand by while my lie gets him in trouble.

I rush to Ryan's side and put my arms around him.

"It's okay, Dalila," Ryan says in a calm voice.

Why is he so calm? Doesn't he care if he gets beaten up by a bunch of men?

"Don Sandoval, please accept my apologies," he says with such dignity and respect my heart is bursting. He wraps his arm protectively around me. "Dalila just wanted to go visit her grandmother and I thought—"

"You have no right to *think* about anything regarding my

daughter," Papá says through gritted teeth. "Dalila, I will not ask you again."

"Go," Ryan urges, taking his arm off me. "I'll be okay."

I know the unspoken words Ryan's thinking. *I'll take it like a champ.* But I don't want him to be hurt. If Papá would just listen to me, he'd realize it was all my fault.

"Promise me you won't hurt him, Papá," I cry out. "He didn't do anything wrong. He was helping me." I can't let go of Ryan until I get a promise. I know I'm publicly disrespecting my father by not following his orders, but I have to take a stand and protect Ryan.

Like he'd protect me.

"Just go in the house," Ryan urges. "Do what your dad says."

"Only if he promises you won't be touched."

"Fine," Papá says. "I won't hurt him."

I tentatively move away from Ryan and take one last look at him. At his reassuring nod, I walk through the gates and enter La Joya de Sandoval. I look around at the colorful artwork on the walls and the mosaic tiles on the floor. Its splendor used to delight me, but right now it feels fake and contrived. This isn't a *joya*, a jewel. It's a facade.

For the first time in my life La Joya de Sandoval doesn't feel like home.

THIRTY-ONE

Ryan

I know I'm about to eat shit. I'm outnumbered by more than a hand-ful of trained muscle. Just by assessing Dalila's father's demeanor I can tell he really does want to kill me.

I don't have a problem with him hating the fact that I spent the night with Dalila. I can't stand the fact that she tried to talk to him and he wouldn't listen. He refused to give her a voice.

With Dalila safe inside the house, I head back to the truck. But two of Don Sandoval's bodyguards block my path.

"I'm not done with you yet," Don Sandoval says in an eerily calm tone.

"You do realize it's six against one, right?" I ask him.

"Rumor has it you're an impressive fighter, and I wasn't about to take any chances. I made sure I have the upper hand." He paces in front of me, probably contemplating how many ways he's going to make me pay for spending the night with his daughter. Truth is, I deserve his wrath. His daughter spent the night in my arms and it wasn't innocent.

With a nod to his henchmen, I'm grabbed and held with iron grips. I struggle against their muscle, but I realize quickly that while I might be able to wrest myself free of these two clowns, four more of them are waiting in the wings.

Don Sandoval walks right up to me, so close I have no choice but to be surrounded by the smell of his expensive cologne. "Listen to me, punk, and listen good," he says through gritted teeth. "You will never talk to or look at my daughter ever again. Do you understand me?"

I look right into his sharp eyes without saying a word. I can't promise that I'll stay away from her. She's become my lifeline. She sees the value in me that I don't even see in myself.

He nods to the biggest dude of the bunch, a guy with oversize biceps and no neck. I remember him as the head of the security detail at Dalila's birthday party, Gerardo.

Gerardo walks up to me and is about to throw a punch. Running on adrenaline, I wrestle myself away from the two clowns holding me back and duck his assault. On pure instinct I connect with a solid right hook to Gerardo's big face before I'm grabbed again. The clowns grip me tighter this time as a furious Gerardo swipes at the blood running down his lip.

Without a word or grunt, he punches me in the gut. His fist

feels like a steel mallet. Fuck, that hurt. I stand tall and show no expression, not wanting any of these guys to know how much that sucked. And it sucked. A lot.

So much for Don Sandoval's promise not to hurt me.

Gerardo punches me in the gut with that mallet fist of his two more times. I don't want to crumple to the ground when the clowns release me, but the pain takes over my resolve and all of a sudden I'm eating dirt. The only satisfaction I have is that the dude will have a big fat lip in the morning because of me.

Don Sandoval kneels next to me. "If I find out that you're working for *Las Calaveras* and luring my daughter into some sick game, I will kill you."

With those words still lingering in the air, they all leave me by the side of the truck and disappear into the house.

Once I've recovered I pull myself up, slide into the truck, and stare at the entrance to the compound. It's got two statues of angels flanking a security gate. What's really hidden inside those gates besides Dalila and her family?

I want to call out for Dalila to come with me, to leave this place behind and spend the rest of her life with me. But I can't do it. Fantasyland isn't real. The past forty-eight hours might as well have been a dream. It's over. For Dalila's safety, I should let her go. Dating me can only bring her more heartache and trouble.

The problem is, this feeling of dread that I've just lost a part of me isn't going away.

I don't even know who *Las Calaveras* are. Is it a cartel that's threatened Don Sandoval and his family? And if Don Sandoval is an enemy to *Las Calaveras*, does that mean he's linked to *Los Reyes del Norte*?

As I drive back to the gym, I don't know what I'm going to say to Camacho when he comes to train me tomorrow. I'm definitely going to get chewed out for breaking his rule about getting involved with girls. When he finds out I've been with Dalila Sandoval, is he going to kick my ass? Or worse, stop training me?

When I reach the gym there are a bunch of cars parked in the lot, which is unusual. My veins fire up when I see my Mustang has its tires slashed and all the windows bashed in.

I step out of the truck and walk over to my car.

Damn.

All my little rusty beater needed when I left here yesterday morning was gas. Now she's a hunk of metal.

"Welcome home, Ryan," a voice calls out from the front of the gym. It's Rico, the last person I wanted to see today. "Did you have a nice time with Dalila last night? Damn, bro. Someone sure did beat the shit outta you."

Six guys are standing behind him, and I feel a sense of déjà vu. Dalila's father might have let me go just to set me up for a show-down with Rico. Rico, as sophisticated and regal as he wants to come across, is just a thug. His designer suits and expensive car are just a cover-up. Underneath all that shiny shit is a piece of crap who thinks he owns people.

Well, he doesn't own me. Or Dalila.

I'm gonna get my ass kicked again. Or possibly even killed. Mateo would have my back, but he's not here. I wouldn't even want to get him mixed up in an unfair fight. The only chance I have of getting out of this is to run.

But I don't run. Not since Willie Rayburn chased me that last time in the seventh grade.

I stand tall even as my bruised gut tells me I can't handle much more today.

Rico steps forward and spits on the ground. "There's a code here in Mexico. Maybe you haven't heard of it yet. You don't go off with someone else's girl."

"She's not your girl, man," I counter. "And from what she told me, she never was."

I casually lean up against my broken car and cross my arms, thinking it might delay them from surrounding me. At least I'll have a fighting chance if they're not sneaking up behind me. Who am I kidding? Rico has flashed his gun more than once since I first saw him. The chances that these cowards will resort to fighting with their fists, giving me a fair chance, is less than zero.

I'm going to die here. And unlike Max Trieger, I won't be dying a hero.

"Rico, face the facts, man. She doesn't want you or your douche-bag sports car," I tell him.

He steps closer and I can practically feel the hatred radiating off him. "When I was a little kid my father sat me down and told me I can have anything I want, Ryan. What did your father tell you when you were little?"

"Nothin', man. He split before I was born." Admitting it doesn't even hurt anymore.

"Oh, that's right." He kicks the side of my car, making a dent in it with his steel-toed boots. "I heard you're just a dirty bastard. Let me tell you something, Ryan. *Bastardos* like you are like dogs. Worthless unless they're begging at your feet or following your orders."

Enough of the insults. Let's get this shit started.

I move off my car and stand toe-to-toe with him. "I must be worthless, then, because there's no way in hell I'm gonna beg at anyone's feet. *Especially* yours." I gesture to the crew he brought to back him up. "And while these guys might follow your orders and help you do your dirty work, it's obvious you're a fucking coward who can't fight his own battles. Fight me, Rico. *Mono e mono.*" I point to my cheek.

He chuckles. "It's actually *mano a mano*, dumbass."

"Whatever, man. Here, I'll even give you a free shot."

He punches me.

"Really, that's all you got? I expected more from you. Hell, you pretended to know what you were doin' when you tried to teach Dalila how to box."

A big laugh escapes from his mouth. "Truth is, I knew exactly what I was doing. Getting close to her meant I was getting close to her father. Sometimes you've got to use people to get what you want." He winks. "With you out of the picture, that *puta* will be all mine."

I punch him so hard he stumbles backward. "Let's go, man," I say. "Right here, right now!" Nobody is going to insult Dalila and get away with it. As long as I've got an ounce of fight left in me, I'm all in.

But Rico saw what I can do to someone at the cage fight. He knows I can take on him and his friends, but not all at once.

So when they all come forward, I take a few of them out before I'm surrounded. I'm not giving up, not even when someone whacks me on the back with something other than a fist. The punches and kicks don't stop, and slowly my body gives up. I think I hear one of them say not to kill me because the Texan wouldn't want me brought back to him dead. I can't figure out what he means. My mind is foggy at this point.

Black out, Ryan, my body tells my brain. But I don't give up. Not yet. I've got to fight to the end.

When Rico bends down to punch my bloodied face one more time, I grab the front of his shirt through the fog. With the last ounce of energy I can muster I say, "If you touch her I'll kill you."

He laughs. "That's funny coming from a dead guy." Then, when he stands back up, he orders, "Put him in the trunk of my car."

I fight them, but my body is drained and useless while I'm shoved into a trunk. I wish I were dead at this point. But my aching body reminds me I'm not.

The engine starts and suddenly we're moving. I'm barely here, wanting nothing more than to escape into the darkness of my mind.

I wish I didn't have any regrets, but I do.

I regret not telling Dalila that I love her. I held the truth from her, because I wanted to keep up a part of the wall I've built up over the years. But she should have known.

She deserved to know.

I also regret not being superhuman—if I were I could have

fought off Rico's gang and I wouldn't be stuck in the trunk of a fucking car right now.

I hear mumbled voices, but I can't make them out. I don't know how much time has passed. It seems like hours, but at this point my brain is so foggy I have no clue.

After a while we stop. Okay, this is it. I wonder if they'll shoot me first, then toss me in the Rio Grande. Or if they'll weigh me down with cement like I heard Capone had his men do in the old days.

When the trunk finally opens, the brightness of the sun makes me wince. Rico and his crew yank me out. I try to stand, but my legs give out and I stumble to the ground. "Don't ever come back to Mexico. Next time I won't be so generous," Rico growls.

After one last kick to my stomach with those damn steel-toed boots, Rico and his gang get back in their car and leave me alone.

I sit up against a brick wall and realize I'm in the back of an alley. Where, I have no clue. A stray black cat jumps off a trash bin and looks at me as if contemplating whether I'm a dead piece of meat. It walks past me when it realizes I'm still alive.

Figures. That black cat crossing in front of me is like a metaphor for my life. I'm doomed.

"Wait around a few hours!" I call out to the cat, but it's gone.

I should be happy to die knowing my body will feed a homeless cat. At least my life, or should I say death, would mean something.

Oh, man, I'm in bad shape if I'm thinking of donating my body to a fucking cat. I chuckle at the thought and the movement hurts my face.

I don't have anything with me, not my dead cell phone or my clothes or that amazing food Abuela Carmela packed for us. It takes me hours to gather up enough strength to walk down the alley to see where the hell I am. To my surprise, I'm back in Texas. Those jerks must have had some shady border agent skip inspecting the trunk of the car when they crossed the border before dropping me off less than a mile from Paul's house. He's gonna freak when he sees the mess I've become.

Wanting to avoid Paul's interrogation, I walk in the opposite direction and head for Pablo's house. It takes me twenty minutes to stumble my way to my friend's house. Luckily Pablo is sitting on the front stoop and rushes over to me as soon as I come into view.

"What the hell happened to you, Hess?"

"I got jumped in Mexico." A knot forms in my stomach as I say the words that don't come easily. "Can you help me without askin' questions?"

"Of course." He puts his arm around my waist and steadies me as he leads me into his house. My entire body feels like it's been through a meat grinder. "Mamá, I need your help," he calls out.

Pablo's mother greets us at the door. She's a short woman with a kind smile who comes to watch every one of Pablo's bouts at the gym. She supports her children as if being there for them is her greatest pleasure. Her eyes go wide when she takes one look at my condition. "Take him to your bedroom, Pablo," she instructs like a surgeon in an operating room. "Javier, help your brother! I'll get some kind of pain reliever for him. Claudia, prepare some food for Pablo's friend!" she calls out to Pablo's sister. They all work together without any complaints or questions.

"I'm sorry," I tell Pablo's mom as she rushes to my side once I'm in Pablo's bed.

"What kind of animal did this to you?" she asks me. "This isn't drug-related, is it?"

"No, ma'am."

Satisfied with my answer, she hands me a glass of water and some pain relievers.

"You're safe here," Pablo's big brother, Javier, tells me before leaving the room.

When everyone is gone and I settle into the pillow, I try to ignore the pain. It's no use, I'm going to feel like shit for a long time. "I wish I had your family," I tell Pablo. He's sitting on a chair with his feet propped up on the bed.

"Sometimes they can be annoyin'," he says. "They're always interfering in my life and givin' me advice about what college I should go to."

"I'll trade families with you."

He smiles. "No thanks, Hess. I'll take my meddling family over yours any day of the week."

Claudia, Pablo's younger sister who's going to be a sophomore at Loveland High in the fall, peeks her head into the room. "I made soup," she says. "Can I come in?"

"Sure," Pablo says.

With a shy smile, she walks into the room and stares at my bruised face as she places the bowl of soup on Pablo's desk next to a big yellow book titled *The Guide to the Best Colleges.*

"Thank you," I tell her.

"*De nada*," she replies, then walks out of the room.

"What have you gotten yourself caught up in?" Pablo asks me. "I want to help you if I can."

"You can't help me. I need to deal with this on my own." I hold my aching side. "I'll be out of here in the mornin'."

"You can stay as long as you need to, Ry. Okay?"

"You say you have my back, but you never ask me for help. I'm always askin' you for help."

He shrugs as if it's no big deal. "I'm not keeping score."

"You should." I glance at the Mexican flag above Pablo's bed and the American flag on the wall above his desk. "Where do you like it better?" I ask him.

He crosses his arms and thinks for a minute. "They're both home to me. I guess my heart and spirit is Mexican but my home is the US. I identify with both and wish there were no such thing as borders. Does that make sense?"

"Yeah."

He raises a brow. "You should stay here, although be forewarned: when you wake up you might feel worse than you already do. Gather up enough strength to go back home when you're ready."

At least I can look forward to that scene when I walk into Paul's house and announce in my bloodied state, "Surprise, I'm back!"

THIRTY-TWO

Dalila

Since I came back a few days ago I haven't been able to talk to my papá. He's been working out of the house most of the time, and when he's home he completely ignores me. He's even got Gerardo and a few other guards following me around the house to make sure I don't go anywhere. My house has truly become my prison. My little sisters have supposedly been sent on a summer vacation, but I suspect they've been sent into hiding for their own protection. I asked about them, but I was shut down.

Gerardo told me that Ryan will be killed if he comes near me again. It's not fair. It's like whatever I think or say doesn't matter. Is it because I'm only eighteen or because I'm a woman? I'm a person. It shouldn't matter how old or what gender I am.

I'm going to see him again. I can't let this empty feeling inside me be my new normal. If Ryan doesn't want to see me again, I have to hear it from him.

I find my mamá in the garden. She's busily clipping dead branches off some of the plants and pulling wilted leaves from their stems.

"Are you still mad at me?" I ask her.

She doesn't look at me. Instead she continues with her task. "I'm not mad."

"Then look at me, Mamá."

She does. "What do you want me to say, Dalila?"

"I want you to say that my choices are respected and that when I say something, I'm heard."

She shakes her head. "Your father provides for us and protects us. He makes rules not because he wants to be a dictator, but to make sure we're taken care of and safe. When you disrespect his rules, you're disrespecting your entire *familia*."

Her words tear little rips in my already-damaged heart. I don't want to cry or be emotional, but my eyes start to well up. The last thing I want to do is hurt my *familia*. "I love him, Mamá."

She goes back to gardening. "Nonsense. You don't even know him."

I know I can't convince her that she's wrong. Ryan and I opened up to each other and revealed so much. Even though we've only known each other for a little while, I feel like I know him inside and out. I can feel when he's hurting and when he's stressed. When he's happy or amused, there's a part of me that bonds with those emotions. It's a connection I've never had with anyone else.

Not even my blood relatives.

"I want to see him."

"No."

"Mamá, I need to go to the gym and see if Ryan is okay." I swallow the lump forming in my throat. I haven't heard from him and I can't be away from him any longer. "I'll make sure Soona and Demi go with me. I won't be alone. I know that Ryan needs me. I *feel* it."

Everyone in his life has treated him poorly or abandoned him. I want him to know that I'll never give up on him.

"Give me this one gift," I plead. "If you think I'm oblivious to everything that's been going on, you're wrong. I know more than you think I do."

"You know nothing, *mija*."

"Lucas would want me to follow my own path, Mamá. He wouldn't want me to follow his. I've tried to be the best daughter I could, but I'm not that perfect child. I can't pretend that I want the life you've forged for me. I can't control what Papá does. Don't control what I need to do."

She stops gardening and sighs. "I'm going out with your father tonight," she says softly. "We're attending a benefit with the mayor and his wife."

With a smile on my face and excitement running through me, I run and give my mom the biggest hug. "*Gracias*, Mamá. I love you so much."

She hugs me back but holds on to me tighter and longer than usual. "If I could turn back the clock and change things, I would."

I leave the gardens and head to my room to pick out my clothes for tonight. I wish I could leave now, but I have to wait.

After my parents leave for their charity dinner, I run upstairs to get dressed. I decide to wear a pretty, white, off-the-shoulder top that shows off my midsection. I think it will drive Ryan crazy. I pair it with a black miniskirt I bought in Paris last year. It's a little short, but it goes perfectly with the top.

My hands are shaking as I put on mascara. The anticipation of seeing Ryan again is rattling me to the point of barely functioning. I need to see him, to feel his touch, to tell him how much I missed him.

To tell him how much I'm there for him.

I climb down into the fields in order to meet up with Demi and Soona, because if the guards know I'm gone they'll definitely alert Papá. I'm not risking that.

After I weave through the fields and shimmy through an opening in the fence on the edge of our property, I see Demi in her car. As a favor to us, Mateo had it fixed by one of his cousins and brought it back to her in perfect condition.

"You're going to get yourself in big trouble one of these days," Soona says as I slide into the back seat.

"She's doing it for love, Soona," Demi chides her. "What's more powerful and worth it than that?"

"Love?" Soona scoffs. "Really? You're in love?"

Before I met Ryan I didn't know what falling in love meant. Love makes you weak and strong. It makes you secure in your feelings and insecure that something will come along to ruin everything. Love makes you have purpose and passion. I'd run to the ends of the earth to find Ryan. If he doesn't feel the same way, it won't matter. For better or worse, my heart is seared with my love for him.

Soona hasn't been in love. Demi is a romantic at heart, but she just hasn't found the right person.

I direct the girls to the gym and notice a bunch of cars in the parking lot. A sharp feeling of dread overcomes me as I notice Ryan's Mustang with its windows shattered and the tires flat.

"What happened?" Soona asks.

"I don't know, but I'm gonna find out."

One car in the lot I recognize as Rico's. Why is he here?

I take a deep breath and lead the girls into the gym. All eyes are on us as we enter.

Rico is standing with another guy in the ring. He's got a strange, cocky smirk plastered on his face as he ducks through the ropes and approaches me. "Hey," he says, grinning from ear to ear. "You and your friends come to watch me?"

Is he serious? "What happened to Ryan's car?"

He doesn't answer.

"I need to talk to Ryan," I say, scanning the gym for him.

"He's not here," Rico says.

"Do you know where he is?"

His smirk turns into a chuckle and it makes me want to step back. But I don't. I need to figure out what's going on. "Ryan went far away. Well, that is if he's actually alive. He didn't look too good the last time I saw him."

My heart starts pounding so hard I can feel it beating against my shirt. "What do you mean *if he's alive*? What did you do to him?" I ask, my voice shaking uncontrollably.

"I just made sure he'd stop interfering in your life."

"What I do with my life is none of your business, Rico Cruz!" I shoot back.

"It is when I make it my business." He looks at me as if I'm some kind of strange creature. "You don't think you two were actually a thing, do you? He was playing you, Dalila. He admitted he was just trying to get into your pants, so I beat the shit out of him and dumped him back in the US where he belongs." He jumps down from the ring and places a comforting hand on my shoulder. "I did it to protect you from that *pendejo*. Aren't you going to thank me for saving you from him?"

No. He's lying.

I'm so confused right now.

My mind whirls with Rico's words.

"Come on, Dalila," Soona chimes in. "Let's go home."

I'm still in a daze as my friends and I walk out of the gym and head for Demi's car.

As if on cue, Mateo's truck pulls into the parking lot. He sticks his head out the window and waves. "Hey!"

"Did you know Rico beat up Ryan?"

A shocked Mateo rushes out of the car. "What do you mean?"

"He's gone."

"I know." Mateo's brow furrows in confusion. "I thought he couldn't deal with the pressure of livin' here and just went back to Loveland. Rico said his car was vandalized after he left. I haven't heard from him."

"So you haven't talked to him this past week?"

"I've been busy with family stuff." He swears under his breath. "I should have been there for him."

I can't just go on with my life pretending that Ryan doesn't exist. "Rico said Ryan is in the US. Can you help me find him?"

Soona sucks in a breath. "Dalila, you can't go. You heard what Rico said. Ryan was just using you."

Demi puts her hands on her hips. "Let me go with you so I can beat the shit out of that lying user, too."

My friends have no clue what it was like to spend time with Ryan. He wasn't using me. I know he wasn't.

Mateo shakes his head. "Whoa. Rico said that Ryan was using you? No way. Ryan doesn't use people."

I know. "Take me to him, Mateo."

"You want me to sneak you across the border? No way," he says, holding his hands up.

"I've got a passport back at home. That's all I need."

"We can't go tonight," Mateo says. "But I can take you tomorrow night if you're up for it."

I'm ready to fight for what I want, even if I'm breaking the rules. Nothing's going to stop me now.

I just have to find a way to sneak out tomorrow night without anyone noticing.

THIRTY-THREE

Ryan

I left Pablo's and came back home a few days ago. My head is pounding and my body still feels completely broken, but that doesn't matter to Paul. He barged into my room this morning and is standing over my bed, wearing his ever-present Loveland sheriff uniform.

"I've left you alone for the past couple of days, but I'm not about to let this go. What happened to you in Mexico, Ryan?" he asks, scrutinizing the mass of bruises and cuts on my body. Not because he's concerned for my welfare, but because he needs to pry.

"I was beat up."

"Obviously."

My mom peeks her head in the room. "Were you involved in drug deals, Ryan?"

"Of course it was because of drugs, Susan," Paul answers like he's some psychic and knows exactly what I've been up to. He puts his hands on his hips, his finger brushing against the butt of his gun. "I told you this would happen."

"Paul, drug test me. I'm not doin' drugs. I got beat up by some thugs, that's all."

He's watching me with a critical squint. "Where's your car?"

"I totaled it." That's not exactly true. Rico totaled my car, but the less Paul knows the better.

"If you would've taken the job at the farm, this wouldn't have happened," he says in an exasperated voice. "If you keep makin' the wrong choices in life, you'll go nowhere."

"You're right."

He leans forward. "What'd you say? Speak up, boy, I couldn't hear you."

"I said you were right." If I spent all summer shoveling shit I wouldn't have been beat up. And I'd still have a car with windows and tires without holes in them. And I wouldn't have ruined Dalila's life. Everything I did was a lost cause.

Mom walks farther into my room. "I can't bail you out every time you get in trouble, Ryan. At some point you're going to have to learn from your mistakes. Paul is here to help you."

I'm gonna play it their way just until I can figure out a plan. "I'll go talk to Mr. Johnson tomorrow," I say just to appease them.

Paul nods, then leaves my room. "You better get your shit together, Ryan. This is your last chance," he calls out from the hallway.

I look over at my mom. "I'm sorry, Ma."

She leans her head against the doorjamb. "Me too. Listen, I know Paul isn't easy on you, but he's the only person I can rely on. He's the only thing I got."

I don't remind her that she's got me, but I never mattered to her.

"Maybe try a little harder, you know," she says. "The grass needs mowing. Show him that you appreciate him taking care of us."

The last thing I want to do is show Paul any gratitude, but causing waves isn't going to get me anywhere. "I'll mow the lawn," I tell her. "For you."

She leaves the house to go run errands and I head out to the garage.

"The loser's back," PJ says as I pass him in the living room. "From those bruises, I can tell you had the best time in Mexico. You definitely came back here with your tail between your legs, loser. Ha ha!"

Man, would I like to punch him in the teeth so hard they all fall out.

In the garage, I pull out the lawn mower.

I'm trying to start the rusty thing when Allen peeks his head into the garage. "Yo, Cinderella!" he calls out. "How about you wash my car after you mow the lawn."

"How about you go suck your brother's dick," I say.

He sucks in a fake horrified breath, as if my words were too harsh for his sensitive ears. "I'm telling my father you said that."

"Go ahead."

I push the lawn mower out of the garage, ignoring the pain the movement causes me. The thing is so old it takes me forever to get it to work. I gather the clippings and toss them in the huge paper bags I found in the garage, the entire time wondering how Dalila is holding up. Is she thinking about me? Is her father making sure she's safe from danger?

Telling myself not to think about her just makes me think about her more. The bossy way she talks, the way strands of her long, curly hair fall into her face, the way she'd roam her fingers over my body as if she wanted to memorize every ripple.

The sun is beating down on me. When I go in the kitchen for a water break, I hear PJ changing channels. He stops on the news.

"*Revenge is the name of the game when it comes to the warring cartels on the Mexican border with the US,*" the reporter on the TV is saying. "*Revenge kidnappings have been a problem here, where families of cartel members have been held for ransom or killed in retaliation. Has the conflict boiled over into the US? If it has, what can authorities here do to stop it? Would they even want to? More on this story at ten.*"

Hearing about the kidnappings makes me wonder if Dalila is safe.

Frustrated, I go back outside to finish mowing the lawn. I'm on my last bag, dumping all the clippings into the trash bag, when the entire thing falls over.

Damn.

I kick the lawn mower and it goes flying to the back wall of the garage. It bashes part of the wood structure and an entire panel of wood comes dislodged from the frame. Oh, great, one more thing to go wrong today.

I'm attempting to move the panel back in place when I realize something's not right. It's a fake wall. I dislodge it even more and see there's an entire space between this fake wall and the back of the garage. I'm thinking the construction on this thing was done by a bunch of idiots. But when I peer inside the empty space, I notice piles of cash. They're stacked up like soldiers.

Bribe money.

So Paul *has* been working with the cartels. He boasts about his reputation as the savior sheriff who'll rid Loveland of the gangs and drugs streaming across the border from Mexico but it's all bullshit. This entire time he's been lecturing me about making the right choices while he's been bought off by the cartels he says he's determined to take down.

I'm done playing his game.

It's time he plays mine.

THIRTY-FOUR

Dalila

Since Lucas died, I've been living my life in honor of him as if that's what would have made him happy. I also hold massive amounts of guilt that it was Lucas who had the heart murmur and not me. That guilt guided me in every one of my goals and the way I lived, pretending it was what I wanted, but I never felt any true purpose or passion.

Until now.

Ryan has pulled me out from a cloud I've been living under. This tension I feel when he's away from me isn't going to go away. I'm going to see Ryan, to find out if he's okay and to let him know that I'm not abandoning him.

I pull out a backpack from my closet and quickly shove a bunch of clothes inside. I'm not going to sit back and let the things that matter to me slip away. Not anymore, when my parents refuse to trust me with the truth. I don't even feel like I'm a part of this family anymore.

With renewed energy, I'm ready to do this. I'm going to cross the border and find Ryan. We're still in this together whether he wants to believe it or not.

I put on jeans and a T-shirt, ready to shove all plans aside and start a new path. One that *I've* created.

Reaching onto the top shelf of the hall closet where my parents hide our passports, I feel around but can't find them. Frustrated, I grab a chair and stand on it so I can see the entire top shelf.

They're not here.

Someone moved them.

I rush downstairs and storm into my father's office. "Where is it?"

He takes his glasses off and looks up at me from his desk. "Where is what, Dalila?"

"My passport."

He raises a brow and eyes me suspiciously. "May I ask what you need your passport for, *mija?*"

"To cross the border. I looked in the hall closet and it's not there."

"Ah, I see." He leans back in his chair. "I will tell you right now that I forbid you to cross the border, so finding it is of no consequence."

Without warning my mamá appears in the doorway. "Your father had nothing to do with it," she says. "I hid the passports somewhere else."

"I need mine."

She shakes her head. "It's locked in a secure place."

Her words make me want to sink to my knees in despair. "No," I say in a defeated whisper.

"It's for your safety, Dalila," she says, then steps closer to pull me into a hug.

I shrug out of her embrace. "You don't understand. This place has become my prison," I tell them. "What's the use in being safe if you can't live your life?"

"The alternative is not having a life," Papá chimes in.

"I'm not happy here."

"You think you'll be happy with that boy from the US?" Papá scoffs. "He's different and mysterious. A novelty. You'll get bored of him and he'll get bored of you soon enough, and then where will you be? In the middle of a cartel war where people want to hurt you."

"Why would they want to hurt me?" I cross my arms on my chest. "Because of you? Be honest with me for once, Papá! You sent my sisters away. You're keeping our home a fortress. You're putting us all in danger. Why?"

"I can't share those things with you," he says.

"You have to trust us that we're making the best decisions for you and your sisters," Mamá chimes in.

I can't blindly trust them, not when it feels like they're the ones putting our family in danger. Somehow, Papá's friendship with Don Cruz and his association with Santiago Vega have something to do with the change in our lives.

"Fine," I say. "You win."

My parents look at each other with wary expressions as I walk out of the office.

This isn't over.

Back in my room, I stare at my backpack lying on my floor. That passport was my ticket across the border to find Ryan. Besides me there are only three people who matter to him: Mateo, Juan Camacho, and his friend from the Shadows of Darkness concert, Pablo.

During dinner, I try to act normal.

"What do you think about traveling this summer?" Papá asks me.

"Where?"

He hesitates as if it'll increase the excitement. "A cruise. There's a friend of mine with a private yacht. You and your mother and sisters can spend time on the ocean and enjoy—"

"What about you?" I ask him. "Won't you be going?"

"Unfortunately I have work and can't take time off. Not this summer, anyways."

I look at my mom, who's busily eating her food. "It'll be wonderful to get away, Dalila. Wouldn't it? No stress, no drama . . ."

No Ryan.

"Sure," I tell them in the most enthusiastic tone I can muster. "Sounds like fun."

I don't reveal that I won't be going on any cruises.

Not without Ryan, anyways. Back in my room, I start making my plan.

I decide to wait until they're asleep to sneak out. It's no use going out the front door, because there are two guards stationed there at all times. The only way out of my prison is jumping off the garden balcony into the fields below.

Ducking through shadows, I stealthily glide through the house trying not to make a sound.

But when I pass my dad's office, I hear him talking to his head bodyguard, Gerardo. "In the morning you'll take Dalila to Casa Nieves," he says. "She'll be safe there."

"She won't want to go," I hear Gerardo say.

"She doesn't have a choice," Papá responds.

But I do have a choice. I'm not going to be hidden away and ordered around like some kind of pawn.

It's not easy ducking out of the house in the dark, especially when a bunch of bodyguards are patrolling our *ranchero*. When one of them goes on break, I sneak into the gardens and jump off the balcony. Running through the fields makes me anxious until I get to the other side of the property. I walk on the edge of the dark roads, hoping nobody realizes I'm gone until the morning.

With one last glance at my home and tears staining my eyes, I silently say good-bye to my home. The life I once knew is gone, replaced by one less known but more meaningful.

I knew where I was going the minute I left. Without a passport, I hop on a bus headed for Sevilla. I keep my head down, hoping nobody will recognize me as the daughter of Oscar Sandoval.

I have to stay under the radar if I'm going to pull this off.

THIRTY-FIVE

Ryan

It's hard to play it cool when I know there's a ton of dirty cash hiding in our garage. So many thoughts have been running through my mind since I found it. Paul is either getting bribes from *Los Reyes del Norte* or *Las Calaveras*, the two major cartels taking over the border.

I'm sitting at the breakfast table with the entire family when Paul blabs about getting some intel on the newest Mexican cartel, *Los Reyes del Norte*.

"They're buying up real estate in Texas," Paul says. "Lots of it."

"Don't you have to be a US citizen to buy property?" Mom asks.

"Nope. Any immigrant asshole can buy US property with the right funds," Paul tells her.

"Any asshole citizen can buy US property with the right funds," I counter.

"Speaking of assholes, did you have any run-ins with the cartels when you crossed the border, Ryan?" Paul asks me.

"No."

PJ and Allen snicker as if they've got some private joke.

"Really?" Paul cocks his elfin head to the side. "Because you were in Mexico for a few weeks and they're recruiting a lot of kids your age. And then you get beat up like you were involved in some kind of drug deal gone wrong. You didn't hear *anything* about them?"

I look him straight in his beady eyes. "No, Paul. I haven't heard anything about them. Why do you keep asking me the same question?"

"Maybe because we think you're a pathological liar," PJ chimes in.

Instead of making him stop asking me stuff or defending me, my mom just zones out.

Paul puts his fork down and sits back. "There's about to be a power shift between the *Las Calaveras*, who have been in control for years, and *Los Reyes del Norte*, the dangerous new cartel taking over territory in the north," Paul says. "We've got intel on the inside and they're telling us that the recruiting has gotten insane."

"You sure do know a lot about 'em," I mumble.

"What's that supposed to mean?"

I shrug. "Just sayin' that you're pretty well informed. Must be nice to have inside intel."

Paul pointedly looks at me as if I'm one of the enemies. "The bad guys always lose in the end."

"Good," I say, then add, "Anyone who cheats the system needs to go down."

He furrows his brow, as if my words trigger him somehow. But he keeps a straight face, even kissing my mother before heading to the station.

Last night I went through every scenario on what to do with the money Paul has stashed in his garage. Stealing all that money to buy Dalila a large piece of land in Mexico would make my dream come true, but then I'd be no better than Paul. I can't go to the police, because I don't know anyone at the station who'd bring Paul down. He's the dictator at the Loveland police station.

When he leaves for work, I pull out the old business card Max Trieger gave me with his contact info on it. My heart is beating fast as I dial Lance's number.

"Lance Matthews, US Border Patrol," the guy answers in an authoritative voice.

"Yeah, um, I was wondering if I could meet with you."

"Who is this?"

I swallow, hard. "Ryan Hess."

"Sheriff Blackburn's son?"

"Stepson."

"Are you in trouble?"

"Not really. I just have some information and wanted to meet with you."

There's a hesitation on the line. "Information? What kind of information?"

"I can't say over the phone. I need to meet you in person. And I need you to keep it confidential."

"I'll be at the border station in Loveland at two o'clock today. Come by then and we can talk."

"Sounds great. Thanks, Officer Matthews."

I hang up and head over to Lone Star Boxing Club, because I can't do this alone. I need my one-man crew.

Pablo greets me the second I walk into the club. "Hey, Ry, how've you been? I've been thinkin' about you and wondering how you've been holding up."

"Life's been crazy," I tell him. "I need you to do me a favor, Pablo."

"Sure, Ry. What do you need?"

"I need a crew, and you're it."

I'm not going it alone this time. When Pablo comes to my house, I show him the money.

"Damn, Hess," he whispers as he peeks his head through the break in the garage wall. "There must be over two million in there."

"I need you to get rid of it for me," I tell him. "If you get caught—"

"I'm not afraid of anyone. Crooked cops piss me off."

With Pablo on board, we secretly load the cash onto his truck. After hauling it away and making a plan of what to do with it, I stand in front of him and shake his hand. "Thanks, man. I couldn't do this without you."

"Despite the color of our skin, we're bros with *fuerza*, Hess. Thanks for trusting me. I mean it." I turn to leave when he calls out, "I think you finally found your cause. I'm proud of you."

After leaving Pablo, I head over to the border patrol station to meet with Officer Matthews. I walk up the brick steps into the place feeling like my entire life has led up to this moment.

Lance recognizes me right away. He's sitting on the edge of one of the desks lined up in the middle of the busy station. He's a good-looking guy, with dark, straight hair combed neatly to the side.

"Thanks for meeting me, Officer Matthews," I say, feeling completely awkward and nervous.

"Not a problem, Ryan." He motions for me to sit in the chair across from his desk. "Sit down."

I look around at the crowd of people in the room. "Can we talk somewhere private?" I'm not about to out the town's sheriff as crooked in the middle of the entire border patrol station.

"Sure," he says. "Follow me."

He leads me to a back room, away from everyone else. I'm immediately on edge as I realize this is an interrogation room. It has one table and two old, metal chairs. I'm aware that there is no camera or recording equipment in the room. A window with blinds overlooks the rest of the station, so anyone can look in and see us. The door automatically locks as we enter the small room, making me feel claustrophobic.

I briefly wonder if this is a good idea, or if I just put a nail in my coffin. If I'm wrong about Officer Matthews I might as well be handing myself over to the enemy.

Officer Matthews takes a seat opposite me and leans forward. "Tell me what's on your mind, Ryan. Are you in trouble?" His words are kind and not judgmental, reminding me of Max Trieger.

I focus on the handcuffs secured in his belt and the gun at his waist. "No. It's nothin' like that. What if I found cash that I suspected was connected to the cartel?"

"How much cash are we talking about, Ryan? Hundreds? Thousands?"

"More than that," I tell him. "A lot more."

He takes a long, slow breath as he sits back in his chair. "Max Trieger was investigating *Las Calaveras* and their connections here in Texas," he says. "He said there was a money trail, but he wouldn't share the specifics with me. He kept me in the dark."

"Why?"

"Because he knew the closer he got to figuring it out, the bigger the target on his back." He shakes his head slowly, as if remembering his beloved partner's doomed fate. "The son of a gun wanted to protect me. He was like a brother to me and there's not a day goes by when I don't want to get revenge for his death."

"What if I could give you—" I glance through the blinds covering the window and my entire body goes numb as I see Paul walking into the station with a furious look on his face. "Why is Paul here? Did you tell him I was comin' here?"

"No," Officer Matthews says. "Did you tell him you were coming to see me?"

I shake my head. "No."

Officer Matthews stands. "Wait here, Ryan."

He walks out of the room, leaving me alone. I would book it out of here, but the door suddenly opens again. Instead of Officer Matthews, it's Paul. He storms in front of me with a menacing scowl. "Where's the money, Ryan?" he says in a low voice so nobody else can hear. We're in a soundproof room, but I'm sure he doesn't want to take any chances.

"I don't know what you're talkin' about."

He grabs the front of my shirt and twists it in his fist. "Tell me where you put my *fucking* money or I will tear your *fucking* heart out," he growls through gritted teeth.

"If you do that, I don't think you'll get your money."

"Oh, yeah?" He lets go of my collar and steps back in an attempt to compose himself. "Let me tell you somethin', you piece of shit. If you don't tell me where the money is right now, I will destroy everything important to you."

"That's not really a threat," I tell him. "You should know by now that I have nothin' of value for you to destroy."

"Oh, really? What about Dalila Sandoval?"

I stand violently, my chair scraping the floor as I get in his face. "What do you know about Dalila?"

"I know *everything*, Ryan. I know you were livin' in Sevilla at that run-down boxing gym and I know you were with Oscar Sandoval's daughter the night before you got the shit kicked out of you. You think you're so smart, don't you? You know crap, Ryan." He points to his chest like a gorilla marking himself as the alpha. "I've been a cop on this border since before you were born. I know everyone and everything on both sides. Give me that money, or that pretty girlfriend of yours is as good as dead."

Every emotion I've ever had rises to the surface now as I get in his face. "If anything happens to her, I'll kill you. That's not a threat, Paul. That's a fact."

"The fact is she's as good as dead. Just like our dear old Max," Paul says in an eerily calm manner as he takes out his handcuffs. "Oh, and by the way, you're under arrest for threatening an officer."

"You're a crook," I tell him. "I'm going to tell them you're crooked."

"Nobody will believe you, Ryan," he says, amused. "You're a bad seed and I'm the beloved sheriff of this town. Don't fuck with me. You won't win."

He pushes me hard up against the wall, attempting to handcuff me. He's not strong enough to overpower me, though, and I end up grabbing the handcuffs and twisting them so I cuff one side on the table leg and the other around his wrist.

While he's screaming at me, I knock on the door. Officer Matthews opens it, wide-eyed as he focuses on the scene in front of him.

"What's going on here?"

"Ask the crooked sheriff over there," I tell him, then rush past him and run as fast as I can out of the station. I don't want Paul manipulating the border patrol or the police to arrest me for something random in an attempt to shut me up and peg me as a troublemaker delinquent. I wouldn't put it past him to frame me.

I run through town knowing I'm finally done with the life I lived before this moment. I might be alone, but I'm not scared. I have a purpose, and that's to make sure Dalila is safe. I call Mateo and tell him to meet me across the border, then run as fast as I can to get there.

Crossing the border into Mexico isn't a problem, even though I feel all eyes are on me, waiting to arrest Sheriff Paul Blackburn's wayward stepson who's gone rogue.

After crossing, I breathe a sigh of relief as I catch sight of Mateo's uncle's red pickup truck. I quickly settle into the passenger seat. "We have to go to Dalila's house," I tell him. "She's in danger."

"She's not there," Mateo tells me.

"Where is she?"

"Nobody knows. She's missing."

THIRTY-SIX

Dalila

"Dalila, you need to get some rest," Juan Camacho says to me as I sit on his sofa and stare at the clock on his wall. He hands me a mug filled with *champurrado*. I breathe in the cocoa and it immediately comforts me.

"*Gracias*, Juan," I say. "I can't sleep. I'm worried about Ryan."

The old man smiles warmly at me, his deep wrinkles and white hair showing every bit of his age.

Last night I came here and told Juan about what happened with Ryan and my suspicions about my father. He said I shouldn't judge before knowing all the facts, but I can't help it. There are just too many things pointing to the fact that my father's engaged in illegal activity with one of the cartels.

"Stop worrying so much, Dalila," Juan says as he shuffles to his rocking chair and slowly takes a seat. "I know your father as a good, honorable man."

"Then why is he involved with bad people?"

"I don't know." He rocks back and forth. "These old bones don't get involved in other people's lives. Not anymore, anyways."

"Were you ever involved in the cartels?"

"No." He takes a long, slow sip of *champurrado*. "The promise of unlimited power lures young men in. It's intoxicating and alluring." He chuckles to himself. "They get duped into thinking they're invincible when they're just dispensable pawns. I'm not anyone's pawn," he tells me. "I never have been."

"Why did you quit boxing?" I ask.

"Something else more important lured me away." He motions to the other bedroom. "She's sleeping in there. When my wife got ill, I stopped dedicating my life to anything else but her."

I think about how tough it must be for him to take care of Valeria. I remember stories of her coming to our house. My mother told me she was an intelligent and vibrant person who lit up a room as soon as she entered it. "I'm sorry about Valeria," I tell him.

"Don't be sorry, Dalila. She has some good days and when she looks in my eyes I still see her spirit. The love doesn't stop even in times of illness."

A knock at the door interrupts our conversation.

"It's Franciso Cruz," a familiar voice bellows.

Rico's dad.

I stiffen at the sound of his name.

"Wait," I whisper, then motion to Juan that I'll be hiding in the other room where Valeria is resting. He nods, understanding that I'm not ready to reveal to anyone where I've been hiding out. Grabbing my backpack, I quickly flee into the other room and hide behind the door as Juan lets him in. If Valeria wakes up and starts talking to me, Don Cruz will surely know something's up.

"I usually don't like visitors," Juan tells him.

"I'm not a visitor," Don Cruz says as he walks inside. "I'm an old friend. Right?"

"*Sí.*" I can hear the clink of Juan's spoon stirring his *champurrado*. He's completely relaxed, as if this is an ordinary visit from an ordinary friend. It's anything but.

"Have you been busy?" Don Cruz asks.

"Not really."

Peeking through the door frame, I see Don Cruz walk over to the mug I'd been drinking out of. "Do you have a guest?"

Juan shakes his head. "Just Valeria."

"How is she these days?"

Juan doesn't answer. Instead he picks up both mugs and brings them to the sink. "It's obvious this isn't a social call, Francisco, and I'm too old and cranky to play games. Why are you here?"

"I need to know if you've had any contact with Ryan Hess."

"What do you want with Ryan?"

"Let's just say he's a wanted man. I have people who said he crossed into Mexico yesterday."

Juan raises a skeptical brow. "Wanted by who?"

"*Las Calaveras.*"

"What crime is the young man accused of?"

"Why all the questions, Juan? Either you've seen him, or you haven't. It's a simple question."

"Nothing is simple, Francisco. We both know that." Juan turns to Don Cruz, his face unreadable. "I was training Ryan at the gym, but from what I understand he went back to Texas. I haven't heard from him since."

"What about Dalila Sandoval? She's missing, too."

"Is she wanted as well?" Juan asks in an almost mocking tone. "The girl isn't a threat to anyone."

After a long, brittle silence Don Cruz says, "Her father betrayed *Las Calaveras*."

There's an unspoken threat in the air and my stomach churns with increasing intensity. My father's involvement put a target on my back. Whether or not I like it, I've been forced into being a pawn.

Don Cruz stares at Juan, a chilling stare that makes me shiver. He takes a business card out of his suit pocket. "If you see either of them, call me. And if you see them and don't call, there's a price to pay. I don't play games either, Juan."

When Juan opens the door to let Don Cruz out of the apartment, I look down at my trembling hands. I know I can't stay here any longer.

After giving enough time for Don Cruz to be out of hearing range, I join Juan in the living room. He's got a somber look on his face.

"I can't stay here," I tell him, trying to keep my voice from cracking. "If I do, your life is in danger."

"I do not fear Francisco Cruz or anyone else."

"You have enough responsibility with Valeria. I won't let you take on more stress." I pick up my backpack. "I'll find Ryan. Maybe Mateo has seen him. Besides you, he's the only friend in Mexico that Ryan has."

"I assume *Las Calaveras* will be contacting Mateo," he says. "It's just not safe to leave right now."

I'm scared, but an eerie calm washes over me. I have a mission to find Ryan. He saved me from danger that first night at the club. It's time I step up and become his heroine.

"I'm sorry, Juan. I have to go. Nothing you say will stop me. Ryan needs me and I'm not going to abandon him. Someone needs to warn him and make sure he's safe from . . . everyone."

He gazes toward the bedroom, toward his sick wife. "I wish I could go with you."

"I know."

The old man heads to the closet and pulls out a big gray jacket. "Put this on as a disguise."

I slip the jacket on and pull up the hood. I can definitely hide my identity this way, just in case anyone is looking for me. I wrap Juan into a big hug and feel his long, scratchy beard on my cheek. "Thank you, Juan."

After I release him, he braces his hands on my shoulders. "I should be calling your father and telling him you're here. But I won't."

"*Gracias.*"

My father helped Juan a long time ago, so there's a loyalty that he's betraying for me. When I arrived in the early hours this morning and knocked on his door, I told him the entire story about my father and his sketchy behavior. He didn't believe that my dad would be involved in the cartels but couldn't rule it out. He said everyone has a price.

"If you can't find Ryan, you come back here or go home. Be skeptical of everyone you meet."

Determined to stay strong, I put my shoulders back and stand tall. I can do this. "You are a wonderful man, Juan Camacho."

"You're one of the strongest people I know, Dalila Sandoval. And I've met some tough *pendejos* in my time."

With the hood covering most of my face, I walk out of his apartment and onto the street. As I duck around corners and head for the grassy trails in the distance, I know where I'm headed.

Right back to the lion's den.

THIRTY-SEVEN

Ryan

After picking me up from the border, Mateo immediately took me to that bar where we met when I first came to Mexico, Mamacita's. Mateo told me that he had heard some guys connected to *Las Calaveras* were asking about me and I needed to keep a low profile. It's obvious that Paul is the mastermind, making sure he covers his tracks so Officer Matthews thinks I'm just a crazy, lying delinquent. I'm hiding out in one of the bedrooms above the bar waiting for Mateo to come back with news about Dalila.

All I know is that she's missing. Dalila is out there somewhere and I need to find her. Every moment that ticks by is torture.

I hear footsteps coming up the stairs and I'm ready for anything that comes at me. The lock on the door squeaks open and Mateo is standing there with a Styrofoam container filled with takeout food.

"Have you heard anything about Dalila?" I ask before he even walks in the room.

"Here," he says as he hands me the container. My mouth waters from the savory scent filling the room. "Eat."

I start chowing down. Food is fuel and the only way I can rely on my brain to work properly. Right now I need a clear head.

"Do you know where Dalila is?" I ask.

"No, man. She disappeared without a trace."

I stiffen. "Why? Do you know what went down?"

He shrugs. "Beats me. You need to be worrying about yourself, Ryan. *Las Calaveras* are looking for you." He leans against the old wooden dresser next to the small window. "Tell me what happened in Texas."

While I'm not used to trusting anyone, Mateo has been on my side ever since we were in the ring at Lone Star.

"I found money hidden in my stepfather's garage," I tell him. "A lot of it."

"How much?"

"Two point two."

He raises a brow. "Are we talking two thousand two hundred?"

I shake my head slowly until the reality sinks into his brain.

"Wow." He lets out a low whistle. "That's crazy."

"Yeah. He's pretty pissed off that I took it."

"I'll bet. Sounds like blood money or bribe money." Before I can respond, Mateo gets a call on his cell and has an entire conversation with someone as he stares out the bedroom window.

When he hangs up, I start packing my stuff. "Listen, Mateo. My stepfather has followed my every move since I came to Mexico. He knows I got close to Dalila." I look at the people walking on the street below and wonder if any one of them is reporting back to Paul. "You think he'll go after her to get to me?"

"People do crazy shit when it comes to money, Hess."

She's out there somewhere and I'm going to find her. "I'm not about to hide in this room all day," I tell him.

"What the hell are you gonna do? Go out there and get yourself killed?"

"My plan doesn't include me getting killed, even though her father would like nothing better than for me to disappear from her life."

"I should probably let you know that I'm working security at her house tonight," Mateo says.

I look up at him with no small amount of shock. "You're serious?"

He shrugs. "Her father's hired extra protection around his place. It pays good. I could probably sneak you inside the compound if you want."

"You could get yourself in a heap of trouble if you help me, Mateo."

"Hell, what are friends for," he says. "Right?"

If he's been working for Oscar Sandoval, he probably knows more about the man than I do. Would he share that info if he had it? "Can I ask you a question?"

"Shoot."

"How much is Dalila's father involved in illegal crap? Dalila told me he's a lawyer, but it's got to be more than that. The guy wouldn't have people shooting at his place and have to hire an army of bodyguards if he were just a lawyer."

A guarded look crosses Mateo's face. "He knows too much," he mumbles.

"About what?"

"I don't know." He takes the food container off my bed and shoves a bite into his mouth. "I just figure if someone's gonna go after him, there's got to be a reason."

"Dalila thinks he might be the head of *Los Reyes del Norte* cartel. El something or other."

"El Fuego? The Fire?"

"Yeah, that's it," I say, remembering when Paul once talked about finding the head of the newest cartel causing problems along the border. "You think it's possible that he's El Fuego?"

"Anything's possible."

I pull on a hoodie and lift the hood to cover my face as much as possible. The fact that I'm sweating like a damn pig doesn't matter.

"Where you goin'?" Mateo asks as I head for the door.

"To find Dalila."

"Let me help you." He pulls keys out of his pocket. "I can take you wherever you want to go until I have to leave for the job at the Sandovals' tonight."

"I don't want you to be involved," I tell him.

He laughs. "If you haven't noticed, I'm already involved. Rico and his buddies came by the gym this morning demanding to know if I'd seen you or Dalila."

"Rico Cruz?" I ask, knowing there are still remnants of bruises from the last time I had the displeasure of seeing Rico and his buddies.

"The one and only. I told him I hadn't seen you or Dalila. You two have sure gotten yourselves into a mess."

"Tell me about it." If we were together and I could ensure she was safe, I'd feel a helluva lot better.

Time is ticking and I need to find Dalila before Rico does. "Can you drive me to Panche? I need to talk to her friends Soona and Demi." They're her best friends. I figure it's the first place to start.

Walking through Mamacita's puts me on edge as we pass the customers sitting at the bar. Who's an enemy and who's there just for a cold beer and camaraderie? I'm sure they can tell I'm not a local just by looking at me.

Mateo doesn't seem to be concerned as he leads me to his truck parked in the back lot. "We're not alone," he says when I slide into the passenger seat and spot two guys by the side of the building watching us. They're pretending to be in a deep conversation, but every few seconds their attention is focused on us. We're definitely being monitored.

On the way to Panche, I'm trying to keep my cool and take cues from Mateo. He doesn't seem worried as we drive, as if we've somehow left the danger behind us.

"How can you be so calm?" I ask him. "You're in a car with someone who's wanted by the Loveland sheriff and Rico Cruz. If you haven't noticed yet, the dude travels in a pack." As I say it, a lightbulb goes off. Rico is Paul's informant. That's why Paul knows what I've been up to since I came to Mexico.

"There's no reason to ditch you because you're a target. I ain't afraid," Mateo says.

"You should be."

"As long as you're in Panche, you should sneak into La Joya de Sandoval after sundown."

I look at him sideways. "For what?"

"Gather clues, make her dad talk." He pauses. "Retrace Dalila's steps. If you don't know where she's been, how the hell do you know where she's going? I'll be there to help, so if something happens, I have your back."

"If I don't get answers from Demi or Soona, I might not have a choice." Her dad threatened my life the last time I saw him, but I'm not afraid. If I have to confront him, I will.

When we drive up to Panche, the landscape has changed dramatically from what we've driven through up to this point. I look ahead at the big mansions on huge pieces of land. Some are protected by impressive iron gates and others are surrounded by solid cement walls so high there's no doubt they're hiding something on the other side.

"I think Rico and my stepfather might be working together," I blurt out.

"Highly likely," Mateo says. "The Cruz family is known to have ties with *Las Calaveras*."

"You think they'd hurt Dalila?"

"If they have motive, those assholes will hurt anyone." He stops in front of one of the compounds. "Which house is it?" he asks me.

"I don't know."

He leans back and faces me with amusement. "You don't have an address?"

I shake my head. "I know they live in Panche and I know their names. I'll figure it out."

"Hess, people aren't going to give some random *gringo* directions to someone's house."

"Everyone has a price," I tell him. "Lucky for me I just came into an unexpected inheritance." I point to a park with a bunch of people milling around. "Drop me off here."

"No way." Mateo parks the car and pulls out his cell. Within seconds he's on the phone with someone. Through the Spanish I hear the words *Soona* and *Demi*. "All right," he says. "I'll take you to Soona's house."

When we get there, Mateo drives up to the gate. They've got this intercom on a post, reminding me of some of the exclusive neighborhoods in the Chicago suburb Winnetka. Mateo pushes the call button and we wait. I'm more than aware of the security camera mounted on the front gate that's probably recording our every move. This place is like a fortress.

Nobody answers.

Mateo rings the call button again.

"This sucks," I say as I get out of the car and look between the iron bars at the house to see if I can see any sign of life. There isn't any.

"My friend told me where Demi lives," he says. With a long, hopeless sigh, I get back in his truck.

"We'll find Dalila," Mateo says. "One way or another."

We finally reach Demi's house. It's a white two-story stucco house with unique rounded doorways and windows. It reminds me of something I'd find on the cover of a magazine.

Luckily Demi is home. After Mateo asks the housekeeper if we can see her, the woman leads us to a room off to the side.

It isn't long before Demi appears with a concerned look on her face.

"Did you find her?" Demi asks me.

"No. I was hoping you knew where she went."

She shakes her head. "She called me crying, but wouldn't say much. She said she felt lost and didn't know what to do. I told her to come here, but she refused."

Any hope I had of Demi knowing where Dalila is crashes down in an instant.

THIRTY-EIGHT

Dalila

Hiding my identity is easy, especially since I've got the hood blocking my face as I walk through town and head home. The problem isn't going home. It's sneaking into my house so I can confront Papá.

When I reach Panche, things look different to me. I always thought my town was beautiful, but now I see a darkness lingering over it. I hide behind trees so nobody will recognize me as they drive by. I know I'm a target, but at least I can be an invisible one.

At the top of the hill I see my house with the gates shut. I might have to go around back and sneak through the wheat fields, but I'll have to wait until it's dark.

I've been lurking in the shadows for about an hour when I see a police car drive up my street. I peek around a tree to see where they're headed, even though I have a dreaded hunch as to their destination.

I can't wait any longer. It's time for me to make my move. I shimmy my way through one of the gates, then run through the side yard while two police officers are at the front door talking to Papá's bodyguards.

As if I'm some kind of daredevil, I find the palm tree that leads to my bedroom window and start climbing it. At any moment someone could spot me, but I'm going on the hope that the police are taking up all of the attention. It doesn't take me long to find my way into my room, but when I hear voices in the courtyard below I tiptoe to the hallway and peek over the balcony.

"I don't know where he is," Papá is saying.

"We think you do," the officer is telling him. "His wife said you were the last person to talk to him, Oscar."

The second officer starts poking his nose into the kitchen. "You sure he's not here?"

"No."

"So tell me," the first officer says as he sits in one of the lounge chairs. "How much does Santiago Vega know about *Las Calaveras*?"

Papá crosses his arms on his chest. "That's confidential information."

"So you're saying you refuse to tell us? We have reason to believe Vega was working both sides."

"I'm going to ask you officers to leave," Papá says. "Unless you have a warrant . . ."

"We'll get one," the officer says. "Good day, Don Sandoval. If you see Santiago Vega, let us know. Here's my number," he says, writing it down on a sheet of paper and handing it to Papá.

When the officers leave, Papá pulls out his cell phone. "Santiago Vega is missing. Get over here right now, Cruz."

My heart starts beating fast. I was going to confront my father, but in reality I don't know this man who raised me. What if he lies or just tries to send me away again?

Does he know where Santiago Vega really is? Does he know where Ryan is?

I watch as he storms into his office and slams the door shut.

The echo of footsteps coming up the stairs startles me. I rush into my room, careful not to make any noise.

And I wait.

Tonight I'm going to find out who my father really is and what information he's hiding. The more I know, the closer I'll be to finding Ryan.

THIRTY-NINE

Ryan

Mateo and I leave Demi's house without any information. It's beyond frustrating.

The problem is that I have to look over my shoulder at every turn. Rico is after me. Paul is after me. Dalila's dad threatened my life if I ever saw her again. It's time to break all the rules, because being hunted doesn't work for me.

The hunted is about to become the hunter.

I leave Demi's house with a renewed sense of purpose. Mateo was right. To find out where Dalila went, I need to retrace her steps, which means there's only one place to start.

La Joya de Sandoval.

Mateo dropped me off behind the property before heading into the house to work as one of the Sandoval security guards. I plan to hide in the fields behind the compound until it's dark. Lurking in the shadows will be easy. Waiting is the frustrating part.

I find a place in the fields, surrounded by waving wheat five feet tall in some places. It's easy to maneuver, but I'm careful not to make my presence known. I'm more than aware that Dalila's father hired bodyguards to patrol the place. But after working there the night of Dalila's birthday, I also know there's a delay of about one to four minutes in between shifts.

I try to ignore the bees that attempt to sting me and the ants that start crawling up my leg. When a fly thinks I'm its perch, I swat it away, but two more join him. Look at me: the guy who vowed never to get involved with a girl is hiding out in the wheat field behind her house on the slim chance he can find a clue to where she's at.

Some things are worth fighting for, I guess. Or maybe I really am a fool who's been hit on the head so many times in the ring I can't think straight.

When darkness finally blankets the landscape, I take off into the thick undergrowth. It's hard to navigate the fields with the wheat scratching my arms like prickly knives, but nothing will keep me from my mission. I stay low and undetected until I see the guard near the flower garden disappear.

I jump over the wall and quickly open the side door that leads to the upstairs bedrooms.

"Everyone knows you've become the enemy by representing Santiago Vega!" I hear Rico's voice call out. I freeze and crane my neck trying to figure out what they're arguing about. "You have to choose a side or else deal with the consequences."

"You have no clue who you're dealing with," I hear Don Sandoval say in a loud, authoritative voice. "Get out of my house!"

Footsteps echo through the hall, reminding me of my mission. Looks like Rico and Don Sandoval are in a power struggle. The last thing I want to do is get caught in the middle of it. I round the hall and head to the stairs. Across the balcony, Mateo is patrolling the second floor. When our eyes meet, he gives me a short nod.

I slip into Dalila's room unnoticed, ready to gather evidence.

But my mission is cut short.

Dalila is standing by her dresser, her hair in wild waves falling down her shoulders. She whips around and gasps when I burst into her room, but I quickly motion for her to stay quiet.

I'm not prepared when she flings herself into my arms. The softness of her skin brushes up against mine. I feel her relief as she relaxes her body in my embrace and I hold her tight.

I didn't come here prepared with a speech. There's so much to say, but I know there's only a small window of time before someone sees us together.

"They're looking for you," Dalila whispers. "You shouldn't be here, Ryan. It's not safe."

I take her hands in mine, this Mexican princess who holds everything dear to me. "I came to find you. I heard you were missing."

"I couldn't stay here any longer and went to Juan Camacho's place last night. I just came back to confront Papá."

"Rico's downstairs. I know his dad was looking for you . . . it's because of me." If he's part of *Las Calaveras*, her father just invited the devil into his home.

"I think they're after me because of my father, Ryan. Not because of you." Tears well in her eyes. "Whatever he's involved in, it's dangerous. He sent my mom and sisters away. You're all I have left."

I'm about to tell her that I'll do whatever's in my power to protect her when a loud gunshot rings out. *Pop!* Then another. *Pop!*

Dalila sucks in a shocked breath and her eyes go wide with panic. "What's happening?" She grasps me tight. "Ryan . . ."

"We need to get out of here." I quickly take her hand and head for the stairs.

We're halfway down the staircase when we come upon a gruesome scene in the courtyard and Dalila screams in horror.

FORTY

Dalila

My entire body goes numb as I see Papá holding a gun. He's standing over a body lying in a pool of blood.

Rico's body.

Papá, wearing a fierce, deadly look on his face, turns and points the gun in Ryan's direction.

"Papá, no!" I scream as loudly as I can. I run toward Ryan in an attempt to shield him.

"Get away from my daughter," Papá growls in a tight, commanding voice. He steps through the pool of blood and walks toward us. "Dalila, move away from him."

"No!"

Ryan pulls me behind a pillar. "Run away with me, Dalila."

I shouldn't.

But with everything that just happened, I know this isn't home anymore. This is my past.

Ryan is my future.

I grab Ryan's hand and nod.

We dodge one of the security guards by rushing up the stairs and running to the second-floor balcony. Mateo is here motioning for us to follow him.

"Go to the edge of the property," Mateo says, his dark eyes wild with adrenaline. "I'll meet you there."

Ryan jumps off the balcony. In a leap of faith, I jump into his waiting arms. Holding his hand with the tightest grip I can, I wind my way through the fields with him.

When we stop at the edge of our property and duck beneath the trees, Ryan holds me close. I don't even realize I've been crying this entire time.

"I'll get you through this," he tells me as I bury my head into his chest and sob.

"Papá killed Rico." The sobs just won't stop as I contemplate what would have happened if I hadn't shielded Ryan. "He was about to kill you, too."

"But he didn't. Look at me." I do. His chiseled face is somber and his eyes are full of determination. "We're going to get through this."

How is everything going to be okay, when my entire life just crashed before my eyes? It's like living inside of a nightmare where you can never wake up. The only bright spot is that Ryan is with me so I'm not alone anymore.

I tense when I hear the sound of tires on the gravel road.

"It's just Mateo," Ryan assures me.

Mateo pulls up to us in his uncle's red truck. We rush into the car and in a few seconds Mateo is driving on the side roads to avoid being followed.

"Mateo, you can't be seen with us," Ryan says. I need to feed on his strength because mine is waning fast. My entire existence is based on greed and death. A part of me knew it, but the truth was so easy to deny.

Mateo says in a panic, "I need to take you farther from the compound. They're going to have *policiá* and bodyguards hunting you guys down."

"Drop us on the side of the road," Ryan says. "We'll figure it out."

"Dude, I can't just drop you on the side of the road. That's crazy!" Mateo is freaking out. His hands are shaking and he's breathing heavy. "You can hide at the boxing gym."

"They'll look for us there. We need another place."

Hide out? We didn't do anything wrong, yet we're being forced to act like fugitives. I hold my head in my hands in shame. "For so long I didn't want to admit it."

"Admit what?"

I look up at Ryan through blurry, teary eyes. "My father must be connected to *Los Reyes del Norte*. He just killed Rico, Ryan. The Cruzes are connected to *Las Calaveras*. All this time they acted like friends when they were bitter enemies."

"What does Santiago Vega have to do with the rivalry?" he asks.

"I think I read somewhere that he was involved with *Las Calaveras*. Maybe he changed sides. I don't know."

"Everyone has a price," Mateo chimes in from the front seat.

I'm hyperventilating now and my mind is racing. Nothing could prepare me for seeing Papá standing over Rico's lifeless body on the floor of our courtyard.

This can't be happening. I squeeze my eyes shut trying to block out reality but it's no use.

The thought of Papá behind bars is making me physically ill, but that's where he should be. What he did to Rico . . . taking his life. I lean over and put my head between my knees while Ryan rubs my back. He says encouraging words that are meant to help, but nothing will help. This feeling of dread I have isn't going away. It's just getting worse.

My stomach starts lurching. "Stop the truck."

Mateo screeches to a halt and I stumble out. Within seconds I'm puking my guts out.

When I settle back in the truck, Mateo's cell rings. We all go silent. I hold my breath while he tells the person on the other line that he's out looking for us. He promises to let the person on the other end know if he finds us. As I set into panic mode again Ryan puts a comforting arm around me and kisses my forehead.

He's all I have right now. He's everything to me.

Mateo ends the call and swears loudly.

"What's wrong?" Ryan asks him.

Mateo turns to us with an apologetic look on his face. It's obvious he doesn't want to share the news. "Before I left, Don Sandoval was ranting to everyone that you killed Rico, Ryan. He just framed you, man. The *policiá* and detectives have been called to La Joya de Sandoval and they're assembling a small army to hunt you down. They said if I find you, shoot to kill."

Shoot to kill?

I want to be the warrior woman I've always said I was, but my emotions are getting the best of me. *Dalila, calm down.* This isn't the end of the world, it's just the end of the world as I knew it. Things change, situations change, people change.

But I don't have to change. I refuse to let my emotions rule me. I'm going to fight for Ryan . . . for us. Even if I have to stand in front of a bullet to do it. Fighting for what's right is more important than standing idly by while injustice takes control.

"Ryan didn't do anything to Rico," I cry out. My mind is whirling with questions. Why would Papá want to frame Ryan? He's not a part of any cartel rivalry.

But his stepfather is.

"Paul is working with *Las Calaveras*," Ryan murmurs. The puzzle pieces are coming together.

"Listen," Mateo says. "I know of a safe house you two can go to. It's in Chihuahua, but I can hire guys to take you there. Or I can take you myself."

"No way. I don't want you gettin' more involved than you are," Ryan tells him. "If they find out you drove us away from La Joya de Sandoval they'll hunt you down as well. I can't do that to you, man. You need to get back to the house as soon as possible or they'll start to get suspicious."

"I'll be fine. It's a safe house, Ryan," Mateo says. "They call it *safe* for a reason."

Ryan puts his arm around me. "We can't risk it. Not now, when they could be combing the highways for us."

Why is my life spinning out of control? I'm so confused, like I'm caught in the middle of a tornado and can't escape.

There is no solution here. I can't go back home ever again. I can't see my family ever again. My father's men will be looking for Ryan. He'll be searching for me. They'll never stop.

Mateo drives off, twisting through old, dusty, unpaved roads hardly used by anyone.

"Let me out here," Ryan says before letting go of me. He takes my hands in his and his gaze locks on mine. "Listen to me and listen good, Dalila. I'm going to be a hunted man and I don't know if I can protect you. You don't deserve any of this, love. Have Mateo take you to your grandmother's. You'll be safe there for the time being. I promise to meet you there when this all blows over." He opens the door and steps out of the car, leaving me behind.

I quickly jump out of the car. "Have you gone completely *loco*? I'm not going anywhere without you, Ryan. Please don't leave me."

He looks pained as he runs his fingers through his hair. "You have to go somewhere you can be safe. I wasn't thinking when I told you to run away with me. Mateo will take you to Abuela Carmela's house. Stay there."

"No!" I rush up to him and cup his face in my hands, his stubble scratching my palms. "We need to be together, no matter what. We fight together, or we lose everything. I'm okay with whatever happens, as long as we're together. My entire life is crumbling beneath my feet." I can feel hot tears falling down my cheeks. "Stay with me."

Ryan holds my hand tight and for a moment I feel like I can get through this. But only if he's by my side.

"Dalila, don't you know how much I care about you? You deserve so much more than to be connected to a fugitive on the run." He looks down the gravel road and tenses. "A car could come by at any minute. Go with Mateo and be safe. Let him take you to your grandmother's."

"No. My safe place is with you." I start walking away from the truck, not caring that Ryan is watching me with a frustrated look on his face. "Are you coming, or are we going to stand around and argue something that's a done deal?"

Ryan shakes his head. "What can I do to change your mind?"

"*Nada.*"

If I'm not strong, I'm going to lose him.

"Well, I guess that's a done deal," Mateo says, then holds a cell phone out the truck window. "Here, it's my uncle's cell phone. Keep it powered off until you find a place to hide out so you don't run out of battery."

Ryan reaches into the car and shakes Mateo's hand—the gesture of two boys who share loyalty and trust in each other. "Thanks. I don't know what I'd have done without you today," Ryan says. "Now go back, before they suspect you're up to somethin'."

Mateo winks at Ryan. "You might not realize it, but we're in this together. Turn on that phone and text me updates. I'll let you know when the heat is off." Mateo points at me. "Take care of him, Dalila."

"I will."

Ryan slips the phone into his pocket as Mateo turns his truck around and heads back to the compound. "Come on," he says. "We need to find shelter and figure out how the hell I'm going to get you to your grandmother's."

"You're going to drop me at Abuela Carmela's and leave? No way." He doesn't answer so I block his path. "I'll agree to lead you to my grandmother's only because I think she can help us figure all this out. She'll help *us*. That means you and me."

"Chances are we'll be dead long before we even get there," Ryan barks out as he grabs my hand again. "Until then, I'm not lettin' you out of my sight."

"Good. Wherever you go, I go." I point him in the direction of Tulanco. We walk along the deserted, grassy landscape until the sun starts setting. My feet hurt and my body is full of dust and dirt, but I keep going. I don't want Ryan to think I can't keep up with him.

It's dark and I hear coyotes in the distance. Papá always told me to stay clear of the mountains at night, because as darkness falls the land becomes alive with predators. We don't have a car this time as shelter.

After a while, Ryan must sense my nervousness because he points to something in the distance and says, "There's a rock formation over there. We can sleep on it tonight so we're not vulnerable to wildlife."

He looks sideways at me, probably expecting me to complain about the less-than-stellar accommodations. I don't want him thinking that I'm afraid or regret my decision to stay with him. I take his hand in mine and we walk together to the boulders.

Ryan clears the area and creates a barrier to make sure our shelter is shielded from any creatures that might want to creep up on us in the middle of the night.

He helps me onto the boulder and then spends time making sure we're well hidden from anyone who might drive by even though we're far from any road. After a while he rests his head in his hands and swears under his breath. I don't talk to him, but I know how he feels. Devastation, like a simmering fire inside me, settles in the middle of my chest.

As if on cue a pack of wolves howls in the distance and Ryan pulls me close. "Lay your head in my lap and go to sleep," he tells me. "We need to get up early and start movin'."

I do as he instructs, but start shaking as the horror of what I saw today comes back. "I can't believe what Papá did. I don't know if I'll ever be okay."

"It'll take time, baby." He puts his finger on my chin and guides it so I'm looking right at him. "You're the strongest girl I've ever met."

"I don't feel very strong right now. I just want to crawl into a hole and cry until I have no more tears left. Ugh, I hate feeling so defeated. What are we going to do, Ryan?"

He looks out at the darkened landscape in front of us. "I don't know, baby." He brushes the hair out of my face and rubs my back as I lay my head on his lap.

As the night wears on and my eyelids get heavy, I mumble, "Just so you know, I won't let anyone hurt you."

He chuckles, then kisses the top of my head. "Do you believe in miracles, my Mexican princess? Because I think we're going to need one pretty soon."

FORTY-ONE

Ryan

I couldn't sleep, and now the bright Mexican sun is rising over the horizon like an obnoxious alarm clock. If it were a different time or place, I'd be mesmerized at the multicolored landscape. Each rock has its own color and the carpet of long green and yellow grass seems to be changing with each movement of the sun. It's so peaceful and quiet here you'd think we were on a boulder smack-dab in the middle of heaven.

I look down at Dalila finally sleeping peacefully on my lap. I heard her cry in the middle of the night and it tore me apart. I don't know how we got here and I sure as hell don't know where I'm going in this beautiful foreign land.

All night I've been going through scenarios of why her dad

would want to set me up. It just doesn't make sense. He thinks I'm the enemy.

Unless her father is El Fuego like she said. But why kill Rico and blame me for it? He said he'd kill me if he found out I was working for *Las Calaveras* cartel. If he knew Rico was a member of *Las Calaveras*, obviously that was enough for him to kill the guy. If he saw me at the compound and thinks that somehow Rico and I were in on some kind of mission to hurt him or his family . . . that's the only reason he could have to justify framing me.

Dalila has to be right.

Don Sandoval is connected to *Los Reyes del Norte*. If he's the head of the cartel, it makes perfect sense to frame me for Rico's death. It takes the big, fat target off of his back and puts it on mine.

When a bird flies over us I notice the sun is rising higher in the sky. I'm tired but determined to get Dalila to a safe place tonight so she doesn't have to sleep on another fucking boulder. I want to protect her so damn bad, but there's no denying we're both in danger. If *Las Calaveras* cartel thinks I killed one of their own and stole money from their crooked Loveland sheriff who is being paid to look the other way, they'll shoot first and ask questions later.

Actually, they'll likely torture me first without asking questions.

Meeting up with Don Sandoval or anyone from *Los Reyes del Norte* won't be any better. I'll definitely end up six feet under if either cartel finds me. And if they don't get me, the Mexican police will likely shoot me or arrest me for allegedly murdering Rico.

"*Buenos días,*" Dalila says, stretching. "Did you get some sleep?"

"Yeah," I lie.

She closes her eyes and takes in a deep breath. Why isn't she afraid of being with me out in the wilderness without any luxuries? No shelter, no food, no hope.

As she sits up, she wraps her arms around herself and shivers.

"You're cold."

"I'm fine."

I can see the goose bumps on her arms. "Come here," I say, pulling her close and rubbing her arms to keep her warm. I notice her eyes are still bloodshot and irritated from crying last night.

"I'm sorry," I tell her.

"I'm going to stay strong," she tells me. "We're going to figure something out. We'll get out of this situation."

"I think I know why your dad framed me. I think it was to take the target off his back. It's the only explanation."

She perks up. "What if I talk to Papá and . . ." She hangs her head low. "I can't do that. I don't ever want to see him again after what he did. I swear the past month he's been a different man than I've ever seen before. Ever since he started representing Santiago Vega."

I convince Dalila that we need to head to Abuela Carmela's house as soon as possible. As we're walking I'm all too aware of our surroundings. We're in a deserted area, but every once in a while we come upon small farm communities. Families with goats and chickens farm their land while their children play in the yards. Most people smile and wave as we pass them. I'm careful to keep a jovial gait, hoping they just see us as typical foreign backpackers walking through their towns instead of two weary, suspicious teens.

Each time we pass one of the small farm communities without causing suspicion, Dalila lets out a sigh of relief.

About two hours into our trek, Dalila slips off her shoes and I notice she's got blisters on her feet. The sight of them makes something sting inside me.

"We need to take a break," I tell her.

"No. Let's keep going. We have to keep going." I don't want to admit she resembles Cinderella before the fairy godmother showed up. Her legs are dirty and her face is solemn.

"You've got blisters."

She keeps on walking. "I'm not the delicate girl you think I am. I'm not the first person to have blisters, and I won't be the last. I'm tough, okay? My emotions might be a mess, but blisters are nothing."

"How are you gonna walk when the brutal Mexican sun heats the ground in another hour?"

"I'll figure it out." Her stomach lets out a loud growl. "We're going to need food at some point."

As soon as she says it, I spot a lone chicken running in the distance. At least I think it's a chicken. Unless my eyes are playing tricks on me, which is entirely possible due to lack of sleep.

"That wasn't a chicken, was it?"

Dalila nods. "That was a chicken."

We run after it as if our lives depend on it. It runs over a little hill and I chase it, dust flying behind me, until I reach the other side of the hill and freeze in my tracks. "There's a house." I motion for Dalila to follow me. "It looks abandoned."

It's the very definition of a shack. Four walls and a roof, but that's about it. At this moment a doghouse would feel like a palace to me.

"You think it's safe?" she asks with a worried look on her face.

"We haven't seen anyone for miles." I look up at the sun. "We need shelter. I'm game if you are."

She nods. "We can do this."

I make her stay back while I scout out the shack. As I open the door and peek inside, it's obvious the place hasn't been occupied in quite some time. Dust has settled in just about every corner. There's a table and chairs that look like they've seen better days. The rest of the furniture is scattered throughout the tiny structure, as if someone hastily abandoned it and never intended on returning.

Dalila and I spend the remainder of the day indoors. I try to chat with her about nothing and everything just to get her mind off what happened yesterday.

It takes me a long time and a great amount of frustration, but I finally catch the lone chicken. I feel sorry for it, because it kinda reminds me of myself . . . a loner without a chance of survival.

But I'm not alone.

I have Dalila, a girl with a heart so big she's willing to risk everything to be with me. I think I'm just about the luckiest guy on the planet to have a girl like her by my side. I don't deserve her, but I sure am glad she doesn't realize it.

Inside, Dalila sets the table as if a small chicken is a feast fit for a king.

I build a fire out back with some old matches I find in the shack and cook the chicken. "If I had some barbeque sauce or spices I bet it'd taste good and mask the charred flavor," I say lamely as I bring the thing inside.

She stares at the chicken with a cocked brow. "I like my chicken well done," she assures me, but I know differently as she pulls apart the leg and takes a small bite. I could watch her all day and never get tired of discovering the little quirks she has. Like when she doesn't like something, her lips purse just the slightest bit. Or when she wants to laugh hard but restrains herself, she covers her mouth with her hand.

I could find a thousand things to admire about her, and that'd be just the beginning.

"Why are you staring at me?" she asks.

"Besides the fact that you're beautiful? You're eatin' that chicken in such dainty pieces you'd think we were at a formal ball." I grab a piece of meat off the carcass and show her how it's done.

She shakes her head. "You look like a caveman."

"At this point I might as well be one."

She laughs, the sound a welcome change from the grim mood we've both had since yesterday. I haven't heard her laugh since we left her house. I know even though she's in her own hell right now that she's worrying about taking some of my misery away. Her smile might brighten up this dingy, dark, abandoned place, but our situation is still hopeless.

After we eat, we're so exhausted from walking in the heat and sun that we lie down on the old couch together.

She wraps her arms around me and I hold her close. She's still got that sweet smell of wildflowers and her lips are soft and welcoming. It isn't long before she settles her head on my chest. The sound of her slow breathing lulls me to sleep. It's been a long day and I don't reckon tomorrow will be any better.

"I love you, Ryan," she whispers as I fall into a deep slumber.

Her words echo through my brain and seep into my soul. For her own safety I'll have to give her up soon, even though I'd sell my soul to feel this content forever. For the moment, though, I let myself enjoy it.

FORTY-TWO

Dalila

When the morning sun shines through the windows, we know it's time to leave. As much as I'd like to stay in this cabin, I know we have to keep moving and cover our tracks.

After packing up our stuff, we trek past the grassy plains near the cabin and enter the harsh, rocky landscape. "You haven't talked much this morning," I say to Ryan. "Did I do something wrong?"

"No. Not at all. I just wish things were different."

"Me too." I manage a small, tremulous smile.

"I hate seeing you so sad." He takes my hand and pulls me into the circle of his arms. With a dip of his head, he kisses me tenderly and my heart turns over in response. "We'll get through this. I promise." After kissing me on my nose, Ryan points to a hill in the distance and is back to the task at hand. "Let's head that way to avoid the main road."

I nod. "I agree. Staying out of sight is best."

Ryan takes my hand and we continue our trek toward Abuela Carmela's house. The strength of his grip gives me an amazing sense of calm.

It isn't long before I hear a car in the distance. It's coming closer and I tense up. "Ryan . . ."

As if he knows what I'm about to say, he leads me up a dirt hill and we hide behind a big spiky bush. He shields me as the car passes.

Ryan's face is tense as he takes my hand again. "Come on, we better keep movin'."

We rush through the mountains, stopping each time there's a boulder to hide behind and looking into the distance for any sign of trouble. I can feel the stress of today radiating off him.

I sense his hesitation. "There's somethin' I haven't shared with you." He stops and pulls me back to face him. "I stole money from my stepfather. A lot of it."

"When?"

"A few days ago. I'm almost certain it was bribe money." He combs his hand through his hair as his face turns stoic. "Or maybe it was to turn the other way when there was a hit on one of the border patrol cops in Loveland."

"Wow." I step back, because my brain needs time to process this. "Why didn't you tell me earlier?"

"I didn't know how to tell you. I took a little for emergency cash and the rest is being divided."

"Divided?"

"Remember my friend Pablo? You met him the night of the Shadows of Darkness concert."

I nod.

"Well, I left Pablo instructions. Most of the money goes to Max Trieger's family. He was investigating *Las Calaveras* and died because of it. My stepfather is taking bribes from *Las Calaveras* so it's only fair his family receives some of it."

"And the rest of the money?" I question.

"Let's just say it's called a power play. In boxing, if you're not the favorite you have to figure out a way to beat your opponent even though the odds are stacked against you. And make no mistake about it, Dalila, the odds are stacked against me. Come on," he says. "Let's keep movin'." He hesitates, then takes Mateo's cell phone out of his pocket. "Unless you want me to call the cops and turn myself in. I'll do that for you."

"No! You're not calling the cops. We'll figure something out, Ryan. I promise."

He doesn't seem convinced, but I'll come up with a plan to right all the wrongs.

We keep winding through the mountains, hoping there's no way anyone can spot us. Ryan doesn't seem concerned for himself, even as sweat soaks his T-shirt. He keeps asking me if I need a break or if I'm hungry.

We're both highly sensitive to every sound and movement to make sure we're not spotted or followed.

The sound of an engine startles me and Ryan immediately pulls me down. "Someone's comin'," he says as he helps me crawl to the nearest boulder. We stay silent and still as a white truck drives across the barren land, dust kicking up behind it.

The truck stops and two guys get out. They scan the horizon as if they're looking for something and I hold my breath and pray.

What if we're caught?

I can't lose Ryan, not now when we've just found each other. Our connection is getting stronger every minute we're together. He must feel it too. I can sense the emotions he's experiencing like they're my own.

The guys focus their attention on the ground. "They're checking for tracks," Ryan tells me.

The sound of a rattle startles me. I look down. Right next to my shoe is a rattlesnake.

"Stay still," Ryan instructs. He slowly bends down and grabs a long, forked stick from the ground as I hold my breath. "Now back up slowly."

I do as instructed, careful to keep the boulder between me and the truck. Ryan holds down the snake until we move away from it. Finally the snake slithers away. We stay hidden for a long time, even after the truck and the snake are out of sight.

I can tell there's a change in Ryan's demeanor. He's completely silent and when I ask him questions he gives me one-word answers.

As the sun starts to set, we head out once again.

"What's wrong, Ryan?" I ask. "You haven't said a word for the past two hours."

"What's wrong is I let you come with me. Look!" he says,

holding his arms out wide. I can feel his frustration. "Look around us, Dalila. I put you in danger and I've set you on this course that could only lead to us runnin' like animals for the rest of our lives. You don't deserve that."

"I don't have anywhere else to go, Ryan. I can handle this rough spot in our lives."

"Rough spot? Baby, you're *delusional*. Havin' an argument about what movie to go see is a rough spot. Forgettin' a birthday or anniversary is a rough spot. This . . . this is a nuclear attack on your life! What happened at your house is a complete and utter breakdown of everything you know and everything that you are."

The truth hits me hard, but it's not because of what Ryan just said. It's what he's not saying that makes me love him more. "You haven't asked me to fix this," I mumble.

"You can't fix it."

But I can. "The only person who was with you when the shots rang out is me. I'm your alibi. You could ask me to go to the police to tell them the truth about everything."

"You can't do that."

He doesn't say it, but I have to. "Because it'll make me implicate my father as Rico's murderer."

"They probably wouldn't believe you. They'll think I've somehow brainwashed you. I'm a foreigner here and your father is very powerful. I'll figure out somethin'." He gazes across the horizon. "But first we need to get you food and water. I've got enough money if we find a place to eat."

Walking all day is exhausting, and tripping on rocks in the dark isn't pleasant, but I keep up a quick pace so we can get as far away as possible from whoever was in the white truck. Night falls and I feel a sense of security under the cloak of darkness.

As if by some miracle, twinkling lights in the distance catch my eye. I grab Ryan's arm and shake it as if I've just spotted a pot of gold. "Look! There's a town up ahead," I cry out. "See the lights?"

We're both dehydrated and weak. With renewed energy, we rush toward the town. I'm not familiar with it, but then again these little towns in the mountains are so out of the way that it's not unusual for them to go unnoticed.

But as we get closer, it's clear that it's not a small town in the middle of the desert. It's a small, exclusive four-star hotel called Estrella.

"We can't go in there," I tell him.

"Call and ask if they have a room available for tonight," he tells me. He pulls out Mateo's phone and hands it to me. After a little searching, I get their number and book a room under the last name Reyes. We wait awhile in the parking lot, then walk into the hotel as if we belong here.

The teenage girl at the front desk hardly looks at us when we enter the lobby. She doesn't even flinch when Ryan pays for the room with American dollars.

Ten minutes later we're in a big, fancy hotel room with plush towels and a bed so soft I feel like I could sink into it. After making sure every door and window is locked and all curtains are closed, shielding us from the outside, Ryan calls room service and they deliver steaming-hot platters of *carne* and vegetables.

My mouth is watering just thinking about the spread in front of us.

"I should feel guilty," I say as I savor every flavorful bite. "But I can't."

After downing four bottled waters and ordering another four, we scarf down our food as if we're not going to eat another meal for a while. By the end, we're both stuffed and fall onto the bed.

"We can't be in this bed together, Ryan," I tell him as I stare up at the ceiling fan above us. "Not like this."

"Like what?"

"We're both dirty." I take his hand, because I don't want to go anywhere without him. "Come shower with me."

FORTY-THREE

Ryan

I look at the girl standing in front of me, this girl who's risking everything just to be by my side. Her usually shiny hair is messed up and dull from our journey. She's wearing ripped, dirty shorts paired with a top that's seen better days. Her cheek has a streak of dirt on it from sleeping on the boulder two nights ago. She's a hot mess.

And she still takes my breath away.

I realize at this moment that I'd love nothing better than to take a shower with her. I should run right out that door and never look back, because the more time I spend with her the more I don't want to let her go. I'm just torturing myself at this point.

"Wherever you go, I go." Dalila leans in close and kisses me. Man,

I could kiss her forever and never get tired of it. "Make me forget reality, Ryan," she whispers when she pulls back the slightest bit. "Make me forget the world outside this room exists."

I never knew I could feel this way about another person. When she looks up at me, the love reflected in her eyes is enough to make me want to shelter her until the end of our days.

There's desire reflected in Dalila's eyes too, but I can't help but notice the sadness that the events of the past two days have inflicted upon her. She wants me to make her forget the outside world. I'm going to do everything in my power to make that happen.

I turn the shower on. Steam quickly fills the room and our eyes cling to each other's. She's leaning against the tile wall and her dark, smoldering eyes roam down to where my body is reacting all on its own. She swallows, hard.

"You undress first, Mr. America," she says. I can almost feel her pulse beat harder and faster as the words leave her mouth.

"Don't you want to make out first?"

She shakes her head. "No."

The side of my mouth quirks up as I slip my T-shirt over my head. I work hard on being fit, but the appreciation showing on Dalila's face as her eyes roam over my chest and abs makes me feel like I'm superhuman.

I place my hands on the zipper of my jeans and pause. I want to make sure she's present in this moment and isn't worrying or thinking about anything else but what's happening in this room. I can feel her eagerness as the seconds tick by.

Her tongue darts out and she licks her lips. "You're teasing me."

"Yeah, I am." I undo the button and slowly move the zipper down, the entire time watching her reaction. I pull my jeans down and kick them away. "You've already seen me," I tell her as I expose the rest of myself.

"I know, but I was too nervous to really pay attention." Her eyes gaze over me and they brighten with a passion that makes me feel like I'm invincible.

I've got her attention now. "Your turn," I tell her.

"Not yet." She steps closer and reaches out, touching my chest with her soft, delicate fingers. Her eyes soften and her mouth twists into a somber frown as she touches my abdomen. "You're still bruised."

I'm trying to keep my emotions in check, but her touch sends my body into overdrive. "I'm fine."

"You sure?"

Her fingers gently glide over my bruises. At first I think she might be repulsed by them, but to my surprise she bends down and her fingers are replaced by her lips. I close my eyes and feel the brush of her gentle kisses on each bruise, starting with my shoulders and moving down to my chest and lower . . .

"I think I'm all healed," I groan, acutely aware that I'm rock-hard right now. "Damn, I should get beat up more often."

A satisfied grin crosses her mouth. As she reaches up on her tiptoes to kiss me, I pull back and cross my arms. "Your turn." I gesture to her clothes. "Take 'em off, baby."

She pouts with those soft, full lips that are driving me wild. "I wasn't finished exploring."

With an amused grin, I shake my head. "Even the playing field, Ms. Sandoval."

She holds her hands up in mock surrender. "Fine." Reaching out for the light switch on the wall, she moves the toggle down so the light is dimmed to where I can hardly see her.

I turn the light back on to full strength.

She dims the light again. "It's too bright in here."

"It wasn't too bright a minute ago."

"A minute ago you weren't about to see me naked." When she can see I'm not about to give up, she adds, "I don't want you to see my imperfections."

"What imperfections?"

"I'm not going to tell them to you. Then you'll focus on them."

"Baby, from where I'm standing you don't have imperfections. Not one." I turn the light back on and step closer, then ease her shirt up over her head. I hear her uneven breathing when I turn her around and unhook her bra as I kiss the back of her neck. "Show me your body, Dalila," I whisper against her skin. Her hands immediately cover her breasts as she turns to face me. I gently take her hands and ease them away, exposing her.

At first she tenses, but soon her hands reach around and grab the back of my neck as she relaxes. "You sure you want to see everything?"

I nod. "Oh, yeah. Very sure."

Her hands go to the waistband of her shorts and I feel like I'm the luckiest guy alive. This isn't the first time we've been intimate, but this feels different. She isn't just gifting me her body. She's trusting me with her inner fears and insecurities. When her panties and shorts fall to the floor, she focuses her gaze on the ground.

"Look at me, Dalila."

When she does, my fingers trace a path from her taut stomach to those perfectly shaped hips and I settle my palms on her amazing backside. I pick her up by her bottom. In one swift movement, she wraps her arms around my neck and her legs around my waist as I escort my beautiful woman to the shower.

"Thank you, Ryan Hess," she whispers against the crook of my neck.

"For what?"

"Loving me."

In the morning I wake up early and turn Mateo's cell phone on. He left me a text that I should come to the gym and he'll drive us to the safe house. He's got it all set up.

I ignore his message because Dalila doesn't need a safe house. She needs her grandmother. Hell, we both need Abuela Carmela at this point, the strong Mexican woman who's paved her own path and survived. She doesn't trust Don Sandoval and who he's become. She'll tell us what to do.

I text Mateo back that we're going to Dalila's grandmother's house in Tulanco and I'll call him when I get there. I don't want him to wonder if we're dead or alive.

Just being in Dalila's presence calms me and makes me want to live in her mind, because she tries to find the positive where I can only see negative. Even last night, she was content to block out the crap situation we're in and focus on the amazing reprieve in this luxury hotel.

While she's in a peaceful slumber, I push away the curtains and peer out our hotel room window. Below us, roaming the pool area as if they're on a mission, are two Mexican police officers. Are they looking for us? My mind starts racing with random thoughts. If they're crooked, are they affiliated with *Las Calaveras* or *Los Reyes del Norte*?

If they're connected to *Los Reyes del Norte*, Dalila should be safe.

If they're connected to *Las Calaveras* . . .

I don't wake her up, but I sit by the door just in case anyone decides to come in uninvited.

"Good morning," Dalila says in a groggy voice as she stretches. When she sits up, I try to act like everything is cool but she takes one look at me and frowns. "What's wrong?"

"Nothing. *Nada.*"

She looks at me sideways. "Tell me."

"I saw two cops around the pool area. I don't know if they're after me or not. We need to get to your grandmother's house. Today. Even if we have to hot-wire a car to do it."

She nods. "Okay."

Luckily the cops leave. We wait for a while, then Dalila asks one of the gardeners to drive us to Tulanco for a hefty sum. After his shift, we get in his truck and head out. He drops us off in Tulanco a half hour later.

"The door is wide open," Dalila announces as we walk up to the front of Abuela Carmela's house. "Why would it be open?"

"Maybe she forgot to close it," I explain. "She's old. Old people forget things."

But as we step into the house, it's obvious something's wrong. The pictures on the walls are all crooked and furniture is scattered on the floor, signaling some kind of struggle.

I step farther into the kitchen and a grisly scene greets me, one more vile than Rico's death.

No.

"Dalila, don't look! Stay outside!" I rush to Abuela Carmela, who's lying on the floor, soaking in her own blood. "Whatever you do, don't come in here!"

It's too late. Dalila's hand flies to her mouth and a helpless cry pierces the air at the sight of her grandmother riddled with stab wounds.

The word *venganza* is written on the floor in blood.

FORTY-FOUR

Dalila

With a pained, piercing scream I fall to my knees next to my *abuelita*. This can't be real. Not her, not now! Her clothes are completely
soaked with blood and her eyes are empty.

She's gone. *Venganza* means revenge, which means she was killed
in retaliation by one of the cartels. There's only one person responsible for this.

I have no strength left for this.

Nausea invades my body. Why her? She was just a frail old
lady . . . my *abuela* who refused to give up on what she believed in
even if it meant not seeing her family.

"No!" Rage like a tsunami engulfs me. "Give me the phone!" I
cry out, grasping at Ryan's jeans for Mateo's cell. I dial my father's

number to scream at him and call him a murderer and threaten every bone in his body, but Ryan rips the phone from my hand before my papá answers.

"Don't call him," he says, hanging up.

"Why? Why can't I tell him the truth, that he's a monster? My father is a monster, Ryan! If it weren't for him, she'd be alive," I sob. "I just know it. *Venganza* means revenge, Ryan. Papá killed Rico, so *Las Calaveras* killed her!"

"Now isn't the time to confront him."

"It'll never be a good time. He's destroyed everything I care about. Everything! If anything happens to my mother, sisters, or you... I'll... I'll..."

I grab a towel and rush to the sink, then wipe *mi abuelita's* bloody face to preserve some of her dignity. Disgust and anger envelope me as I cradle her head in my lap, unwilling to let her go. Unable to accept this. I'm shaking while uncontrollable sobs rip from my lungs. Ryan kneels beside me and holds us both.

"Why? Why? Why?" I chant over and over as I break down. I don't know what I would do if he weren't here for me, to be my support when I feel like my own life is draining from my body.

"I'm calling the police," Ryan says.

"No! What if they're the ones who did this? What if it's another ploy to frame you?" I look at him, my eyes blurry and stinging from crying so much. "Why did they do this?" I say in a weak, defeated voice.

Ryan sighs. "I don't know," he finally says.

The devastation will never end. My emotions are running

rampant. I was strong and determined to fight for my independence but now I feel like giving up.

I take in my now-bloody clothes and bloodstained hands. "What are we going to do? No police, Ryan. I don't know who we can trust at this point."

"I can try calling someone in the US." He looks as defeated as I feel. "But I don't know if that'll make things worse."

"We're alone in this, aren't we?"

He nods. "Yeah. We're alone. I mean, I can call Mateo and see what he says but I'm sure he's gettin' grilled by your dad or Rico's crew by now. Or the police. I don't want to get him killed for associating with us."

"He said he knew of a safe house. I know you don't want to admit that we need it . . ." I lean into him for strength. "But we need it, Ryan. We need to be safe. Together. Wherever you go, I go."

As long as we're together, that's all that matters. I have nothing left. Nothing, besides the man standing in front of me.

"You don't deserv—"

"Stop saying that! We're family now. Nothing else matters. We're not safe here. If this was some sort of setup, they'll be back, Ryan." I take the phone from him. "Call Mateo. Tell him we're ready to go to the safe house. After we're there maybe I can send for my mom and sisters. You can't protect me on your own. I know it's not your nature, but don't be afraid to ask for help. It doesn't make you less of a man. I promise you that."

As I sit on the stoop of Abuela Carmela's house, I hug my knees to my chest and rock back and forth. Ryan reluctantly calls Mateo. He tells Mateo everything that's happened. Mateo admits that he's been interrogated by members of *Las Calaveras*. They've been asking questions about Ryan and his whereabouts. In the end, Mateo agrees to meet us here so he can get us to the safe house where we can be invisible.

Ryan kneels in front of me. "I need to wash the blood off you," he tells me in a calm, gentle voice. "If we're questioned, we can't be seen with blood all over our clothes and hands."

"I can't do this." I look into his kind, loving eyes. "I can't function."

"Yes, you can." He rubs my palm gently with his thumb, the sensation reminding me that I might be completely numb inside but I'm still alive. "I'll get some clothes you can wear from inside the house. Okay? You can do this. I'll help you."

I nod.

With tender hands, he leads me to the water tank on the side of the house. As I stand here, barely aware of what's going on, he washes all the blood off me carefully and slowly as if I could break at any moment. I feel fragile and want to shut my mind off. I don't even protest when he dresses me in a pair of my grandmother's shorts and a T-shirt that still carries her sweet scent.

After I'm clean, he instructs me to sit on a rock not far away. He kneels in front of me again and makes me look at him. "I'm going to bury her," he says, his face full of compassion.

"No," I cry out as I clutch his shoulders in a desperate attempt at blocking this entire scene out of my head.

"I don't want to leave her like this, love. She deserves a proper burial." He points at the horizon. "Just look across the horizon and think of that house we talked about building. Remember that house? I can almost see it if I focus hard enough."

As I stare across the land, he kisses me on my forehead before taking on the daunting task of laying Abuela Carmela to rest. By the time Mateo pulls up in his uncle's red truck an hour later, we're all cleaned and have said our teary good-byes to her.

I climb into the back seat and insist on Ryan sitting next to Mateo in front. We need help, and Mateo is the only person who can help us right now.

We can't do this alone. Not anymore.

"I can't believe what happened," Mateo says. "It's insane!"

"Yep," Ryan murmurs. "Tell us what to do, man. I'm out of ideas."

"Well, I didn't want to tell you this, Ry," Mateo says with a slight groan. "It's pretty bad."

"What's going on?" Ryan asks. "Hit me with it."

"You sure?"

Ryan puts his hands in the air, exasperated that there's more bad news. "Nothin' could surprise me at this point."

"All right." Mateo keeps driving, his eyes focused on the road as he hesitates. "*Las Calaveras* have put a hit out on you. I guess your stepfather is going to try to come from Texas so he can get the job done. Without concrete evidence, there's no way they'll lock him up."

The reality of it all is too much. Ryan's stepfather is out to kill him?

No, it can't be.

But when I look at Mateo's serious expression I know it's true.

FORTY-FIVE

Ryan

Every time life has thrown crap my way, I've dealt with it. It's been nonstop my entire existence.

The fact that my mother's husband wants me dead is chilling. I look back at Dalila, who's staring at me, wide-eyed. "We'll figure this out," she says. "I'll think of something." She sounds so determined and sure of herself. I'd love to be able to tell her that everything will be okay, but I can't.

I swear under my breath. While I can't say my mother has been a loving parent, I still can't leave her to be manipulated by her crook of a husband. "I'm going to the US to bring him down," I tell them. "Mateo will take you to the safe house. I'll go to Loveland and—"

She shakes her head. "No. You're not leaving me."

"I can't let him get away with what he's doing." Max Trieger wouldn't hide out in some safe house if he knew that an officer was dirty. He'd fight for what was right, no matter what. I'm tired of running.

Dalila shakes her head again. "You're not leaving me."

Driving through the now-familiar landscape, I'm careful to shield myself so nobody can recognize me as one of the most wanted men in Mexico. I'm finding it hard to wrap my brain around all the players and what their motives are.

All I know for sure is that I'm caught in the middle of it.

"So here's the plan," Mateo says as we get close to Sevilla. "We'll wait at Mamacita's until ten tonight, then I'll drive you to the safe house. It's better to travel in the dark."

I turn around. "You okay with the plan?"

Dalila, still in shock from the turn of events, nods. "You're staying with me, right?"

"Yeah. I'll be with you," I tell her. At least until I figure out a plan.

I think she's in survival mode, just breathing to live. I squeeze her hand to let her know I'm here. I'll be here for her as long as I can.

After we pull around to the parking lot in the back of the bar, Mateo and I rush Dalila through the back door and up to the second-floor apartment. Mateo sits at the kitchen table and starts making phone calls to his buddies who can help us when I remember I left my duffel in the car with a big stash of cash inside. I don't want to leave it alone for one second. "I have to get my stuff from the car," I tell Dalila. I grab the keys Mateo left on the counter. "I'll be right back."

"Hurry," Dalila calls out as I rush to the parking lot.

My duffel is in the front seat where I left it. As I grab it, I remember the little heart-shaped rock Dalila gave me for good luck the last time we drove this truck. I open the glove compartment to retrieve it, but when I reach inside something sharp slices through my finger. Rummaging inside, I notice a bloodstained cloth. As I pull it out, a knife falls into my hand.

Abuela Carmela's jewel-encrusted, one-of-a-kind heirloom knife with her great-grandfather's initials carved into it. A gun is hidden inside the glove compartment as well.

The only explanation I can come up with makes my entire body fire up. Don Sandoval didn't instigate this war between *Las Calaveras* and *Los Reyes del Norte*.

Mateo did.

He killed Abuela Carmela. But why?

With adrenaline running through my body, I quickly pull out the cell phone he gave me and call Officer Matthews.

"Matthews," he answers.

"This is Ryan Hess, Paul Blackburn's stepson."

"Where are you?"

"Mexico." I hesitate, because I'm not 100 percent I can trust him. "Something's going down here and I need help. Oscar Sandoval is involved with some guy named Santiago Vega and I think they're part of *Los Reyes del Norte*. Mateo Rodriguez killed Oscar's mother for revenge, but I don't know why. My stepfather is connected to Francisco Cruz and *Las Calaveras*. I think they were involved in Max Trieger's death."

"Whoa, slow down."

"I can't. I don't have much time to talk." I look over my shoulder at the bar, hoping that Mateo is still preoccupied.

"Oscar Sandoval is working with us," Officer Matthews tells me. "His client Santiago Vega has been an informant. They're on our side, Ryan. We just don't have confessions or evidence."

Dalila's father is helping Vega bring down the cartels. He isn't one of them. Her dad is one of the good guys. A sense of relief rushes through me.

"Meet me at the boxing gym tonight in Sevilla," I tell him. "Ten o'clock. I'll make sure everyone is there. I'll bring evidence and try to lure out confessions."

"Don't try to be a hero, Ryan. Stay out of it. They're dangerous people who kill for a living."

"It's too late for that. I'm already involved," I tell him, then hang up.

I call my one-man crew and tell him what's going down. I instruct him to call Camacho and make sure the old man stays clear of the boxing gym tonight. I don't want him getting caught in the crossfire.

"I got you. Be safe," Pablo says before hanging up.

Afterward I make my last call.

"Sheriff Blackburn," he answers.

"It's Ryan."

"Where are you, Ryan?"

"I'm in Mexico. I have the money but there are people after me," I say in a shaky voice so he thinks I'm scared. "Can you come get me?"

He hesitates. I can hear his labored breathing on the other end. "Yeah, I can come get you. Tell me where you are."

After I tell him I'll be at the boxing gym in Sevilla at ten, I hang up and pray I haven't just signed my own death sentence. I'm bringing all the players together to one location. If I can get them to confess in front of Officer Matthews, this nightmare will be over.

I need to go back in the apartment and pretend I didn't find the knife and gun. *Play it cool, Ryan. The only way to save Dalila is to play it cool.* I was such a fool thinking Don Sandoval was the one who killed Rico. It was Mateo. I remember what he looked like when he picked us up after the shooting. His eyes were wide and he was too hyped up afterward, like he got a high from the kill.

"Hey," I say as I walk back into the small apartment.

Mateo ends his phone call and looks at me suspiciously. "Why'd you go outside?"

I hold up my duffel. "It's the only thing I've got left, bro." I toss the keys to him.

Mateo smiles warmly, but now I can see through that facade to the blackness of his soul. How many times did he say he had my back? Too many to count. I wanted to believe him, so I did.

I want to fight him so damn bad, but I can't. Not now, at least.

Dalila is anticipating going to a safe house. I feel like the biggest asshole for bringing her to this place. This is the opposite of a safe house and I need to get her out of here. I've only got one play left to get the upper hand.

"You okay?" Mateo asks her.

"Now I am." Dalila looks up at him and breathes a sigh of relief. Damn, she has no clue we just walked into a trap. "Thanks for being such a good friend to Ryan."

"I always have Ryan's back." He pats me on the back. "Right, bro?"

My hands ball into fists at his words. No, he doesn't have my back. "Right," I say with very little emotion. "Listen, I need to tell you somethin'. It's really important."

Mateo raises a curious brow. "What's up?"

I pull Mateo aside. "I hid the money at the gym and need to go get it."

"The two mil?" He almost chokes on the words.

"Two point two. I'm gonna give it to you for helpin' us out." I pat him on the back. "Listen, without you I'd probably be dead."

He chuckles. "That's for sure."

There's hidden meaning behind those words that I only now understand. I have to sweeten the pot, because I need to make sure this works. If he's who I suspect he is, two million isn't a lot of money to him. "I've also got a list of the people Paul has been working with. I figure if you could give that list to the police, they could bring down *Las Calaveras*."

Mateo agrees. When it gets dark he drives us back to the gym, but it's still too early. Nobody is here. "Why don't we spar one last time, Mateo?" I say. "For old times' sake."

Dalila shakes her head in confusion and grabs my elbow. "What are you doing, Ryan? You can't fight now. We have to leave."

"I'm good," I tell her. "Boxing is my life. You know that, baby." I turn to Mateo. "Our little mission can wait, can't it?"

He checks his watch, then shrugs. "I guess."

Standing beside Dalila, I get into gear. "You need to get out of here," I whisper to her. "Now."

"What are you talking about? No. I won't leave you," she says.

I lean in to kiss her. "Save yourself, baby. This fight is for you," I say in a quiet whisper so only she can hear, then kiss her tenderly. With a last glance hoping she'll understand, I turn and face my fate.

She backs toward the exit as Mateo and I get into the ring, but she doesn't leave. We spar and I let him get in some shots. I'm just trying to kill time, but as he starts getting aggressive, I start pounding on him.

Mateo puts his hands in an X. "Time-out!"

"No. No time-outs today, Mateo." I punch him again and again. I can feel myself losing control. "This is for Rico, for Abuela Carmela . . . for me and Dalila."

He holds his hands in front of his face, shielding my target. "You don't get it, Ryan."

I throw down my gloves. "Why did you do it, huh?"

"*Venganza.* Revenge." His mouth twists into a wicked grin. "*Las Calaveras* killed my cousin two years ago and I vowed revenge, so I started *Los Reyes del Norte*, the new movement. I needed you to rely on me so you could lure Paul onto my turf to bring him and *Las Calaveras* down. You've got to admit my brilliance. Disabling Demi's car, lending you my truck." He looks cocky when he says, "Have you heard of a remote-control shutoff? Genius, right?" He winks at us then stands in the middle of the ring as if he's the champion. "I made the car stall knowing Dalila's Papá would want to kill you. Rico beating your ass was just a bonus, Ryan, but he ruined my plans when he dumped you back in Loveland. We got even with him, though, didn't we?"

"You didn't have to kill him," I say.

"Hell yeah. I smoked his ass. Bonus when Don Sandoval found the body and saw you first. He didn't frame you, bro. *I* did. I'm El Fuego, Ryan. Not Don Sandoval. In the end, I always win."

"You'll never win this one, Mateo," Camacho says as he appears from the back room.

Suddenly a barbell is flying through the air. It hits a surprised Mateo in the arm. "You're done," Dalila says, appearing from the shadows.

Mateo laughs, a maniacal laugh that echoes in the gym. He pulls out a gun from his pocket. "I've got a gun, *puta*. I can smoke all three of you."

"You mean four of us," Pablo says, popping up from behind the front desk with a nine millimeter in one hand. He points the gun at Mateo.

Mateo sneers at Pablo. "Who the fuck do you think you are?"

"I'm Ryan's crew, *pendejo*. There's no way out of this."

Where's Officer Matthews? If he doesn't come through, we're all dead.

"Just so you know, I've got backup," Mateo warns. "A truckload of guys from *Los Reyes del Norte* are on their way here with instructions to shoot up this place and everybody in it." Mateo flashes a sick grin. "Besides me, of course."

"How does Santiago fit in with all of this?" I ask.

"Santiago Vega is a snitch. I kill snitches and everyone associated with them. You think your stepfather is any different? Blackburn killed that border patrol guy. Shot him right in the face and got two mil for the hit because the border cop was about to expose him."

"Yeah, but nobody will ever know because we're going to blow this place up," Paul says, suddenly appearing from the back room with Francisco Cruz right behind him. "Ryan, where's the money?"

I eye my duffel in the middle of the gym. "That's not all of it," I tell him.

Paul walks toward the duffel while Cruz blocks the entrance. Pablo points to a cell phone that he rigged in the corner of the room and signals to me that he's been secretly recording everything this entire time. It's all the evidence Officer Matthews will need to take them down.

"Where is the rest of the cash, Ryan?" Paul pulls a gun out and points it at me.

Cruz is pointing a gun at Pablo, then at Camacho.

Mateo points his gun at Dalila.

Helicopters are flying overhead now and the sound of sirens can be heard in the distance. We're about to be surrounded. I can tell by the fire in Mateo's eyes that he's not ready to be taken down. Not by a long shot.

In the ring, desperate men do desperate things. We're all feeling desperate. If I don't move quickly, it's either my crew or me.

It's time to take one for my team.

I walk over to the cell phone and pick it up. "This has been recording the entire time," I tell them. "All I have to do is send it to the authorities. Put the guns down and I won't do it."

All guns are now pointed at me.

As I press Send, Mateo curses at me and I see the fire flash out of the barrel of his gun. I'm not surprised I hear the loud *pop* before I actually feel anything. Something cold pierces my gut and my shoulder. I know I've been hit.

Paul and Cruz attempt to escape, but more shots ring out as the doors burst open. US and Mexican forces fill the gym. They're finally here. I breathe in, but a sharp pain makes me wince.

Dalila is suddenly next to me. I can tell by her gasp when she moves my hand away from the wound that it's bad. "Why did you do that?" she says through uncontrollable sobs.

"I had to. He was gonna shoot you. All of you." I reach out for her hand and tell her what I should have said a long time ago. "I love you, Dalila."

My girl, her eyes glazed over with fury, stands in front of me as if she's some shield. I try to pull her back, but my energy is waning fast and I'm starting to have trouble hearing. It's like I'm in a fog.

"I'll kill you," Dalila growls at Mateo.

Mateo grabs her and attempts to run out with her as his shield, but Don Sandoval walks in and growls. "Step away from my daughter or the authorities have orders to shoot."

"Not if I've got faster reflexes, old man," Mateo warns. I hear shots ring out. Mateo falls to the ground, his body riddled with bullets. He's dead.

Everything is so foggy and distant, as if I'm not even here. All I know is that Dalila is safe now. My own mind is fading fast. This isn't how it's supposed to end . . . when I feel like my life just began.

I hear Dalila crying as she clutches me.

"I'll always go where you go . . ." I manage to say. I want to say more, but I feel like I'm slipping away into nothingness.

"Stay with me, Ryan! Please!" she pleads.

"I can't."

"No! Don't leave me. I need you!"

"I wish . . ." I try to get out the words but I'm feeling so weak right now. I know I don't have much time. "Live for me . . ."

"I can't," she sobs, her tears falling on our entwined fingers.

"You're the strongest girl I know, baby . . . the strongest . . ."

The last thing I hear is her voice telling me she's with me and she's never letting me go. The last thing I feel is her touch, her love . . . finally giving me a sense of peace.

FORTY-SIX

Dalila

"Dalila, are you ready?" Margarita asks me as she peeks her head into my room. She's wearing a pretty skeleton costume with a white tutu and black leggings. "Mamá says we're leaving in a few minutes."

I'm wearing a colorful dress today, because it's *Día de los Muertos*, the Day of the Dead. I'm trying not to become emotional as I gather everything I'll need for tonight.

When I walk downstairs, a crowd of people is waiting for me in the courtyard. Soona and Demi are carrying the sugar skulls we decorated this afternoon. Mamá is holding a handful of *cempasúchil* flowers that she grew in her garden. My sisters are helping Lola carry trays of fresh tamales she just made.

Papá walks into the courtyard lugging a gym mat. "Are you sure you don't want us to bring pillows and blankets? Ryan's spirit has a long journey ahead of him. Maybe he'd be more comfortable resting on something softer."

I shake my head as I pat the gym mat. "No. This is perfect, Papá. Thank you for getting it."

"You ready?" Mamá asks.

"Yes." As ready as I'll ever be.

We arrive at the cemetery near Sevilla. There are already people gathered around the gravestones. Music is playing, and it's like a big party has begun. I don't have to search for Ryan's gravesite. I've been here more times than I can count in the past four months since he passed that fateful summer night.

This isn't a day to mourn him, I remind myself. It's to celebrate his life. I called his mother last week and invited her to join me today. She said she might, but I haven't heard from her since.

After Papá sets down the familiar gym mat for Ryan's spirit to rest on after his long journey, I set the *cempasúchil* around his gravesite, which will be a welcoming sight as his spirit is guided back to me. Soona, Demi, and I set the sugar skulls on top of his gravestone. Mine has colorful flowers painted on it because I remember him telling me how he liked the bright colors of our paintings and murals. I also added hearts into the eyes, because I saw love reflected in his eyes long before he told me he loved me.

"Don't forget the tamales!" Coco calls out as Galena places the platter of tamales on top of his now-crowded stone.

Who knew when we joked about me putting tamales on his grave that it would become a reality not long after? Every day since

Ryan was killed I've wanted to give up, but he wouldn't want that. He'd want me to soldier on, to fight like he did in the ring and out of it.

So I am.

I reach into my bag and pull out the little heart-shaped stone I found on the ground when we were stranded that first night we made love. He said the stone was good luck. The stone must have summoned Ryan, because it led him to the truth about Mateo. I kiss the stone, then set it on the gym mat.

"We've got to go," Mamá says. "It's a long drive to Abuela Carmela's house. We have a lot of things to bring to her gravesite. And then we'll be visiting Lucas's grave in the morning."

"I know." I hug my parents and sisters. "Thank you for being here."

Since Ryan passed, my parents have helped me cope with the loss of the boy I fell in love with. I'll never lose faith in them again. My father lost his way at one point and got blinded by money and bribes. He wanted to redeem himself and make Abuela Carmela proud by helping Santiago Vega and the authorities take down *Las Calaveras* and *Los Reyes del Norte*. He had to keep it all a secret to protect us. Now Papá is lobbying to be a judge. I'm really proud of him. The night Ryan died, his stepfather was arrested along with Francisco Cruz thanks to the evidence recorded on the cell phone. If it weren't for Ryan bringing all of them together, they wouldn't have been arrested so soon and the war between the cartels would have raged on.

After my family leaves the cemetery, I close my eyes as I hold

Demi's and Soona's hands. I feel a calm wash over me as I imagine Ryan's spirit coming home to me.

"I'm starting at the university in January, Mr. America," I say out loud, hoping Ryan can hear me. I'm trying not to choke up, because today is a celebration of his life. It's not a time to be sad. "I'm going to study law and become an advocate for underprivileged kids like Sergio." I never want kids to feel alone in this world. Making my country the best it can be will be my life's mission.

"Something's missing here," a voice calls out above the music playing.

I look over to see Pablo walking over to us with a Lone Star Boxing Club towel in his hand. "Hess will need this," he says, placing the towel on the gym mat. He stares at Ryan's gravestone for a long time. "We met at the club the first week he moved to Texas. I thought he was a *gringo* who couldn't box." He chuckles to himself. "I was wrong. He beat the crap out of me. Ryan was a damn good fighter and could have been one of the best. A legend, like Camacho."

"Did someone mention my name?"

Juan, with his gray hair neatly combed and his gait a little lighter than when I last saw him, is wearing a big smile on his face. He's also got an old championship belt slung over his shoulder. The shiny metal glitters in the moonlight. "This is for Ryan. I won it many years ago," Camacho says as he places the belt in front of Ryan's grave. "You'll always be a champion to me, *mi hijo*."

"I'm glad you're here," I say, hugging the old man tight. "Ryan will love your gift."

After Juan tells stories about the first time he met Ryan at the gym, I hold up a hand. "You'll have to humor me, everyone," I say as I set up little speakers and plug in my phone. I press Play and Atticus Patton's voice fills the air, clashing with the traditional Spanish music at the other end of the cemetery. "Shadows of Darkness was our favorite band. We met at the concert."

"We didn't even have a ticket to that concert," Pablo chimes in. "We snuck in posing as caterers. You almost didn't meet."

"It was fate," Soona says as she takes Pablo's hand in hers.

As we all dance and sing to the music, I step back and see that Ryan had a crew. These are the people who cared about him most. He thought he was alone in this world, but he had more than a lot of people can boast about.

Being independent was my goal in life, but I was wrong. It's about making meaningful connections with people who'll stick up for you and be your champions.

Sometimes you never know what's missing in your life until it's right in front of your face.

I never thought I needed a hero, until I met Ryan Hess.

ACKNOWLEDGMENTS

First and foremost, I would like to thank my editor, Emilia Rhodes, for her unending support and encouragement while I wrote many versions of this book. I'll never forget your faith in me and I am so happy to be working with you and your entire staff. I feel so honored to be part of the HarperCollins family!

I would like to thank my amazing agent, Kristin Nelson, for always cheering me on and continuing to make sure my books find the best homes possible. And to Pete Harris, who held me up and never let me fall. Your emails that said simply "Call me, I'm here for you!" throughout this process helped me more than you will ever know. You're a wonderful person and I definitely owe you a drink and a spa day the next time I come to LA!

Dalila and Ryan came alive due to some very important people! Claudia was a great sensitivity reader who provided valuable insight on the Latino community and Mexican culture to make this book the best it could be. Maria Perez-Chavez was a fan who became my beta reader who helped so much with the book. You are an amazing woman and I am so thankful for your input! And to my fan Jose Ibarra and his stunning wife, Natalie, who helped when I was out of ideas. I miss you both and am still honored that I stood up as a bridesmaid in your wedding!

I am in awe of Margie Longoria, a devoted librarian from Texas who has dedicated her life to putting books in the hands of teens. Your input helped make Dalila and Ryan's journey magical. Margie, you are a role model for all librarians and I wish everyone had your passion. You are a true gem!

I don't know what I'd do without my friends Cynthia Singer, Nanci Martinez, and Mindy Berman. You are all strong, incredible women who give me strength, comfort, and a shoulder to cry on when I need it. Nasien, thank you for your encouragement and support.

Finally, I want to thank my mom, Fran, who is annoying and crazy and wonderful and my rock. My children, Brett and Samantha, make sure my life is never dull. You both challenge me and drive me nuts but I'll go to the ends of the earth to make sure you're safe, happy, and healthy.

I love interacting with my fans on Twitter, Facebook, and Instagram, so come find me! You can find my website at www .simoneelkeles.com.